PRAISE FOR THE NAT_____
NEST BOO_

A Si____

"The second Raven's Ne_____
love interest, Rick Sanders, right in the ____
Clara's personal interest in solving the crime adds to the
plausibility of her actions, and characters and relationships
are further fleshed out in this novel."   —*RT Book Reviews*

"An entertaining, amusing whodunit as the two cousins who
are BFF 'sisters' land in one mess after another . . . Fans
will enjoy this lighthearted, well-written mystery."
    —*Genre Go Round Reviews*

Mind Over Murder

"A delightful read . . . [A] winning addition to the cozy paranormal mystery realm."
    —Yasmine Galenorn, *New York Times* bestselling author

"The breakout must-read mystery of the fall season. [It] is
a definite contender for best new cozy series of 2011 . . .
Kingsley's inhabitants are a sensational cast of players with
exhilarating and quirky personalities that vibrantly jump
off the page, engaging the reader immediately."
    —*Seattle Post-Intelligencer*

"A fun paranormal amateur sleuth . . . The story line is fast-
paced throughout, regardless whether the plot focuses on
the whodunit or the men wanting to date lofty Clara. It is a
sure bet that fans will want to return to the Raven's Nest
Bookstore for more Quinn Sense sensational stories."
    —*Genre Go Round Reviews*

"Fast-paced and a quick read. This is a puzzling cozy that
will appeal to a wide audience."   —*Once Upon a Romance*

Berkley Prime Crime titles by Allison Kingsley

MIND OVER MURDER
A SINISTER SENSE
TROUBLE VISION

Trouble Vision

Allison Kingsley

BERKLEY PRIME CRIME, NEW YORK

THE BERKLEY PUBLISHING GROUP
Published by the Penguin Group
Penguin Group (USA) Inc.
375 Hudson Street, New York, New York 10014, USA

USA | Canada | UK | Ireland | Australia | New Zealand | India | South Africa | China

Penguin Books Ltd., Registered Offices: 80 Strand, London WC2R 0RL, England
For more information about the Penguin Group, visit penguin.com.

TROUBLE VISION

A Berkley Prime Crime Book / published by arrangement with the author.

Berkley Prime Crime Books are published by The Berkley Publishing Group.
BERKLEY® PRIME CRIME and the PRIME CRIME logo are trademarks of
Penguin Group (USA) Inc.

For information, address: The Berkley Publishing Group,
a division of Penguin Group (USA) Inc.,
375 Hudson Street, New York, New York 10014.

ISBN: 978-0-425-25198-0

PUBLISHING HISTORY
Berkley Prime Crime mass-market edition / June 2013

PRINTED IN THE UNITED STATES OF AMERICA

10 9 8 7 6 5 4 3 2 1

Cover illustration by Griesbach / Martucci.
Cover design by Laura K. Corless.

ALWAYS LEARNING   PEARSON

To my husband,
Bill, for being my knight in shining armor.

Acknowledgments

Many thanks to my editor, Michelle Vega, for being such a joy to work with and for making me look good.

Thanks to my agent, Paige Wheeler, for knowing what I want before I know it myself.

Deepest thanks to my good friends Sam and Alan Willey, for all your help with the research and for all the wonderful stories that brighten my day.

And to Mr. Bill, my heartfelt thanks for watching over me and making me smile.

1

"Quiet!" The sound of a mallet pounding the podium accompanied Madison Cheswick's shrill voice. The strident shouting of the crowd gradually faded away, until all that was heard was the shuffling of feet and a nervous cough or two.

Seated at the back of the conference room, Clara Quinn exchanged a meaningful glance with her cousin. On the way over to the town hall, she and Stephanie had speculated on how well the new mayor would handle the crowd, given the controversial subject of the meeting. So far, things had been somewhat rowdy.

Clara recognized several of the people sitting around her. Some of them were customers of the Raven's Nest, the bookstore owned by Stephanie and run by the cousins, with the help of Molly, their young assistant. Normally,

Clara would be working there until eight p.m., but this being a Tuesday, her day off, Molly was taking care of the bookstore.

Weary of the constant bickering on TV about the construction of a hotel resort at the edge of their coastal Maine town, Clara had been reluctant to go to the meeting. Stephanie had begged her to go, saying that as a local business owner the project affected her and she needed answers. As usual, Clara had found it hard to say no to her cousin.

Stephanie had recently changed everyone's schedule, as business at the bookstore had shifted since they'd opened. If she'd still had Wednesdays off, Clara thought, as she tried to get comfortable on the hard chair, she would have had to work until eight tonight, giving her a good excuse not to come to the meeting. Then again, Stephanie would probably have asked Molly to fill in. Stephanie was used to getting her way.

Leaning back, Clara studied the new mayor. Madison Cheswick's cheeks glowed in the harsh light from the stage. She'd swept her dark hair back from her face into a tight bun, which made her brown eyes seem enormous. In her mid-fifties, the mayor was still an attractive woman, with a slim figure and a flashy sense of style that only a confident professional could pull off.

In many ways, Madison reminded Clara of her mother. Jessica Quinn was about the same age, and just as fashionable and feisty. Jessie would have whipped this lot into shape before they'd even sat down. Clara waited with interest to see how the mayor would manage the restless crowd.

Now that she had silenced the room, Madison laid down her mallet and spoke quietly into the microphone. "As I was saying, the complaints from the owners of the construction site on the bluff are disturbing. I've had reports of sit-down protests, confrontations and on more than one occasion, an incident where blows were exchanged. I don't have to tell you how this reflects on our community."

Another bout of muttering began, but the mayor shot her hand up in the air. "I understand," she continued loudly, "your concerns about the new construction. A resort hotel and golf course is a huge project that will certainly bring some changes. I've seen the design plans, however, and I'm confident that the Cliff Top Resort will be a tasteful and beneficial asset to the town. The hotel buildings are charming and will blend in with the scenery along the coast road, while the golf course will be a half mile from the bluff and hidden by trees."

A young man with straggly red hair and heavy stubble on his chin rose to his feet. "What about the wildlife? Who's going to protect them?"

"Yeah," an elderly woman echoed. "They're using up all that land. Think of all those people tramping all over the bluff, not to mention the cars. The whole thing will be an ugly mess spoiling the view of the entire coast road."

Several people murmured in agreement.

"I assure you," Madison said, "that once the project is

completed, you will be pleasantly surprised. Just try to think of the benefits. Finn's Harbor relies a great deal on the tourist season, and the resort will bring in more money for the town. More money means better services for our citizens. It also means more funding for our schools, our local businesses and our recreational programs."

A hoarse voice answered her, thick with anger. "That's a load of bull! All that place will do is put money in the owner's pockets. What about the extra traffic? Already we've got trucks rumbling through town every day. What about when the resort opens? We'll be stuck in traffic all day. Before long, there'll be drunks wandering around at night, and crime in the streets. You wait and see." The burly gray-haired man shook his fist at the mayor. "I say shut down the project and give us back our safe and quiet town before it's too late."

The younger man next to him shot to his feet, his face red above his thick, scruffy beard. "My father's right! Shut down the resort! We don't need it." He turned to wave an arm at the crowd and began chanting, "Shut down the resort. Shut down the resort!"

Clara and Stephanie exchanged uneasy glances again as a few halfhearted voices joined in.

Once more Madison raised a hand. "I think you're overreacting—" she began, but was rudely shouted down by the elder of the two protestors.

"You don't want the truth to come out! How much did those land-grabbers pay you to support them?"

"Yeah," added his son. "What about what the people of this town want? Where's your loyalty to your citizens, Mayor?"

The murmuring grew louder, and Madison's pleas for quiet were drowned out by the continuous bellowing of the two men. Finally, much to Clara's relief, Deputy Tim Rossi stepped in.

She couldn't hear what Tim said to the men, but it must have been a stern warning, as they stomped out of the room, calling out a parting shot or two before the door closed behind them.

"Whew!" Stephanie wiped imaginary sweat from her brow. "I thought they were going to start a fight."

"Me, too." Clara frowned. "Those two seemed really belligerent. I think they're just troublemakers."

"You could be right." Stephanie glanced at her watch. "I hope this meeting is over soon. George is probably going nuts by now trying to keep the kids under control."

Clara had to sympathize with Stephanie's husband. Knowing their father lacked the strong arm wielded by their mother, the three kids took advantage of him every chance they got, and invariably created havoc when Stephanie was away from home.

Fortunately, Madison took that moment to bring down the mallet one last time on the podium. "I think it's time we adjourned. I'm asking all of you to think about this new project with an open mind. Trust in your town leaders. We have discussed this at length and we are all in agreement that the Cliff Top Resort will do nothing but good for the town. I must warn you, however, that disruptive and abusive behavior on the site will not be tolerated. Feel free to e-mail us with your concerns, and we will do our best to give you answers. Thank you for your time."

Stephanie rose to her feet, yawning behind her hand. "Well, I'm not convinced. How about you?"

"I don't know." Clara scooped up her purse and slung the strap over her shoulder. "I don't think anyone can be sure until the resort is built and in operation."

"By that time, it will be too late." Stephanie stepped out into the aisle and waited for her cousin to join her. "I just hope that the mayor is right and that the benefits will outweigh the problems. Otherwise I can see riots happening in the streets."

"I sure hope it doesn't come to that." Clara stood and paused as a wave of darkness suddenly swirled around her. Voices began whispering urgently in her head, insistent and impossible to understand. It felt like a cold hand clutched the back of her neck while she fought off the sensation. *Evil.* It was all around her, and close by.

She grasped the back of the chair in front of her, and met Stephanie's gaze. Her cousin's eyes were wide open with expectation.

"It's happening, isn't it?" she whispered.

Clara blinked, and the world returned to normal. "Let's get out of here," she muttered, and pushed past her cousin into the aisle.

Once outside in the darkness, she stood on the steps

of the town hall and filled her lungs with cold, salty ocean air. People streamed by them, some arguing, some with heads down, apparently deep in thought. Stephanie paused two steps above her cousin so that their faces were level.

"You had another vision. Right?"

Clara hesitated, reluctant to admit that the infamous Quinn Sense had struck again.

She and Stephanie had been born two months apart, and had grown up together closer than most sisters. They'd shared everything from toys to clothes to hair-raising adventures that had terrified their respective parents.

One of the things they hadn't shared, much to Stephanie's intense disappointment, was the family inheritance of a sixth sense. Most women in the family possessed it to a certain degree, while one or two men had admitted to having it. The cousins had eagerly waited for the day when they would be able to predict the future and read minds.

It hadn't turned out that way. Clara had inherited a certain amount of the Quinn Sense, though it was unpredictable and unreliable. It usually appeared when she least expected it, and rarely when she needed it. Worse, it made her feel like a freak, to the extent that she had left Finn's Harbor to live in New York, hoping to escape the wretched curse, as she called it.

Stephanie had never quite forgiven her cousin for deserting her, and never got over the fact that Clara had the Sense while she did not. When a personal heartbreak had brought Clara back to Finn's Harbor, the cousins had renewed their close relationship, though the subject of the Quinn Sense was still a source of controversy at times.

Clara did her best to ignore it, while Stephanie fervently watched for any sign of its appearance. Right now, she was staring at Clara with a giddiness usually reserved for small children on Christmas morning. "You did, didn't you?"

Clara sighed. "Okay, but it wasn't a vision." She hesitated. "More of a feeling, that's all."

"What kind of feeling?"

Clara glanced over her shoulder. Below her, a small group of people surrounded the long-haired young man who had seemed so concerned about the habitats of wildlife on the bluff. He was talking earnestly, waving his arm about to emphasize his words. Whatever he was saying was obviously what the crowd wanted to hear, as there were several cries of "Right on!" and "Let's do it!"

Clara stared at them for a moment, but felt nothing except an uneasiness that could easily have been brought on by the belligerence of the protestors. "It was a nasty feeling," she said, turning back to her cousin. "Like something bad is going to happen, but I don't know what. It's gone now."

Stephanie pouted. "You never seem to get to the good part. Are you sure you don't know, or are you keeping stuff from me?"

They'd had this argument before. More than once. Clara crossed her arms. "Stephanie Quinn Dowd, for the last time, I'm not keeping things from you. As I've told you numerous times, the Sense comes and goes, and I don't have any control over it."

She started down the steps, trying to control her irritation. She was not a lover of the family curse. If she could, she'd give it to Stephanie in a heartbeat and be rid of it once and for all. It had let her down when she'd needed it the most, and she hadn't trusted it since.

"Wait!" Stephanie flew down the steps behind her, catching up with her just as Clara passed by the group of protestors.

"So when do you want us to meet, Josh?" someone asked, while someone else added, "Yeah, let's do it soon."

The redheaded man put his arm around the pretty blonde next to him and drew her close. "How about tomorrow?"

There were choruses of enthusiastic agreement from the crowd.

Clara kept walking, with Stephanie bouncing along by her side.

"Sounds as if they're planning another protest," Stephanie said, sounding out of breath.

Clara slowed her steps. "I don't know what good it will do. They can protest all they like; it's not going to stop the construction."

"I just hope nobody gets hurt," Stephanie murmured.

They were walking across the parking lot now, to where Clara had parked her car. As they reached it, the dark cloud wrapped around her again. The sensation of danger was so intense, she shuddered and gripped the handle of the car door.

Luckily Stephanie had walked around to the passenger side, and by the time they were both settled in their seats, Clara's mind had cleared again. Still, remnants of the premonition lingered, and she was thankful when they reached Stephanie's house and she could park the car.

"Are you coming in?" Stephanie paused in the act of climbing out. "The kids would love to see you."

Clara shook her head. "Not tonight. I still have to take Tatters for a walk and I promised my mother I'd help her with her tax return. She's expecting a refund and wants to get it in early."

Stephanie wrinkled her nose. "Ugh, taxes. We always put them off until the last minute. Anyway, we still have two months to worry about it." She opened the door wider, and shivered. "I hope it's not going to snow. We just got rid of the last lot."

Clara smiled. "That would slow down the resort project again."

"At least the protestors would be happy." Stephanie waved good-bye and slammed the car door.

Clara waited until her cousin was inside the house before pulling away from the curb. She didn't want to think about protests, or problems that might arise from the new construction. Or what had caused the strange feeling of impending doom that had attacked her twice that evening.

All she wanted to do was take Tatters for a walk, check her e-mail, maybe watch the news on TV and go to bed.

The thought of Tatters waiting anxiously for her to get home made her smile. The big, shaggy dog had become so much a part of her life, she couldn't imagine existing without him now. Tatters belonged to Rick Sanders, who owned the hardware store across the street from the Raven's Nest.

Rick's ex-wife had dumped the dog on him, and when he had threatened to send Tatters to the pound, Clara had offered to take care of him. Since she didn't have to be at the bookstore until noon, and her mother arrived home around four, it meant far less hours that the dog was alone than Rick could manage.

Tatters, it turned out, had a zest for activity and a mind of his own—a combination that, given his size, was quite a challenge for both Clara and her mother. Jessie, however, seemed to have found a way to control the turbulent animal, much to her daughter's surprise and admiration.

Arriving home, Clara opened the front door to be met with a huge furry body and a floppy, wet tongue. After assuring the dog that she would take him for a walk just as soon as she changed her shoes, Clara looked into the living room. Her mother sat in front of the TV, a folded newspaper on her lap and a half-empty glass of wine at her side.

"Oh, there you are." Jessie took off her glasses and peered up at her daughter. "So, how did the meeting go?"

Clara walked into the room, followed closely by Tatters, his breath warm on her calves. "It was a bit unruly."

"I've just been watching it on the news." Jessie picked up the remote and switched off the TV. "Seems as though you had some excitement down there. I saw Tim escorting Bob and Eddie Hatchett off the premises. They were both making too much noise, as usual."

Clara raised her eyebrows. "You know them?"

"Bob Hatchett is an electrician. As a matter of fact, he was the one who wired that new chandelier in the dining room a month ago." Jessie reached for her wine. "While he was here, his son came looking for him. He seemed upset about something. I could hear them shouting at each other out in the driveway even with the front door shut." She took a sip of her wine and put the glass down. "That son of his has a nasty temper."

"I got that impression listening to him tonight. He was still shouting when Tim ushered him out the door." Clara headed back to the hallway. "I'm going to take Tatters for a walk."

"Well, dress warmly. I wouldn't be surprised if it snowed again."

Clara wrinkled her brow. She'd had enough of the snow. Roll on summertime, when she could shed her heavy coat and boots and frolic with Tatters on the beach.

Walking briskly down the street a few minutes later, she felt a sharp longing for the warmer weather. Summer in Finn's Harbor was a joy—lots of sunshine, clean, fresh air and sea breezes to make the heat bearable. The winters, however, could be brutal, when temperatures often slipped below zero and stormy winds lashed the coastline.

These were the times she missed New York the most—the lights, the crowded sidewalks, the spacious restaurants and shops where she could always find refuge from the cold. Thinking of New York, however, brought back memories she'd sooner forget, and she shut her mind to them.

Turning up the collar of her coat, she shook Tatters' leash. "Come on, big fella, let's run."

The dog obediently took off, so fast she had trouble keeping up with him. She let out the length of the leash and he tore around the corner, then sat waiting for her, tongue hanging out the side of his mouth. She stumbled to a stop, gasping for breath. "I think it's time we went home," she said, when she could find her voice.

Just when it was getting exciting. Tatters stood, raised his nose in the air, then trotted off, leaving her staring after him.

Pulled along by his leash, she shook her head. Of all the surprises the Quinn Sense had given her, none matched the discovery that she could read Tatters' mind. It unnerved her, and although it didn't happen that often, she lived in dread that Stephanie or her mother would realize the fact. Either one would be a disaster. Her cousin would be constantly asking her what the dog was thinking, while her mother would finally find out that her daughter possessed the Sense.

So far, Clara had managed to hide it from everyone except Stephanie, who had sworn on pain of death to keep her cousin's secret. Even though she couldn't understand why Clara was so intent on ignoring her gift, when Stephanie would have traded her firstborn to have it.

Clara had done her best to explain that she couldn't stand the idea of people thinking she was nuts. She hated how the Sense came and went without warning, disrupting what she was doing and forcing her to cover up what was happening to her.

Worst of all, she had started to rely on it until she hadn't known if it was the Sense or her own instincts working, and in the end she hadn't been able to trust her instincts when she'd needed to the most.

Letting herself into the house, she called out a goodnight to her mother and went directly to her room. She had long ago given up on persuading Tatters to sleep in the utility room, and now he shared the bed with her every night. Although shared was perhaps too generous a word, since he took up most of the room. She'd become used to his warm body now, and knew she would miss him if he wasn't there.

She spent the next hour or so on the computer, then got ready for bed. Tomorrow she would be back at the Raven's Nest for her regular shift. At first she'd been reluctant when Stephanie had offered her the job. She'd hoped to get a teaching position when she'd come back to Maine, but when nothing suitable had come up the first few weeks she was home, she accepted her cousin's offer.

Although the bookstore carried mainly paranormal literature, and Clara tended to avoid anything remotely mystical or magical, she'd managed to come to terms with the idea and soon settled down. Now she enjoyed her job so much she couldn't imagine doing anything else. At least, not in the immediate future.

She enjoyed talking to the customers, and seeing Rick Sanders across the street every day didn't hurt, either. Thinking of him put a smile on her face, and she fell asleep with it still there.

———

The next morning, Clara arrived at the Raven's Nest shortly before noon to find a line of customers waiting at the counter to be served. Business had started to pick up on Wednesdays, and today was no exception. Molly was frantically bagging books, her red hair flying around her face as if she'd been caught in a windstorm.

Stephanie was nowhere to be seen, presumably taking care of a customer somewhere in the aisles. Clara hurried over to the counter, dragging off her coat on the way. There would be time to hang it in the stockroom later. Right now, Molly could use her help.

Clara smiled at the elderly woman standing second in line. "Mrs. Riley! How nice to see you again. Are you feeling better? The last time you were in here, you had a nasty cold."

The wrinkles on the woman's face deepened. "It took me weeks to get rid of it." She moved forward to the counter, sniffed and hunted in her pocket until she drew out a wad of tissues. "It still hasn't gone completely."

"I'm sorry to hear that." Clara held out her hand for the purchase, hoping there weren't any germs on it. "Ah, I see you have *The Child Hunters*. It's at the top of our list of fantasy novels."

Mrs. Riley blew her nose. "I need something good to keep my mind off what's happening out there on the bluff."

Clara nodded in sympathy. "People seem really worried about the effect the new resort will have on Finn's Harbor."

"We have a right to be worried." Mrs. Riley stuffed the tissues back in her pocket. "That whole project is bad luck and it will bring nothing good to the town. I always knew something really bad would happen up there and now it has."

Clara's hand froze as she took the credit card the woman handed her. The voices started whispering in her head, warning her of imminent bad news. She had trouble phrasing the question, and waited for an answer she already knew. "What happened?"

Mrs. Riley stared at her. "You don't know? They found the foreman's body up there last night. They say he fell from the scaffolding."

Still trying to absorb the shock, Clara could think of nothing to say. Molly appeared at her side, muttering in a low voice, "It's all over town. Scott Delwyn's wife called the police when Scott didn't come home from work. Dan found him at the foot of the scaffolding."

Mrs. Riley nodded. "Slipped and fell right off that

thing. Always knew it was bad luck." She scowled at Clara. "Are you going to swipe that card or not?"

The voices. They were clamoring in her head now, like the chattering of squirrels on the hunt for food. She couldn't move. Couldn't breathe. After a moment or two, one voice came through loud and clear: *He was murdered.*

2

Seconds ticked by while Mrs. Riley stared at Clara as if she were looking at some kind of apparition. Clara briefly closed her eyes, and felt Molly's fingers on her arm.

"Are you okay?"

As if they'd been shut off by a remote, the voices stopped. All Clara could hear now was a passing truck outside, and the quiet murmur of conversation from a couple of women at the cookbook table. Quickly she swiped her customer's card and bagged the book.

Just as she handed the package over, Stephanie emerged from the middle aisle and darted over to the counter. "We need to talk."

Clara glanced at Molly.

"It's okay." Molly gave her a little push. "I can handle this."

Clara smiled her thanks, then followed Stephanie down the aisle to the Reading Nook. Finding two customers sitting there sipping coffee, Stephanie kept going and pushed open the door to the stockroom.

"In here. We need privacy."

Clara followed her into the dimly lit room, where cartons and stacks of books lined the walls. She was still shaken by the news she'd just heard, and entering that room with its cold floor and dark shadows didn't help. Not too long ago, she'd found the dead body of Ana Jordan, the owner of the stationers next door, lying on that floor, right where Stephanie was now standing.

Shuddering, Clara stared at her cousin. "Did you know? About Karen Delwyn's huband?"

Stephanie nodded. "I didn't get a chance to tell you until now. I suppose Molly gave you the news."

"Actually it was Mrs. Riley." Clara rubbed her upper arms. "How did you hear about it?"

"Customers. They must have seen it on the news this morning." She tilted her head to one side. "That feeling you got the other night at the town hall meeting. It was about Scott, wasn't it? You knew this was going to happen."

"I felt something bad was going to happen. I didn't know it would be another murder."

Stephanie's gasp seemed to echo around the room. *"Murder?"*

Clara silently cursed her slip of the tongue. "I thought that's what Mrs. Riley meant."

Her cousin narrowed her eyes. "Dan ruled it an accident. No one said anything about a murder."

Clara shrugged. "Then Dan must be right. It was an accident."

Stephanie stepped closer. "You had a vision, didn't you?" She slapped a hand over her mouth. "Oh my God. Scott was *murdered*?"

"Shhh!" Clara glanced at the door. "You can't say anything about this. I could be wrong."

"You're never wrong. At least, the Quinn Sense is never wrong."

Clara uttered a cynical laugh. "That's a debatable point."

"If you're talking about what happened to you in New York, you can't blame the Sense for that. You said yourself you ignored the warnings."

"I don't want to talk about that now." Clara reached for the door handle. "Isn't it time you left? Your mother will be waiting for you to pick up the kids."

"The kids are in school." Stephanie crossed her arms. "What are we going to do about the murder?"

"*We* are not going to do anything. If it was murder, Dan will no doubt find out and he'll investigate. After all, he's the chief of police. It's his job."

"I told you, he believes it's an accident."

Clara let out her breath on a heavy sigh. "What do you propose I do about it?"

"At least go and tell Dan what you know."

"Tell him what? That voices in my head told me Scott was murdered? Imagine what he'd say to that."

Stephanie frowned. "You don't have to tell him that. Think of another way."

"There isn't another way. I don't have the slightest reason to suspect it was murder, except for the stupid Sense in my head."

"Then we'll have to find a reason. We can't let a murderer get away with killing Scott Delwyn. Think what his family must be going through right now."

Clara struggled with indecision, knowing she was fighting a losing battle. Whenever Stephanie got a bee in her bonnet about something, it usually ended up getting them into trouble. Still, her cousin had a point. "How would we even get started?"

A slow smile spread across Stephanie's face. "The same way we solved two other murders: by asking questions."

Clara groaned. "Oh no. Not again. Have you forgotten the messes we get into when we do that?"

"Remember what our parents always said when we were kids? Trouble is our middle name."

"Yeah, and they were right. No matter how good our intentions were, we always managed to screw things up."

Stephanie got that faraway look on her face that meant she was about to dredge up yet another childhood memory. "Like the time we helped that old lady get across the street and onto the bus."

Clara couldn't help a rueful smile. "Well, she did say she was trying to catch the Mittleford bus. How were we to know that she meant the bus coming from Mittleford and not going to it?"

Stephanie nodded. "I shall never forget her banging on the window as the bus drove by."

Clara laughed. "Well, at least the driver stopped and let her off before she got too far. Good thing she realized she was going the wrong way before she got all the way into Mittleford."

"Not so good that she yelled at us and nearly chased us down the street." Stephanie tilted her head to one side. "So, we're going to check out Scott's death?"

Clara gave in. "All right. I'll think about it. But let's wait a day or two and see what happens with Dan. If he hasn't changed his mind about it being an accident by then, we'll ask some questions, though I haven't the faintest idea where we'd start."

"I'm sure the Sense will tell you."

Clara jumped as the door suddenly opened and Molly stuck her head in. "Things have calmed down a bit now," she said, opening the door wider. "I'm going to take a break."

"Right." Clara shot what she hoped was a warning look at Stephanie. "We were just discussing the spring sale. I'll take over for you now."

"And I have to go home." Stephanie followed her outside. "Call me later?"

Clara gave her a nod and headed up the aisle to the counter.

She was busy enough most of the afternoon, which helped to keep her mind off the death on the construction site. It was during the dinnertime lull that she finally had time to take a break in the Nook.

Seated in a deep, comfy armchair, a mug of steaming coffee by her side, she stretched out her aching feet. Now that she had the opportunity to dwell on it, her heart went out to Scott Delwyn's wife. Karen Delwyn was a frequent customer at the Raven's Nest. Both her daughters were avid readers and loved all things paranormal. The sixth and seventh graders loved the Raven's Nest.

Every time they came in they checked out the lifesize figure of the fortune-teller, gazing into her crystal ball, hoping to see something in there. They fingered the rows of colored beads, and called out to the stuffed raven perched on the light fixture. They fought each other to stand in the reflection of the swirling crystals on their golden cords, and often their mother would have to order them out of the store when it was time to leave. In a lot of ways, they reminded Clara of her childhood and growing up with Stephanie.

Clara felt a deep ache spread across her chest. How awful it must be for them all, to lose a husband and father. Her fingers curled in her lap. Stephanie was right: if Scott Delwyn's death wasn't an accident, they must find whoever was responsible and make him pay for depriving those little girls of a father.

Her throat grew tight. She'd lost her own father a few years ago, and she still felt the pain at times. She could hardly imagine the agony Scott's family was going through now.

So deep in thought was she that she failed to notice the chime of the front doorbell or the customer approaching until a deep voice murmured, "Well, there you are. I thought you'd all gone home."

Looking up, her heart gave the little leap it always did at the sight of Rick Sanders. She and Rick had become good friends, drawn even closer now that she was taking care of Tatters. Although she had practically adopted the dog, she still thought of him as belonging to Rick. Part of that, she knew, was because she enjoyed the bond it formed between them.

It was a comfortable bond—close enough that she could take pleasure in Rick's company without the pressure and uncertainties of a romantic involvement. She'd been content with that, for a long time. She'd returned from New York with a broken heart, and she wasn't ready to trust it again to anyone. Not even to a hunky, good-looking hardware store owner with a flair for cooking that threatened to add inches to her waist.

Lately, however, she'd started wondering what it would be like to be in love with someone like Rick. Not that she intended to do anything that crazy, but it didn't hurt to fantasize now and then.

She grinned, happy to see him. "Just taking a break. How about you? Closing the store early tonight?"

"Nope." He walked over to the armchair next to her and flopped down on it. "My new assistant started today, and I figured he could handle things for ten minutes while I steal a cup of coffee."

He started to get up again, but she stopped him with a hand on his arm. "I'll get it. I need a refill, anyway." Walking over to the table that held the coffeepot and an assortment of pastries, cookies and cheese crackers, she added, "How's he working out?"

"Pretty good. He's got a lot to learn about hardware, but he seems willing enough."

"He's young?"

"Early twenties, I guess."

She carried the steaming mug over to him. "Want a snack?"

"No, thanks." He took the mug from her. "I suppose you heard the news about Scott Delwyn."

The moment Rick spoke the deceased's name, the voices started whispering again. She shut them out and sat down, cradling her mug in her hands. "It's awful. I feel so bad for his family."

Rick took a sip of his coffee and put the mug down on the side table. "He was a really nice guy. He came into the store a lot. He loved to talk—he was big on camping and fishing—and was crazy about his family. I'll miss him."

Clara hesitated, then said cautiously, "I heard he fell from the scaffolding."

"Yeah." Rick stretched his long legs out in front of him and studied his shoes. "It was raining last night. Must have been slippery up there."

"I'm surprised no one saw him fall."

Rick shrugged. "From what Dan said in the past, he was usually the last one to leave the site. He liked to check things out after everyone had gone. He must have fallen while he was doing his last-minute rounds."

The Sense crept over her like a thick, menacing cloud of evil. She resisted, trying to think of something to say that would banish the vision before it had time to form. She was helpless in its grasp, however, and she could only wait for the image to appear.

Vaguely she heard Rick's voice in the distance, still talking in normal tones. Praying that he wouldn't notice her detachment, she concentrated on the swirling fog surrounding her. The walls of the Nook melted away.

She was outside, in the dark. The wind caught her hair and whipped it around her face. She could feel the icy rain stinging her cheeks, and the boards creaking beneath her feet. She was up high, the ground maybe thirty feet below her.

Panic caught her under the ribs, and her fingers closed around a cold, wet railing—all that stood between her and the ground below. She jerked up her chin and saw two figures in front of her. They were carrying something, half dragging it along the boards to the end of the scaffolding.

As she watched, the taller figure dropped his end of the object they carried. And now she could make out the shape. It was a man, his head lolling back, his arms flopping around. For a moment the two figures paused, as if unsure what to do next. Then, with one quick movement, they shoved the man off the edge of the scaffolding.

Clara closed her eyes as she heard the *crunch* of the body hitting the ground below. She felt sick, dizzy and deathly afraid. She gripped the railing harder and prayed the two figures wouldn't see her.

"Are you all right?"

Her body jerked, and she opened her eyes. She was back in the Nook, and Rick was staring at her as if she had turned purple.

For a moment or two she couldn't speak, but nodded at him instead. Her right hand gripped the arm of her chair, while the other still held the coffee. She carefully put the mug down on the table, relieved to find her fingers relatively steady. Her voice, however, shook when she finally was able to speak.

"A bout of indigestion. Too much coffee, I guess." She forced a grin.

He still looked worried. "You've turned pale. Sure it isn't something more serious?" He leaned forward. "You're not having a heart attack, are you?"

Now she was able to laugh. "No, I'm fine." To her immense relief, the bell on the front door jingled. "Well, there goes my break. I'd better go and take care of my customer."

She got up, and he leapt to his feet with her. "Are you sure you're okay?"

"Positive." She patted his arm. "It was nothing. I'm fine. Really. Why don't you stay and finish your coffee."

"No, I'd better get back and see what Tyler is up to over there. He's probably waiting to go home to eat." He looked at her and smiled. "Speaking of which, when are you coming over for dinner again?"

She turned to leave, looking back at him over her shoulder. "When you ask me." She flapped her hand at him then headed up the aisle to the front of the shop.

Her customer turned out to be a middle-aged woman who Clara dimly recognized as a previous shopper, though she couldn't remember her name or what she'd bought. As the woman explained what she was looking for, Rick passed them by on his way out.

She met his gaze just before he closed the door, and felt a surge of warmth when he winked at her and blew a kiss. It went a long way to restoring her shattered nerves, though she couldn't quite put the incident out of her mind, and she was still thinking about it as she closed out the register at the end of her shift.

Arriving home, she spent a few minutes doing her best to calm Tatters down before joining her mother in the living room.

"I left a pot of stew on the stove," Jessie said from her usual spot in front of the TV. "Put what's left in the freezer when you're done."

"I will. Thanks." Clara crossed to the kitchen with Tatters hot on her heels.

"I already fed the dog," her mother called out after her. "Don't give him any more. He's putting on too much weight around his middle."

Look who's talking. Tatters sat down on the kitchen floor.

Unsettled by his thoughts once more speaking in her head, Clara wagged a warning finger at him. Opening the fridge, she found a half bottle of wine and poured herself a glass. She took a hefty sip of the pinot before setting the glass down on the table.

The stew smelled heavenly, and in spite of all the upset earlier, she was actually hungry. She ladled a good portion onto her plate and sat down at the table. Tatters settled himself at her knee, his golden gaze searching her face.

Sighing, she fished a cube of steak off her plate and dropped it in his waiting mouth. His tail swept the floor as he licked his lips.

She was rinsing her plate under the faucet when her cell phone buzzed. One glance confirmed what she'd expected. It was Stephanie, obviously too anxious to wait for her cousin's nightly call.

Ignoring the vibrations in her pocket, she finished cleaning up the dishes, then walked back out into the living room, just as the news anchor announced that the autopsy on Scott Delwyn showed no signs of foul play. "Finn's Harbor's chief of police, Dan Petersen, is satisfied that the death was an unfortunate accident. Questions have been raised, however, about the safety of the construction site, and all activity there will be shut down until the premises have undergone a thorough inspection."

"Such a dreadful shame," Jessie murmured. "They really should be more careful. I've seen the way those construction workers scramble all over the scaffolding. It's a wonder more of them don't fall off."

Clara shuddered, the memory of her vision still hovering in her mind. "I've got some work to do on the computer," she said as she crossed the room.

"Well, don't sit up half the night." Jessie switched channels on the TV, allowing an auto dealer's commercial to blare across the room.

Clara lifted her hand in response and escaped into the hallway. Closing the door to her room, she ordered Tatters to lie on his pillow, then quickly thumbed Stephanie's speed dial number on her cell phone.

Her cousin answered on the first ring. "There you are. I called you a little while ago."

"I know. I was in the kitchen. I didn't want to talk within earshot of my mother."

"Oh, good thinking. So, what's the plan?"

"What plan? You're usually the one with all the ideas. I just get to follow along, remember?"

"Well, you don't have to sound so bitter. I don't have the freedom that you have."

Clara relaxed her shoulders. "I know. I'm just tired."

Her cousin's voice changed to one of concern. "What's wrong? Has something happened? I saw on the news that Dan still thinks Scott's death is an accident. Did you know they're shutting down the construction site for inspection?"

"Yes, I heard."

"Clara, something's going on with you. I can tell."

After another moment's hesitation, Clara told her about

the vision. Stephanie kept gasping and exclaiming all the way through it, especially when Clara got to the bit about Rick worrying about her having a heart attack.

"Do you think Rick suspects anything?" Stephanie asked when Clara was finished with her tale.

"No, how could he? He doesn't know anything about the Quinn Sense."

"There are quite a few people in Finn's Harbor who know there's something odd about the Quinns. Some of them might know the truth."

"But no one knows I have it, except you." She paused, then added, "I think it's getting stronger."

Excitement bubbled in her cousin's voice when she answered. "You do? Why?"

"I've had visions before, but I've always been on the outside, sort of looking in, like watching a movie. This time I was actually there." Clara shivered at the memory. "I could feel the rain and the wind, and I heard the sound of Scott's body hitting the ground. I was actually standing on that scaffolding, high up in the air. It was terrifying."

"Oh, *how* I wish I could do that!" Stephanie made a sound of disgust in her throat. "It's just not *fair*."

Having heard all that before, Clara muttered, "Believe me, I wish I could transfer it all to you. I *never* want to do that again."

"Could you tell what these people looked like?"

Clara closed her eyes, seeing again the two dark figures sending a husband and father to his death. "No, it was too dark and misty with the rain."

"Well, you just *have* to tell Dan now." Stephanie gasped, then sounding farther away from the phone, added, "What? No, I was talking about the spring sale." She spoke into the phone again, her voice almost a whisper. "That was George. He wanted to know what we had to tell Dan."

"Well, for heaven's sake, don't say anything to him about this." Clara brushed dark bangs out of her eyes with impatient fingers. "If it makes you feel better, I'll think of something to tell Dan, though I don't know what I can say to him. I'm sure as hell not going to tell him about the Sense. Not that he'd believe a word of it, anyway."

"When will you go see him?"

"Tomorrow, before I start work. I'll let you know what happens when I get to the bookstore."

"I should go with you."

"No, it's better if I go alone. Less conspicuous."

"Okay. I take it everything went all right at the store?"

Clara spent the next five minutes giving Stephanie a report of the afternoon's business. After wishing her cousin a good-night, she sat down at the computer, but found it impossible to concentrate.

Images from her vision kept coming back to torment her. She let go of the mouse and leaned back in her chair. Dealing with the family curse had been bad enough when the voices had interrupted her, or she'd seen vague pictures in her mind. Being snatched away from her surroundings and dumped into a murder scene was something entirely different.

If that happened too often, she could just imagine the havoc it would cause in her life. Even worse, keeping her secret would become that much more difficult. There were a lot of people she'd rather not have learn about her weird abilities. Right at the top of that list was Rick Sanders, and that thought disturbed her most of all.

Was she starting to care a little too much for Rick despite her efforts to prevent it? If so, she was in more trouble than she thought.

3

Many years ago, before Clara was born, the building that now contained Finn's Harbor's police station had been a small theater. All that was left of the original interior was the ornate ceiling, where huge baskets of roses and rainbows had been carved into the plaster. The Rainbow Theater, as it was called, had been built before the turn of the twentieth century, and once, when Clara was a lot younger, while visiting the police station on a class project, she'd noticed an overpowering odor of stale tobacco and perfume. It had shaken her to discover that she was the only one who could smell it.

She half expected to confront it again as she walked inside that morning, but all that greeted her was the faint, musty scent of damp wood and aging carpet. The ghost, or whatever it was that had disturbed her so much, must have long departed.

The sloping floor led down past several cubicles to Dan's office in the rear, and when she knocked on the door, his booming voice answered her.

"Yeah?"

She opened the door and poked her head in the gap. "Hi, Dan. Got a minute?"

He leaned back in his chair and dropped the pen he was holding. "I've always got time for a pretty lady."

She smiled and opened the door wider.

Although Dan was the chief of police, he never let his position get in the way of his attitude toward the people he served. He was a big man, both in build and attitude. He greeted everyone with a smile and a friendly word, though his pale blue eyes never stopped probing and assessing what he saw. Nothing much got past Dan, and he'd earned a great deal of respect from the residents of Finn's Harbor.

He was watching Clara now as she walked toward him and took the chair in front of his desk. "What brings you here this morning?" he asked as she tried to relax her shoulders. "Not trouble, I hope?"

She shrugged, doing her best to appear unconcerned. "Depends what you mean by trouble. I heard about Scott Delwyn's . . . accident."

He must have noticed her slight pause. His bushy gray eyebrows shot up. "What does that have to do with you?"

She shifted on her chair, feeling like a wayward student hauled in front of the principal. "I was just wondering if you'd considered the idea that it might not be an accident?"

Now Dan was frowning. Not a good sign. "That's always a possibility in a case like this. I did a thorough investigation, however, and I'm satisfied that it was an accident. The M.E.'s report confirmed that." He laced his fingers together and leaned forward. "Do you have any reason to suggest otherwise?"

She swallowed. "Er, well . . . I was just thinking, you know, with all the protests going on and all the bad feelings between the construction workers and the protestors, that perhaps. . . ." Dan's gaze was slicing through her head and she let her voice trail off.

"Do you have any evidence whatsoever to support your suspicions?"

She dropped her chin. "No. I just thought—"

Dan groaned. "Clara, Clara, Clara . . . what am I going to do with you?"

Now she was actually squirming. "I just had this really strong feeling. . . "

"Uh-huh. And you thought now was a good time for Clara Quinn, the intrepid investigator, to step in."

Again she shrugged.

Dan leaned back in his chair again. "Clara, honey, listen to me. I know you've had a couple of good results from poking your cute little nose into police business"—Clara winced—"but that doesn't mean you should go off on a crusade every time someone dies. If you're that anxious to be a crime-solver, why don't you apply for a position with the police force? You can work your way up to detective in no time."

Annoyed that he was being more than a little patronizing, Clara got up from her chair. "Believe me, I wouldn't be a cop if they paid me a million dollars."

Dan grinned. "Very wise, m'dear. Very wise."

She reached the door and paused when he added, "Don't worry about Scott Delwyn. It's sad and tragic, and devastating for his family, but it was an accident, pure and simple. These things happen."

She gave him a brief nod and closed the door. So much for letting Dan know what she knew. Scowling, she trudged up the tilting floor and walked out into the stiff, cold wind blowing off the ocean. There was only one thing she could do now and that was find some evidence to convince Dan to open an investigation. Easier said than done.

Stephanie was near the counter, stacking books on a shelf when Clara arrived at the bookstore. She pounced the minute Clara walked inside. "Well, did you see Dan? What did he say?"

Aware of customers who were browsing nearby, Clara shook her head in warning. "Later. I'll call you tonight."

Stephanie frowned. "He didn't believe you."

"No, he didn't." Clara glanced over at the counter, where Molly was holding the phone with one hand and checking something out on the computer with the other. "We'll talk tonight."

"What are we going to do?"

Sighing, Clara beckoned Stephanie to follow and headed down the aisle to the stockroom. Once inside, she closed the door behind her cousin, saying, "Molly is going to wonder what on earth we are up to, if we keep closeting ourselves in here."

Stephanie waved a hand at the unopened cartons. "It's not like there's nothing to do in here."

Clara groaned. "I forgot it was delivery day. I'll get to them as soon as I can."

"Not until you've told me everything that Dan said."

Clara repeated the conversation, or what she could remember of it.

Stephanie's frown deepened as she listened. "Sounds as if he wasn't too thrilled about your visit," she said when Clara was done.

"It could have gone better. Let's face it: he's never going to take us seriously unless we have something solid to give him."

"So how are we going to do that?"

"I don't know." Clara glanced at her watch. "I need to think about it. I suppose we should look for some kind of evidence that at least suggests Scott may have been murdered."

Stephanie snorted. "It will have to be really good evidence to convince him. He thinks we're just a couple of busybodies who got lucky a couple of times."

Clara had to smile. "That's pretty close to the truth."

"Hey! More than once, we've put ourselves in the line of fire to catch those killers."

"Yep, we have. Even though neither of us really knows what we're doing. It's been more by luck than good judgment that we've come out of these escapades unhurt. I'm afraid that if we keep this up, sooner or later our luck is going to run out."

A cloud of concern passed across Stephanie's face then she shook her head. "Nah, not when we have the Quinn Sense and Tatters to protect us."

Clara laughed in spite of her niggling worry. "Okay. You win. We go looking for evidence."

"Where?"

"I guess a good place to start is with the protestors. They're the most likely to have caused trouble. Maybe Scott took a swing at somebody and it got out of hand."

"Good idea. Which ones?"

Clara frowned. "What do you mean, which ones?"

"Well, there's Josh Millstone and his girlfriend. They're the leaders of the conservation group that are protesting the construction because they're afraid the builders will destroy the habitat."

Remembering the meeting, Clara's frown cleared. "You mean the guy with the straggly red hair? How do you know him?"

Stephanie shrugged. "He's a new teacher at the kids' school. I recognized him when we came out of the meeting the other night and heard them talking about protesting. Ethan's always talking about Mr. Millstone and his fight to save the endangered species." She smiled. "I think Ethan is taking an interest in environmental concerns."

"Okay, so there's a place to start. Who else were you talking about?"

"Lionel Clapham."

Clara raised her eyebrows. "The owner of Searock Inn? Why him?"

"He's heading a group of the local businessmen in a protest. According to something George read in the paper, Lionel's been causing trouble up at the site. He got into a fistfight with someone. George says that Lionel's afraid the new resort will take his business."

Clara pursed her lips, then murmured, "That's a pretty good motive to get steamed up about the construction."

"Have you met him?"

"No, but I have a feeling I'm about to." She paused, working out in her mind the questions she might ask.

"There's just one thing," Stephanie murmured. "Josh and his protestors were at the meeting the night Scott died."

"But Scott supposedly fell at the end of the shift when he was doing his rounds. That would be what . . . around six or so?"

"Something like that."

"The meeting didn't start until seven thirty. Plenty of time for someone to kill Scott and get to the meeting before it started."

Stephanie's brow cleared. "You're right. You're not going to see these people without me, I hope?"

"Do I have a choice?"

"Nope." Stephanie grinned. "How about tomorrow

Allison Kingsley

morning? Molly can take care of things. I'll meet you here around nine; that'll give me time to open up. Maybe we can talk to both Josh and Lionel and still get back here for your shift at noon. "

Clara sighed. "There goes my beauty sleep again."

Stephanie gave her a hefty nudge. "You don't need it."

"Thanks." She looked at her watch again. "I'd better get out there. Molly will be wondering what the heck I'm doing all this time."

"You're unpacking cartons." Stephanie nodded at the boxes. "I'll tell her. She can let you know if she needs your help. It's pretty quiet out there right now."

Clara headed for the cartons. Opening the boxes was her favorite part of the job. She loved the smell of brand-new books, the colorful covers, and the smooth feel of them in her hands. Although she'd probably never read any of them since most of the titles were paranormal, just knowing that great adventures awaited their eager customers put a smile on her face.

She heard the door close behind Stephanie, then silence settled over the room. She pulled the first box toward her and reached for the box cutter on the shelf. Seconds later, she pulled back the flaps to reveal rows of flashy blue covers with a white-faced vampire snarling at her.

Blinking, she lifted one of the books for a closer look. The title screamed at her in red letters dripping with blood: *The Games Vampires Play*.

Clara shivered and took out another four of the books. Stephanie liked the books to be stacked five deep on the shelf, replacing them as they were sold. Clara dropped the books onto the rollaway carts they used to transfer the books from stockroom to aisles.

As she did so, she heard a faint scuffling in the corner of the room by the rear door. Skin prickling, she peered into the shadows but could see nothing but cartons, a vacuum cleaner, a box of cleaning supplies and a ladder.

She waited, muscles tensed to leap for the inner door if anything moved. All was still, and gradually she let her shoulders relax. Either she'd dreamed it, or the Raven's Nest was harboring mice.

She made a mental note to mention it to Stephanie. Mice ate books, didn't they? Or was that rats? Either way, she'd rather not come face-to-face with them. She started cutting open the cartons with a feverish speed, hauling books onto the rollaway until it was full. Then, with a last look over her shoulder, she opened the door and shoved the loaded cart out into the aisle.

———

Stephanie was waiting for Clara when she arrived at the bookstore the next day. She must have been watching from the window, since she met Clara on the doorstep with her coat collar turned up and a scarf wound around her head.

The bitter wind swirled dust and dried leaves around their feet as they walked back down the hill to the parking lot. "You could have called me from the car," Stephanie said as they crossed the lot to where Clara had parked her car.

"I need the exercise and fresh air." Clara pressed her key to open the doors. The car answered with a faint *beep* and the *click* of locks releasing.

Stephanie trudged around to the passenger side, raising her voice as the wind buffeted her face. "If the air gets any fresher, we'll be blown right off our feet."

Clara laughed as she slid onto her seat. "It's good for you. Cleans out your lungs," she said when Stephanie climbed in next to her.

"My lungs can manage perfectly well without a gale blowing down them." Stephanie pulled the scarf from her head, letting her fair hair billow around her face. "Where are we going first?"

"To the inn." Clara started the engine and pulled out of the parking lot. A half-dozen cars coasted down the street, and she followed them down toward the harbor. The row of souvenir shops and art galleries, which were so crowded in summer, were mostly deserted, with just a couple of brave souls wandering down the hill.

"You missed all the excitement this morning," Stephanie said as they turned onto the coast road. "Molly caught a mouse in the stockroom."

"So that's what I heard yesterday." Clara put some pressure on the gas pedal. "How did she catch it?"

"Well, it wasn't planned, exactly. She was backing away from it and smacked into the table, which was loaded with books. Some of the books fell off and the mouse must have panicked. It ran right into them."

"Ouch." Clara tried not to visualize what happened after that. "I hope you got rid of it."

"Wrapped it in a plastic bag and deposited it in the garbage."

"Poor thing."

"You wouldn't have said that if it had run over your foot."

Clara shuddered and concentrated on the road ahead. The inn lay farther up the coast road, a half mile or so before the construction site. On one side, the mountains, dotted with pines, rose stark against the sky. On the other side, the gray ocean churned up frothy waves to race onto smooth, empty beaches.

As Clara rounded the bend and saw the outline of Searock Inn in the distance, she muttered, "I don't have a good feeling about this."

Stephanie's voice was sharp when she answered. "The Sense is telling you that?"

"No, my own instincts. I think."

"Why? All we're doing is asking a few questions."

"About a murder. If Lionel Hampton is guilty, he's not going to be too happy to have us nosing around."

"In which case, you'll know and we can sic Dan on him."

Clara shot her a dark look. "You know it's not that easy."

Stephanie sighed. "I know, but I keep hoping the Sense will step in and tell you all we need to know so that we don't have to go around ruffling people's feathers."

"If I remember correctly, this was your idea in the first place."

"Maybe it was, but now that we're actually doing it, I have to admit I'm having second thoughts."

Clara gripped the wheel a little tighter. "We can always turn back. Let everyone think Scott's death was an accident. Maybe it would be better if Karen didn't know her husband was murdered."

Stephanie was quiet for so long, Clara thought she might actually agree. She really wasn't surprised, however, when her cousin said quietly, "You know we can't do that."

"Yes, I do." As if to convince herself, Clara pressed her foot farther down on the accelerator. The sooner they got this over with, the better.

It took several minutes to track down the owner of the Searock Inn. The quiet-spoken woman behind the front desk seemed reluctant to notify him that someone wanted to speak with him. She kept smoothing back a lock of her straight blonde hair from her forehead, while her startling blue eyes looked everywhere but directly at the cousins. "I don't know where he is," she insisted when Clara again asked to see him. "He's never in one place for very long."

"I assume he has a cell," Clara said, sounding a lot more confident than she felt. "Call him on that."

The blonde's gaze wandered up to the chandelier hanging over the entrance. "He doesn't like salespeople. You'll have to talk to the manager."

"We're not salespeople." Clara exchanged a glance

with a worried-looking Stephanie. "We're here on personal business."

The receptionist met Clara's gaze for the first time. "You're family?"

"Not exactly." Clara hesitated. "Look, just tell him that a couple of sympathizers want to talk to him."

Creases appeared in the young woman's forehead. "Sympathizers?"

"He'll know what that means."

With doubt written all over her face, the receptionist picked up the phone and dialed. Seconds later, a sour-faced man with a partially bald head and a beer belly hanging over his belt barreled through a rear door and charged into the foyer.

"Who are you and what do you want?" he barked, sending Stephanie back a nervous step or two.

Clara was happy to note she was taller than Lionel Hampton by at least two inches. Sometimes earning the high school nickname of "Lofty" had its advantages. "We'd like a private word with you, sir," she said, trying to sound forceful.

Lionel's gaze darted from her to Stephanie and back again. "What it's about?"

"It's about the construction on the bluff."

Clara's heart thumped as Lionel's brown eyes bore into hers. Finally, he nodded and beckoned as he turned away. "Come on."

Stephanie's face looked drawn as she followed her cousin behind the counter and through the rear door.

Lionel led them down a narrow hallway and into an office stuffed with papers, files, books and an assortment of coffee mugs scattered about the room. A globe on a stand, covered in cobwebs, stood in one corner. Apparently Lionel didn't have his office cleaned too often.

The owner grunted as he squeezed behind the desk in the corner and lowered himself onto a chair. "Now, what's this all about? I'm a busy man, so make it short."

Clara had rehearsed her speech the moment she'd climbed out of bed that morning. She'd learned from past experience that it helped to have her questions locked into her mind. That way, she could fire them off without giving the other person time to think too long about the answers.

"We're doing a survey of people's opinions," she said, giving Lionel an expansive smile. "I understand you're not in favor of the project."

Lionel's face was creased in suspicion. "So what?"

"We'd like to know your reasons."

Scowling, Lionel leaned forward, his fingers gripped together in front of him. "My reasons are the same as everyone else's in this town: we don't need the traffic, the congestion, the destruction of our scenic highway, or the problems a dump like that will create."

Clara widened her smile. "The resort can hardly be called a dump, Mr. Hampton. From what I hear, it will be a very upscale, expensive establishment, bringing lots of money into the town."

Lionel's dark brows drew together in a fierce line. "We

don't need that kind of money. Finn's Harbor has always done well and will go on doing all right without some fancy new resort taking over everything."

"Well, it seems that not everyone shares your views. The town council for one, and I'm sure the construction workers are happy they have a job in this economy."

Lionel made a sound of disgust deep in his throat. "They're a bunch of money-grabbing traitors, that's what they are. All they care about is their take-home pay. They don't care a damn about the damage they're doing up there."

"Is that why you had that argument with Scott Delwyn?"

Lionel stood up so suddenly, his chair crashed against the wall behind him. "What's that got to do with anything? Who the hell are you? Are you a cop? If so, where's your ID?"

Stephanie shot out of her chair and retreated to the door, while Clara got up more slowly. "I'm not the police, Mr. Hampton. I'm just a friend of Scott's wife, wanting to know what happened to him."

"He fell off the scaffolding, that's what happened to him." Lionel seemed to recover his former belligerence. "That's all I know, and all I'm going to say. Except maybe he was asking for it, strutting around that construction site like he owned the place. I wasn't the only one who got in his way. There were plenty of others."

In the act of turning away, Clara paused. "Like who?"

"Never you mind."

She held his gaze for a moment. "Are you suggesting that Scott's death wasn't an accident?"

"I never said no such thing." Lionel waved his arm at her. "Now, get out of here before I bring charges against you. Pretending to be taking a survey while all the time nosing into other people's business—that's got to be illegal."

Stephanie opened the door and darted out into the hallway.

Clara raised her chin. "I'm just a concerned citizen, trying to get at the truth." She spun around and crossed the room to follow her cousin.

Just as she reached the door, Lionel called out, "If I were you, lady, I'd stay out of things that don't concern you. People get hurt that way."

Clara shut the door behind her with a little more force than necessary. Following Stephanie down the hallway, she muttered, "He's a nasty piece of work. It wouldn't surprise me at all to find out he killed Scott Delwyn."

Once outside in the brisk salty air, she felt she could breathe again. Stephanie was already in the car when Clara reached it. She pulled open the door and climbed in next to her cousin.

"Boy," Stephanie said, reaching for her seat belt. "I thought he was going to call Dan and complain about us."

"He might still do that." Clara started the engine. "On the other hand, if he's got something to hide, he won't want to go whining to the police about us."

"How did you know he had an argument with Scott?"

"I didn't. The mayor said there'd been some fighting

up at the site, and since Lionel Hampton led a group of protestors, he'd be the logical one to confront Scott."

"Do you think he killed him?"

Clara shrugged. "I don't know, but he's right at the top of my list."

"The Sense didn't tell you anything back there?"

"Nope." Clara pulled out onto the coast road. "Guess we'll just have to rely on our own instincts."

Stephanie sank back on her seat. "Crap. I was hoping we'd strike gold on the first try."

"Well, maybe your teacher friend can tell us something helpful."

"I don't know him all that well." Stephanie sounded worried again.

"I thought you said he was Ethan's teacher."

"No, he teaches third grade. Ethan must have heard him talking about the environment at some point. I see Mr. Millstone now and then when I'm at the school, but I've never spoken to him."

"Well, now's your chance."

"Me? You want me to question him?"

"Well, you're the parent of kids who go to his school." Clara squinted as a ray of sun broke through the clouds. "It'll be easier for you to get in to see him."

"I don't see how. None of my kids have him for a teacher."

Clara sighed. "All right, we'll go in together and I'll do the talking. It would help, though, if you backed me up now and then."

"You always seem to manage fine without me. Besides, you're the one with the Sense."

Detecting an underlying resentment in her tone, Clara glanced at her cousin. Stephanie was gazing out the window, however, her expression bland. Deciding she must have imagined it, Clara concentrated on the task ahead.

She had questioned enough people over the past year or so that she was getting used to it. Still, she was fully aware that so far they'd been lucky. Although they'd met with hostility and suspicion now and then, they'd emerged without damage. That could end at any time, and she could only hope that wouldn't be the case with Mr. Josh Millstone.

4

"We should make it in time for morning recess," Clara said as she parked the car behind the school. "Otherwise we'll have to wait until lunchtime, and that would make me late for my shift at the bookstore."

"We won't have to wait. There's Mr. Millstone." Stephanie nodded at the play area, where kids ran around yelling at each other, while others stood in little groups, absorbed in whatever they were doing.

The guy Clara had seen the night of the meeting stood by the fence, reading a sheet of paper that flapped in the wind. He'd tied his hair back into a short ponytail, and his shoulders were hunched against the cold.

Thankful she didn't have to find an excuse to visit him inside the school, Clara approached the fence. When she spoke his name, Josh Millstone spun around, his eyes wide with surprise. He had dark freckles all over his face, and his eyebrows were so flimsy and fair they almost disappeared.

He looked at Clara as if she'd appeared out of the ground. "Can I help you?"

Clara dragged Stephanie closer to the fence. "This is my cousin, and her kids go to this school. Her eldest, Ethan Dowd, is a huge admirer of yours. He's always talking about your fight to protect the wildlife."

The teacher glanced across the playground, then at Stephanie. "I'm sorry. I'm not familiar with his name."

"Oh, he's not in your class," Stephanie said, looking flustered. "He just knows about your interest in the environment."

Josh seemed pleasantly surprised. "Really? So how can I help you?"

Clara smiled. "We just wanted to ask you about your protests up at the construction site on the bluff."

Now wariness crossed the teacher's face. "What about it?"

"Did you know Scott Delwyn?"

He didn't answer at first, but stared at Clara as if trying to figure out what she was getting at. Finally he said, "So that's what this is about. You think my protest group had something to do with his death?"

Clara met his gaze. "Did it?"

For another long moment he seemed about to explode in anger, then to Clara's surprise and relief, he laughed. "Nothing like coming straight to the point."

She shrugged. "Just asking."

"I thought Mr. Delwyn's death was an accident."

"We're just making sure, that's all."

"Aren't the cops supposed to do that?"

"Yes." Clara smiled at him again. "But you know as well as I do that no matter how good the cops are, sometimes they miss things."

His frown reappeared. "Are you saying it wasn't an accident?"

"We're not saying anything; just asking a few questions, that's all."

Josh nodded. "Well, okay. For what it's worth, I can assure you that none of my people would resort to violence of any kind. We'll protest, yes, and now and again we'll try to disrupt things if it helps to emphasize our cause, but violence?" He shook his head. "Not on our agenda. I'll vouch for everyone in the group on that. Besides, most of us were together the night Scott died. We all met in the diner before the meeting."

She couldn't be sure if he knew every one of his followers well enough to vouch for them, but he obviously thought he did. "I guess that's good enough for me. Thank you, Mr. Millstone. We appreciate you taking the time to talk to us."

"Yes, thank you," Stephanie added breathlessly, suddenly springing to life.

Josh raised his hand. "My pleasure. Say hi to your son."

"I will." Beaming, Stephanie stepped away from the fence.

Clara was about to follow her when Josh called out, "Oh, by the way. I don't know if this means anything, but if you're looking for someone with a grudge against Scott Delwyn, you might want to talk to Eddie Hatchett."

Clara blinked, trying to remember where she'd heard that name before. Then it dawned on her: he was the son of her mother's electrician. One of the men escorted from the meeting hall the other night. "Yes, I know he's upset about the project. Then again, so are a lot of people."

"He's more than upset." Josh moved closer to the fence and lowered his voice. "He was working at the construction site when Scott fired him for turning up to work drunk. I was there when Eddie threatened Scott. I can't remember exactly what he said, but it wasn't pretty."

Clara felt a stab of excitement. "Thanks! I'll check into it."

"Be careful. Guys like Eddie are usually all talk and no action, but you never know."

"I'll be careful." She waved at him and chased after Stephanie. Her cousin had reached the car and stood with the passenger door open, looking in her direction.

Clara sprinted across the parking lot to join her.

"You don't think he had anything to do with it?" Stephanie asked anxiously. "He seems like such a nice man. Ethan will be devastated if he turns out to be a killer."

"No, I don't think he's a killer." Once more, Clara slid in behind the wheel. "But he did give me a lead on someone else." She told her cousin what Josh had said about Eddie Hatchett. "His father is an electrician," she said, as she drove out into the street. "They were both in our house a month ago."

Stephanie frowned. "Eddie Hatchett. I know that name, but I can't think where I heard it."

"He and his father were the two guys yelling at the meeting the other night."

Stephanie seemed not to hear as she stared at the road ahead. "I know I heard it somewhere. Eddie Hatchett. I'm sure I know that name."

"Maybe you hired his father. Have you had any electrical work done lately?"

Stephanie shook her head. "George does most of that stuff. It pays to marry a handyman."

Clara grinned. "I bet it does."

"Ah!" Stephanie bounced on her seat. "I know where I heard Eddie's name."

"Where?"

"He's a good friend of Molly's ex-boyfriend. You know, Jason, the one with the motorbike? When Molly was going out with him, she was always talking about Eddie, and how he was a troublemaker and she wished Jason wouldn't hang out with him. Of course, Jason was no prize, either, but she couldn't see that. Not until she caught him cheating on her, anyway. I think—"

"So Molly knows Eddie Hatchett?"

"Yes, she does, but—" Stephanie gasped. "You're not thinking of asking her to question him, are you?"

"She just needs to talk to him and see if she can find out where he was on the night Scott died."

"That would mean we'd have to tell her we think Scott was murdered."

"Yep, I guess it does." Clara glanced at her cousin. "She's helped us before."

"I know; it's not that. I just wonder what reason we're going to give her for thinking that."

"Good question. I'll think of something."

"I don't know if we should ask her to question Eddie. He could be a killer. What if he attacked her? I'd never forgive myself if something bad happened to her."

"We'll have to make sure she meets him in a public place. I could go with her and just stay out of sight while she talks to him."

Stephanie made a face. "Like where and when?"

"I'll work on it."

Clara pulled up in front of the Raven's Nest a few minutes later. "I'll let you off here. I have to go shopping for dog food before I come back to work. I still have about an hour left. That should give me plenty of time to get done what I need to do."

Stephanie opened the car door. "Promise me you won't do anything risky on your own?"

Clara smiled. "I promise. I'm just going to do some shopping, that's all."

Stephanie nodded, then hurried into the bookstore without looking back.

Clara spent the next hour picking up food and treats for Tatters, and checking out the spring fashions in Finn's Harbor's one and only clothes store. She usually shopped in nearby Mittleford at the outlet center, but she rarely missed an opportunity to check out the latest styles at Jasmine's Boutique, most of which she couldn't afford.

She arrived back at the Raven's nest just as Stephanie was leaving. "We're busy in there," she said as Clara passed her in the doorway. "Molly's waiting for you."

"I'll call tonight." Without waiting to talk further, Clara headed for the counter.

Molly was arguing with John Halloran, a somewhat crotchety individual who now and again helped Rick in the hardware store.

John had once owned a candy store called the Sweet Spot farther down the street, but had ended up losing his business and his wife in the same year. He had never been a really cheerful man. Clara remembered him from when she and Stephanie visited his store as kids. Her cousin had been convinced John was an evil wizard, just waiting for a chance to turn them into toads.

Watching him now, Clara had to admit the elderly man did look a little forbidding, with his bowed shoulders, balding head and thick black-rimmed glasses. Years of disappointment and resentment had etched deep furrows in his forehead, and his cheeks sagged on either side of thin lips and a stubbly chin.

"We keep a file of everyone's orders on the computer," Molly said, raising her voice. "We put them in as soon as the customer gives it to us, so I couldn't have forgotten to order your book. You must have forgotten to ask for it."

"I did not forget," John said, his voice gruff with annoyance. "You young people today don't know how to run a store. In my day—"

Clara decided it was time to butt in. "Can I help you, John?"

He turned, pale eyes glaring through the smudged lenses of his glasses. "This girl doesn't know what she's doing. I ordered Paul Wiley's latest book two months ago and now she's telling me I didn't order it." He glared at Molly again. "But I *did*."

"Well, I'm sure we can find you a copy," Clara began, but he interrupted her with a swift flap of his hand.

"No, you can't. It's all sold out, which is precisely why I ordered it in the first place." He sent another glowering glance at Molly. "It *always* sells out."

Clara walked behind the counter and pulled up the file on the computer. "I see we've ordered more copies. They should be here by the beginning of next week. I'll make sure we have a copy for you." She smiled at him. "I'll even give you a call when it comes in. I'm sorry you have to wait for it."

"Not your fault." John tugged up the collar of his coat to cover the back of his neck. "It's *her* fault. I distinctly remember asking her to put in an order for me." With a parting lethal glance at Molly, he turned and stomped out of the store.

"I know I would have put the order in if he'd asked me," Molly said, sounding close to tears.

"Don't worry. John's getting old. He gets confused a

lot." Clara finished making a note to hold a copy of the Wiley book for John and closed out the file. "He's a good customer, though, which is why we put up with him."

"I know. The customer's always right." Molly heaved a noisy sigh. "Sometimes it's hard to remember that."

Clara grinned. "Why don't you go grab a mug of coffee? I can handle things for a bit."

Molly's frown disappeared. "Thanks. I could use one right now." She took off, disappearing down the center aisle.

Clara spared a brief thought to how she would approach the subject of Molly's help, then had to forget it as customers began lining up at the counter.

It was an hour or so before the store emptied out and Clara finally had a few moments to take a break. She found Molly in the Reading Nook, tidying up a stack of magazines that had been scattered all over the tables.

Pouring herself a cup of coffee, Clara said casually, "How would you like to help Stephanie and me catch another killer?"

Molly paused, a magazine dangling from her fingers. "Really? Cool!" Then her expression changed. "Wait a minute. Who got killed?"

"Scott Delwyn."

"But I thought that was an accident."

"Officially it is, which is why we have to be careful."

Molly's eyes widened. "You think someone killed him?"

"I think it's possible. Stephanie and I want to look into it, just in case."

To Clara's relief, Molly was so thrilled to be included in the investigation, she didn't ask for details. "You two should open up a detective agency," she said as Clara carried her coffee over to an armchair and sat down.

Clara laughed. "Thanks, but that'd be a little too much excitement for me. I don't know why we keep getting caught up in this stuff, anyway. It always seems like a good idea at the time."

"Because you and Stephanie are great at it." Molly dropped the magazines on a table and sank onto the adjacent armchair. "That's why you should open up an agency."

"I think we've got our hands full enough with the bookstore." Clara took a sip of her coffee and set the mug down on a side table.

"So what do you want me to do?"

Clara hesitated, then decided that as long as she accompanied Molly, their assistant would be safe enough. "You know Eddie Hatchett, right?"

Molly raised her eyebrows. "Eddie? Yes, I know him. He's a buddy of Jason's." She gasped. "You think he killed Scott? I'm not really surprised. I never liked him. He's a mean dude. He's always, like, arguing with someone over something. I could never understand why Jason hung out with him."

"We don't know, yet, if anyone killed Scott," Clara said quickly. "We're just asking questions, that's all. Finding out where people were that night and what they were doing. Eddie is just a name on a long list of suspects.

There are an awful lot of people who hate the construction on the bluff and any one of them could have let their temper get out of control."

"Enough to kill?" Molly frowned. "Didn't they say that Scott fell off the scaffolding? I can't imagine too many people would climb up there just to have an argument."

"We think it's possible someone killed Scott and then pushed him off the scaffolding to make it look like he fell."

Clara waited, hoping Molly wouldn't ask too many questions.

"So," she said at last, "you don't really know for sure."

"I guess we just want to make certain that it really was an accident. Eddie was heard arguing with Scott and threatening him. That's why he's on our list."

She let out her breath when Molly nodded. "Okay. So what can I do to help?"

"I was hoping you could talk to Eddie and find out where he was that evening. According to the police report, Scott died soon after his shift ended, around six or so. If Eddie has an alibi for that time, we can cross him off the list."

Molly stared down at her hands. "I really don't like the guy. I haven't talked to Jason in months. I don't even know if Eddie still hangs out with him."

"I know it's a lot to ask." Clara paused, choosing her words carefully. "It's important, Molly. Eddie knows you. He's a lot more likely to talk to you than me. We'll have to try and catch him in a public place, and I'll be with you. Just out of sight, that's all."

"Well, that's easy." Molly looked up, her face still creased in doubt. "If Eddie is still hanging with Jason, they'll be at the pool table in the Laurel Street Tavern. They used to go there every Friday night."

Clara winced. "Oh please, not that place again. The last time we were there, we almost got into a brawl."

Molly grinned. "I remember. Some dude got all twisted because you were questioning his girlfriend."

"And what about the biker-babe manager who was all set to throw us out of there?"

"And the female wrestler waiting on tables?"

They both laughed, though Clara didn't feel at all like laughing. Just the thought of going back to that tavern gave her hives. "Well," she said reluctantly, "it's Friday. What are you doing tonight?"

Molly crossed her arms. "I think I'm going to pay a visit to the Laurel Street Tavern. How about you?"

"Sounds like a good idea."

"What about Stephanie? Is she coming, too?"

Remembering how close they'd come to getting into trouble the last time, Clara doubted it. "I'll ask her," she said, "but it's not always easy for her to get out. When you've got three kids and a husband to take care of, last-minute invitations are out of the question."

"I know." Molly sighed. "Kind of puts me off the idea of marriage."

As she got up from her seat, Clara patted her assistant's

arm. "You'll change your mind when you meet the right guy."

"How come you're not married?" Molly reached for the pile of magazines and stood. "Or is that a rude question?"

Clara managed a smile. "Just never met the right guy, I guess."

"What about Rick Sanders?"

Luckily Molly was walking away from her and couldn't see the expression that Clara knew had crossed her face. "What about him?"

"I thought you two were getting cozy." Molly looked back over her shoulder. "He's a hunk. I'd grab him before Roberta gets her claws in him."

Clara made a face. Roberta Prince owned the stationer's next door, and had made no secret of the fact that she intended to snag Rick for her next husband. She'd actually purchased the store just so she could be on his doorstep every day.

The fact that Rick wasn't too thrilled with her interest didn't seem to bother her. In fact, Roberta took it as a challenge, and was always scheming to find ways to spend time with him. She was a formidable opponent, consistently dressed in the latest fashions with perfect hair and makeup. She could put down the toughest critic with her sharp tongue, and never missed an opportunity to take a verbal swipe at Clara.

"I'm not worried about Roberta." Clara picked up her mug and carried it over to the sink. "Rick would never get involved with someone like her. She sounds too much like his ex-wife."

"Ooh, he's talked to you about her?" Molly spun around. "What did he tell you?"

Wishing she'd kept her mouth shut, Clara shrugged. "Not much. It was mostly when she gave him Tatters. He made a couple of comments that made me think of Roberta, that's all. He never talks about his marriage."

"Did they have any kids?"

"No, they weren't married that long." Uncomfortable with the way the conversation was going, Clara added, "I'd better get into the stockroom. I want to unpack a few more boxes before you leave."

Molly glanced at the clock. "Well, you still have a couple of hours."

"Call me if you need help." Clara escaped to the stockroom, thankful for once to be alone where no one could ask her awkward questions.

After making sure the door was closed, she flipped open her cell and thumbed Stephanie's number.

Her cousin answered on the second ring. "Is something wrong?"

Clara rolled her eyes. Stephanie wasn't happy unless she was worrying about something. "Everything's fine here. I just called to let you know that Molly and I are going to the Laurel Street Tavern tonight and wondered if you'd like to tag along."

Stephanie's disgust came through loud and clear. "Why on earth would you want to go there?"

"Molly thinks Eddie Hatchett will be there with Jason."

"Oh." Her tone lightened. "I'd love to come, but I don't know if I can get away. Not without a good excuse."

"Okay, I just thought I'd ask. I know how you hate to be left out of things."

"Oh, I *do*." Her voice had become a wail. "Let me see what I can do. What time are you going?"

"Right after I leave here. Around eight fifteen."

"Right. Save me a seat just in case. That place is probably packed on a Friday night."

Thinking of the clientele they'd run into the last time they were there, Clara shuddered. "You're right. We may be standing at the bar."

"It only gets better." From somewhere in the distance, a high-pitched yell echoed down the line. "Oh, crap. That's Michael. He's probably fighting with Olivia again." Her voice sounded farther away as she yelled, "Olivia! Michael! Quit that. *Right now!* Gotta go," she added into the phone. "Hope I see you tonight."

The line clicked, and Clara closed her cell with a rueful grin. Her conversations with her cousin were constantly being interrupted by Stephanie's youngest two kids. Ethan, the eldest, couldn't be more different that Michael and Olivia. He rarely spoke, preferring to communicate via the computer or texting on the smartphone his parents had reluctantly given him last Christmas. Clara adored all three of them, even though her visits to her cousin's house tended to be unpredictable and sometimes exhausting.

She opened up a book carton, wondering how she would cope if she had three kids. Sometimes it was all she could do to keep up with Tatters, what with walks, feeding and watering, and keeping him quiet so as not to disturb her mother when all he wanted to do was romp around and bark for attention.

Smiling, she tried to imagine herself in a park, watching three toddlers while Tatters bounced back and forth barking at everything that moved. When Rick Sanders walked into the picture, however, she quickly shut off the image. She definitely wasn't ready for that. Not now, maybe not ever.

5

Stephanie's idea of a quiet evening was anywhere without her kids. Even the tavern, where rock bands blasted music so loud everyone had to shout to be heard, would be more bearable than the screaming match between her two youngest offspring.

Michael, it seemed, had taken Olivia's video game and hidden it somewhere. Olivia kept yelling at him to give it back, and Michael kept insisting he'd forgotten where he'd hidden it.

Stephanie took the two of them into the kitchen so that George could watch the news in peace. After prying Olivia's pigtail from Michael's fingers, Stephanie bent down until her face was level with his. "Now, Michael, you will tell me where you hid Olivia's game."

Michael's eyes filled with tears. "Don't remember."

"I'll make you remember," Olivia said, her voice low and fierce.

She lunged at the boy, and Stephanie grabbed her daughter, hauling her backward. "I will handle this, Olivia. Stay put and don't move." She turned back to her son. "If you can't find the game, you will have to buy another one for your sister out of your allowance."

Tears rolled down his cheeks, and Stephanie had to steel herself against the urge to hug him. "I spent my allowance."

"Then you'll have to save every week until you have enough to buy another game."

"That'll take *weeks*," Olivia protested. "I can't wait weeks for my game. I want it *now*!"

"Then you'll have to help him find it." Stephanie gave the little boy a stern look. "Now, Michael, think. Where are your favorite hiding places?"

Michael started muttering something unintelligible.

Olivia suddenly shrieked, making Stephanie jump. "You put my game in the washing machine?"

Stephanie rolled her eyes. "Wait here. I'll go and look." She started for the door, then paused to look back. "Don't either of you move one inch or speak one word until I get back." Hoping that was enough to hold them, she flew into the laundry room and opened up the washer. The video game lay at the bottom of the drum. Muttering to herself, Stephanie hooked it out and took it back to the kitchen.

Neither child had moved, though Olivia's face was red with temper and Michael was staring at his feet.

"Here. Take it and go." Stephanie handed the game to her daughter, who took it and with a last, sinister glare at her brother, fled from the room.

Stephanie crossed her arms. "That was very bad of you to take your sister's game. No TV for you tomorrow."

The boy's face crumpled. "But it's *Saturday*. My favorite shows are on."

"You should have thought of that before you took Olivia's game. If I'd done the wash early this week, it would have been ruined. You have to take responsibility for your actions, Michael. Now go to your room."

Bursting into a flood of tears, Michael rushed out the door. She could hear him crying all the way to his room, until the door slammed and peace was restored once more.

George looked up when she walked into the living room. "What was that all about?"

"The usual. Michael took something of Olivia's and hid it. I don't know why that boy torments his sister like that."

"Probably in retaliation for something she did to him."

Stephanie sat down on the edge of the couch. "Were you mean to your sisters when you were his age?"

George looked at her from under lowered eyelids. "I was terrified of my sisters. I kept out of their way."

Stephanie grinned. "Coward."

"Guilty as charged."

She took a deep breath. "Now that I've restored order in the house, would you mind if I popped out for an hour or so?"

He looked surprised but said mildly, "Of course not. As long as you're not chasing after men. Or murderers."

Her stab of guilt made her cough. "Honey, you know you're the only man in the world who could interest me."

He gave her a look that made her wonder if he could possibly read her mind. "Unless, of course, he happens to have killed someone, then you'd be all over him."

"Well, I'm certainly not expecting to find a killer tonight." She got up, telling herself that wasn't really a lie. "I'm just going to have a beer with Molly and Clara."

"Somebody's birthday?"

"Nope, just a girl's night out."

"Okay, then. Go ahead. You deserve a break."

A sudden rush of warmth propelled her over to his chair. Flinging her arms around him, she murmured, "I'm the luckiest wife in the world. I won't be late."

"Just don't come home drunk."

She drew back in mock horror. "Have you ever known me to come home drunk?"

"There's always a first time." He planted a kiss on her nose. "Slightly tipsy would be okay. Could make things interesting."

"Just like a man. Only one thing on his mind." She tripped over to the door. "See you later, then."

He raised a hand at her, then settled down on his chair to watch the rest of the news.

Feeling decidedly guilty, she checked on all three kids, then slipped into her coat and walked through the house to the garage. What was it she'd said to Michael? *You have to take responsibility for your actions.* She could only hope that she wouldn't have to eat those words before the night was over.

———

Clara had just finished closing up the store and was pulling on her coat when Molly walked in, carrying something that smelled wonderful. "Pizza," she said, holding up the carton. "I remembered the greasy-looking food they had at the tavern, and last time we went you didn't get to eat until really late, so I thought you might want something this time to like, soak up the beer."

Clara grinned. "Good thinking. Thanks! The beer's on me tonight. Share this with me?"

"I already ate." Molly laid the carton on the counter. "You can eat it in the car while I drive us over there. I parked outside, so we'd better get going before I get ticketed."

She led the way out the door, and Clara flicked off the lights, shivering as a cold blast of wind whipped her face.

Munching on the pizza as Molly drove a little too fast for comfort down the narrow streets, Clara hoped the evening would turn out to be less nerve-racking than their last visit. The tavern was on the outskirts of town, and had the dubious reputation of being a hotbed for trouble.

According to what she'd heard, fistfights were common, and belligerent drunks had to be hustled out of there on a weekly basis. Having seen some of the customers that patronized the place, Clara could readily believe the rumors.

She was relieved when she and Molly found an empty

table in a corner by a window. Not exactly secluded but a lot less conspicuous than the table from their previous tavern trip. The familiar odor of beer and sweat seemed even more potent than last time. The wooden floor seemed to vibrate with the thump of bass guitars, and the garbled wave of voices rose in competition.

The same server who had waited on them before strode over to the table, her tattooed arms bulging beneath the tight sleeves of her red T-shirt. Her bleached hair stood up in spikes all over her head. She looked as if she'd stuck her finger into a live electric socket.

Clara ordered two beers, and the woman grunted something as she scribbled on a pad, then took off across the room to the bar.

Molly giggled and raised her voice to be heard above the din. "I remember Stephanie calling her Miss America." She slipped off her coat and draped it over the back of her chair. "Is she coming tonight?"

"She said she'd try." Clara took her coat off, taking a good look around the room. "Can you see Jason anywhere? Or Eddie Hatchett?"

Molly shook her head. "If they're here, they'll be in the pool room at the back. I'll have to go over there and take a look."

They were shouting to hear each other. Even then, Clara could barely catch Molly's words. "Let's wait until we've got our beer. Maybe we'll get lucky and you'll see them come out of there."

"That's if they're here at all."

"Just be careful, okay? From what I've seen of Eddie, he can be really vicious."

Molly gave her a weak grin. "I'm not worried about him, although he is pretty awful. It's Jason. I just hope he doesn't go all ballistic on me. He was really steamed when I broke up with him."

Clara felt bad for her. "I'm sorry, Molly. Maybe I shouldn't have asked you to do this."

"No, it's okay. It's been a few months. He's probably all over me by now." Her face brightened. "There's Stephanie!"

Surprised to see her cousin, Clara waved to get her attention.

Stephanie caught sight of them, jiggled her hand in response and hurried over to the table. "I don't remember it being this noisy," she yelled, sliding onto the empty chair. "I can't hear myself think."

"You get used to it after a while." Clara noticed the server battling her way through the tables toward them, a tray balanced on her hand. "Here comes our beer. You want beer or wine?"

"Beer, I guess." Stephanie looked around. "Any sign of Eddie Hatchett?"

Clara shook her head.

Molly got to her feet. "I'll check out the pool room."

Clara got up, too. "I'll come with you."

"No, it'll be better if I go alone."

"I'll wait for you at the door."

Again Molly shook her head. "I'll be fine. Really. Just enjoy your beer and I'll be back in a little while."

She left, dodging between tables and people, her red hair making her stand out in the crowd.

Clara watched Molly go, uneasiness gnawing at her stomach. "I don't like her going in there by herself. We should be there with her."

Stephanie flapped a hand at her. "Sit down. She'll be fine. Jason adores her. He won't let anything happen to her."

"He might have adored her once, but now they're broken up, who knows what he's thinking."

"You worry too much." She smiled at the server, who was dumping two glasses of beer on the table. Froth ran down the sides of the glasses and formed little puddles on the table.

"Wanna tab?" The server transferred a wad of chewing gum with her tongue to the other side of her mouth and poised her pen over her pad.

"No, I'll pay." Clara fished in her purse for her wallet. "I'd like another beer for my friend, please." She handed the server a twenty.

"You want me to take it out of this?"

"Yes, please."

"I'll bring your change with the beer." The server took off, shoving a scruffy-looking man aside as she barged between the tables.

Stephanie said something Clara didn't hear. She leaned forward. "What?"

"I said, good luck with that."

Clara picked up her beer. "Take Molly's beer. She can have the one I ordered."

Stephanie reached for the glass. "I hope all this is worth it. This stuff tastes like cat's pee."

Clara sent an anxious glance at the spot she'd last seen Molly. "If she's not back soon, I'm going after her."

"What?"

Clara shouted it again.

Stephanie frowned. "We'll both go. Give her a few more minutes."

Tired of shouting everything, Clara leaned back and nursed her beer, her gaze fixed in the direction of the pool room.

Seconds ticked by without any sign of Molly returning. The server appeared out of the crowd with a loaded tray, slammed a glass of beer on the table, dropped a couple of bills in front of Clara and disappeared into the mob again.

Clara shifted around on her chair, trying to get a better look at the door to the pool room. She could hear voices raised in argument from across the room. Putting her glass down on the table, she shot to her feet. "I'm not waiting any longer. I'm going to see what's happening in there."

"Wait, I'm coming with you." Stephanie started to get up, then paused. "Wait, what about the coats? Are we just going to leave them here? What if they get stolen?"

Clara pulled hers off the back of the chair. "We'll take

them with us. Grab Molly's, too, and bring it with you." She headed off to toward the rear of the bar without waiting for her cousin.

She was halfway across the room when a muscular arm shot out in front of her, grabbing her around the waist. A bearded face grinned at her, the eyes bloodshot and bleary. "Hey, pretty lady, what's your hurry?"

Clara came to an abrupt halt. Pushing her face up close to his, she tried not to breathe in the toxic fumes of whiskey. "Get your hands off me, or I'll knee you where it hurts the most."

The guy dropped his arm and stepped back, his hands in the air. "Whoa, lady, take it easy. I meant no harm."

She wasted no more time on him, but plunged through the crowd, hoping Stephanie was close by. Finally reaching the door of the pool room, she turned to see if her cousin was there. Stephanie was right behind her, a huge grin on her face.

"Whatever did you say to him?" She jerked a thumb over her shoulder. "He looked as if he'd been bitten by a snake."

Clara shook her head. "Never mind him. Let's find out what happened to Molly." She shoved open the door and stepped into the pool room.

There were three tables, all with people standing around them. The lights had been dimmed and it was hard to distinguish faces. Clara was still scanning the room when Stephanie gave her a nudge.

"There's Molly over there."

Clara followed her cousin's nod. She saw Molly at the far table talking to a guy she recognized from the meeting the other night: Eddie Hatchett. A tall, dark-haired young man stood on the other side of Molly, his gaze fixed on her face.

"That's Jason next to her," Stephanie said just as Molly turned to leave.

Jason grabbed Molly's arm, pulling her back.

All of Clara's instincts went on alert, but after a moment or two, Molly pulled herself free and marched across the floor toward the door. Catching sight of the cousins, she gave them a quick shake of her head.

"Come on," Stephanie muttered. "Let's meet her outside."

She opened the door, letting in a blast of noise as Clara followed her back into the bar. Glancing over her shoulder, she was reassured to see Molly following them across the room. To Clara's relief, there was no sign of the bearded guy who'd grabbed her earlier.

Reaching their table, which by a miracle was still open, Stephanie threw the coats across the backs of the chairs. Molly joined them, and immediately picked up her glass and took a few swallows of the beer.

"Are you okay?" Clara peered anxiously into Molly's face. "Jason didn't hurt you or anything?"

Molly shook her head, took another swig of beer and sat down. "He wanted us to get back together. I told him no."

Stephanie sat down next to her. "What about Eddie Hatchett? Did he tell you anything?"

Molly nodded. "Let's get out of here. I can't hear myself think."

Abandoning the rest of their beer, they made their way to the door and out into the chilly darkness.

Leaning against Molly's car, Clara let out her breath on a long sigh. "I hope we don't have to go there again. I hate that place."

Stephanie buttoned her coat and turned up the collar. "Me, too." She turned to Molly. "Tell us what Eddie Hatchett said."

Molly shivered. "Let's get in the car. It'll be warmer in there." She unlocked the doors and the cousins scrambled inside.

Turning on the engine, Molly sighed. "That's better. My ears are still ringing from all that noise."

Stephanie leaned forward from the backseat. "Okay, so spill it."

Molly turned so she could look at both cousins. "You can take him off your list of suspects. He was in the ER in Mittleford the night Scott died. Apparently Eddie started working with his father when he got fired from the construction site. He was on his way home on his bike around five thirty that night. It was getting dark and he hit the curb going around the corner. He fell off and sprained his wrist. His called his girlfriend, Stacey, and she drove him to the hospital."

Clara frowned. "Do you think he was telling the truth?"

Molly shrugged. "I guess so. His wrist is all bandaged up."

"Do you know this Stacey?"

"I've seen her a couple of times, that's all."

"Oh, well, I guess that gives us one less suspect." Clara gazed out the window. Mist swirled around the streetlamp, casting an eerie orange glow against the night sky. "Looks like it's back to the drawing board."

Stephanie laughed, though it sounded a little hollow. "You really didn't think it was that easy, did you?"

Molly looked from one to the other. "Are you two sure about this? I mean, about someone killing Scott? It could have just been an accident, like they said, right?"

Stephanie gave Clara a look that clearly asked, *What did you tell her*?

Clara cleared her throat. "Look, Molly, all we can say is that we have good reason to believe that Scott was murdered. We can't tell you any more than that right now. We're just asking you to trust us, and not to say anything to anyone about our suspicions, okay?"

Molly nodded so hard a thick hank of her red hair fell across her forehead. She tossed it back with a flick of her head, saying earnestly, "Of course I trust you both. I want to help as much as I can. If Karen's husband was murdered, I want to see the killer in jail. Which reminds me, the funeral is tomorrow afternoon. Are you both going?"

Stephanie gasped. "Is it that soon? I didn't know." She raised her chin and stared at the roof of the car for a moment. "I think we should close the bookstore for the afternoon, so that we can all go. I'm sure our customers will understand."

Molly smiled. "That's nice. The service is at two o'clock, at Marlowe's Funeral Home."

"I'll be there." Stephanie glanced at her watch. "Guess I'd better be getting back. See you two tomorrow."

"I'll get to the store early," Clara promised as her cousin climbed out of the car, "since we're closing for the afternoon."

"Thanks." Stephanie waved a good-bye and headed off to her car.

"Wait until she's heading out," Clara said, as Molly slid the gear into drive. "I want to be sure she's on her way."

Molly gave her an odd look. "What are you afraid of?"

"I don't know." Clara hunched her shoulders. "I just don't trust some of those guys in there."

Moments later, Stephanie's car pulled away from the curb, and Clara could relax again. Molly chattered all the way back to the bookstore, but Clara listened with only half an ear, murmuring an answer now and then when it seemed necessary.

Her mind was on her vision and the two people struggling on the scaffolding with the body of Scott Delwyn between them. How she wished she could have seen their faces. The darkness and the rain had made it difficult to see much at all. She couldn't say now if they were short or tall, thin or fat.

She closed her eyes, seeing again the shadowy figures heaving the body over the edge to the ground below. Deep in concentration, she jumped violently when Molly spoke.

"Are you okay? You're awfully quiet."

"Oh, yes, I'm fine." She managed a light laugh. "Just tired, I guess."

"So what are we going to do now? Look for another suspect?"

Clara hesitated, reluctant to get Molly any further involved in what could very well be a wild-goose chase. After all, the Sense hadn't been too reliable in the past. Even as she thought it, she was dismissing the doubts. She knew what she'd seen.

She'd been there, on that scaffolding, watching a murder unfold. Whether Scott Delwyn had been unconscious or dead when he was shoved off, those two people were responsible for depriving two little girls of a father, and a young woman had lost her husband.

She was probably the only one, besides the killers, who really knew the truth and nothing or nobody was going to get in her way, Clara vowed, until they were safely behind bars.

6

The following afternoon, Molly and the cousins sat near the rear of the room in the funeral home, listening to the glowing and sometimes tearful remembrances of Scott Delwyn. It was hard for all in attendance. Molly had tears running down her cheeks, and Stephanie kept dabbing at her eyes with a tissue.

Clara managed to hold her emotions in check, though she ached with sadness for the weeping widow and her young girls. Scott, it seemed, was well-liked in the community, judging by the number of people present at the service. Neither Lionel Clapham nor Josh Millstone had chosen to join the mourners, which really didn't surprise her. Neither one of them had shown much regret over Scott's death.

After the service and burial, everyone was invited back

to the widow's house for a celebration of Scott's life. Clara would rather have gone home from the cemetery, but Stephanie and Molly wanted to go to the reception, and not wanting to appear unsociable, Clara tagged along.

Standing in the crowded living room, Clara listened to Stephanie and Molly making small talk with a couple of the bookstore's customers. Now and again she managed to get a word or two into the conversation, but after a while she became restless. Chatting with comparative strangers was never her strong point, and she longed to be out of there and home with Tatters.

Some of the men in the room could possibly have been Scott's coworkers. If so, she would have liked to talk to them. Since Scott died as he was finishing up his shift, one of those guys must have been the last person to see him alive. If she could figure out who that was, she might be able to find out something helpful.

She was tempted to go around asking questions, but somehow this didn't seem the right time or place. Besides, the last thing she wanted was for Karen to find out her husband had been murdered.

Deciding that her questions would have to wait, she managed to signal to her cousin that she was leaving and started edging to the door. As she passed the kitchen, she spotted Karen, standing by herself in front of the sink, looking out the window. Scott's widow looked lost, staring into space as if unaware of all the commotion going on around her.

So far Clara had avoided talking to her, worried that she would say the wrong thing and arouse the woman's suspicions. She could hardly leave, however, without saying something to the grieving widow. Reminding herself to monitor her words, she walked into the kitchen.

Karen must have heard her footsteps, and she turned around, her eyes red and puffy from weeping. "Clara, it was good of you to come." She held out her hands. "Thank you."

Clara nodded, and grasped the cold hands in hers. "I'm so very sorry," she said quietly. "I know it sounds trite, but if there's anything I can do. . ."

"Thank you," Karen said quickly, pulling her hands from Clara's fingers. "We'll be fine. We have to make some adjustments, of course. The girls—" Her voice broke, and she swallowed, tears once more spilling down her cheeks.

A fierce stab of fury took Clara's breath away. Whoever did this deserved to be hung, drawn and quartered. She put an arm around Karen's shaking shoulders. "Call me if you need help. In any way. I mean that sincerely."

"I know you do." Karen tugged a tissue from her pocket and dabbed her eyes. "Stephanie, too. You're both good friends."

Afraid she'd bawl if she stayed, Clara gave her a tight nod and hurried out of the kitchen. Blinded by tears, she smacked full tilt into a short, tubby woman, almost sending her to the floor.

"I'm so sorry!" Angry with herself, she peered down at the woman, who was straightening her glasses. "Are you all right?"

"Sure I am, honey!" The woman smiled, baring tiny

white teeth. "I have plenty of padding to help me bounce right back."

Clara couldn't help smiling.

"I'm Thelma Hogan," the woman added, crinkling her forehead. "I don't think we've met."

"Clara Quinn." She held out her hand and it was immediately squeezed by thick, warm fingers. "Are you a relative of Karen's?"

"Oh, no." The woman's gray curls bounced as she shook her head. "We live next door. Me and my son, that is." She flicked her fingers at the middle of the room. "That's Ray, over there. Making a pig of himself, as usual. I don't know how that man eats so much and stays so thin."

Clara followed the gesture and saw the back of a lean man with a dark ponytail at the refreshment table.

Before she could comment, Thelma added, "Such a dreadful shame about Scott. He was such a nice man." She shook her head, her face lined with sorrow. "He was always offering to do things for me. Real clever with his hands, he was. Not like my son." She tossed her head in the direction of the table. "Useless when it comes to fixing things. He's out of work and has the time. Just doesn't have the know-how. I don't know what we're going to do now that Scott's gone. We can't afford to pay repairmen, not with what they charge nowadays."

Clara nodded in sympathy, feeling more uncomfortable by the minute. She could tell that Thelma loved to talk, and Clara was in no mood to listen to a stranger's life story.

She made a big production of glancing at her watch. "Wow, is that the time? I'd better get going." She smiled at the woman. "Nice talking to you."

Thelma, it seemed, having snagged a listener, wasn't ready to let her go. She beamed up at Clara. "Are you a friend of Karen's?"

Eying the door, Clara figured she'd have to shove the woman aside to get there. Right now Karen's neighbor was wedged between a group of people and a big-screen TV. Hoping someone would move, and soon, Clara murmured, "Karen's a regular customer at the Raven's Nest bookstore, where I work."

Thelma's eyes lit up. "Oh, I know where that is. Right at the top of the hill on Main Street, right? There's a knitting shop across the street a little ways down."

Clara nodded.

"Yes, well, I haven't been inside your store. I don't read much. Prefer to watch TV. A lot less hard work." She laughed, a deep-throated gurgle that shook her body. Then the amusement on her face vanished, to be replaced by sadness again. "Scott fixed my TV when it broke down. Didn't cost me a dime. He was in my house the day before he died, fixing my dishwasher." She shook her head again, making her curls bounce once more. "He was a good soul. I'm going to miss him, that's for sure."

Clara caught sight of Stephanie watching her from across the room and pulled a face. Her cousin caught on at once and started toward her.

"It's been really nice talking to you," she said quickly as Thelma opened her mouth to say something else. "I really have to run now. I hope you find someone else to fix your appliances."

Stephanie arrived at her side and took hold of her arm. "What are you still doing here? I thought you'd left ages ago."

"I'm just leaving." Clara nodded at Thelma. "I've been talking to Karen's neighbor. This is Thelma . . . I'm sorry, I forgot your last name."

"Hogan." The woman beamed at Stephanie.

"This is my cousin, Stephanie Dowd. She owns the Raven's Nest bookstore."

Again the woman's face lit up. "Really? We were just talking about that. I was just saying . . ."

Clara saw a space open up as someone from the group in front of them left. "I'll call you later," she said, and before her cousin had a chance to answer, she slipped through the crowd and out of the door.

Tatters was waiting for her as usual when she arrived home, and the wet and furry welcome chased away her depression. Jessie had left a note to say she had gone out to dinner, and had left a salad in the fridge.

Clara found the plate of greens loaded with hard-boiled egg, ham and cheese and carried it into the living room. Switching on the TV with the remote, she tuned into the local news and settled back to watch.

Halfway through the program, the anchor mentioned Scott Delwyn's funeral. At the end of the brief account, he added that the construction site where Scott had worked had passed the inspection and the crew expected to report to work on Monday.

Clara stared moodily at the screen as the cameras switched to the sports announcer. So that was the end of it. Scott Delwyn was dead and buried, and everything was going to go back to normal. How normal would it be for Karen and the girls? How could anything be normal for them again?

She finished her salad, only half listening to the weather forecast. It was the end of February. She didn't need a weather expert to tell her there was still a month of winter left. Tatters whined and got up from the rug where he'd been lying ever since she'd sat down.

She looked him in the eye and he wagged his tail. "What's the matter, boy? Want to go out?"

What do you think?

She put down her plate with a grunt of disgust. "Don't *do* that! It's unnerving."

Tatters slowly waved his tail back and forth, and she felt bad. He didn't know she could read his mind. Or even if he did, it wasn't his fault she had the stupid Sense. She got up and carried her plate out into the kitchen.

A glass of wine sounded good, but first she needed to get out of the house and give both herself and the dog a breath of fresh air. Tatters waited eagerly by the front door as she dragged her coat on again and wound a scarf around her neck.

"Come on, then." She opened the door and Tatters shot

through it, only to be brought up short when she yelled at him. "You know I have to put your leash on, or you'll be under the wheels of someone's car." She fastened the leash, and was nearly pulled off her feet as Tatters leapt forward. "Wait!"

He paused, looked back at her, then set off at a quick trot. Following behind him, past lawns shriveled by frost and trees barren of leaves, she thought about the news anchor's words. The construction crew was going back to work on Monday. Next week would be a good time to question some of the guys who worked with Scott.

She made a mental note to talk to Stephanie about it, then put it all out of her mind. Right now she needed some breathing space. All she wanted to think about was how to keep up with a determined dog that seemed intent on breaking all speed records on his way to the beach.

Clara enjoyed Sundays in the bookstore, despite the fact that she was there on her own. When she'd agreed to work for Stephanie, she'd also agreed to take just one day off a week, thus giving her cousin Sundays off to be with her family. Molly had Sundays and Mondays off, and Clara took Tuesday as her day off. The arrangement seemed to work well, since early in the week was usually quiet in the store.

Sundays, on the other hand, kept Clara busy most of the day, and that's how she liked it. It was a short day. She opened at noon and closed at five, and the time quickly passed. This Sunday, however, for some reason was unusually quiet.

After tidying and stocking the shelves, Clara decided to unpack some more books, leaving the door open so she could hear the front doorbell. She had just opened the first crate when she heard the faint jingling from the front of the store.

Hurrying up the aisle, she felt the familiar flutter in her stomach when she heard Rick's voice calling out. "He-ll-o-o! Anyone home?"

By the time she reached the end of the aisle, she had everything under control. "Hi, yourself." She flashed him a smile. "What are you doing here? Looking for new cookbooks?"

He grinned back at her, and waved his hand at the cookbooks table. "I'm always on the lookout. Got anything interesting?"

"Of course. All our cookbooks are loaded with fascinating ideas." She paused by the table to pick up one of the heavy volumes. "Like this one, but I think you saw this the last time you were over here."

She handed him the book and he flipped through the pages. "Yeah, I did. Recipes for the diet-conscious." He put the book down again. "If I had to worry about diet when I cooked, I'd hang up my chef's hat."

She laughed. "That would be a terrible loss f r your lady friends."

He had a glint in his eye that made her fidgety. "What makes you think I have lady friends?"

Wishing she hadn't made such an idiotic remark, she shrugged. "Oh, I don't know. Eligible bachelor, great car, small town. . . ."

He nodded. "Ah, yes. Now if only I had the wealth and fame to go with it."

"Not every woman wants a wealthy playboy."

He gave her a look that she felt all the way down to her toes. "No? What about you? What are you looking for?"

She stared at him, trying desperately to think of something cute and flip that would defuse what felt like a serious turn of the conversation. "I'm not sure I'm looking for anything in particular."

"Uh-huh. So just any old thing that walks through the door would work for you?"

The doorbell rang again at that moment, and in walked John Halloran.

Clara took one look at him and burst out laughing.

Rick chuckled, too, and John looked from one to the other with an expression of pure bewilderment.

"What's so funny?" He plodded over to the counter, shoulders hunched and hands buried deep in the pockets of his overcoat. "It's cold enough out there to freeze the gates of hell. I'm going home to a warm fire and a good book." He scowled at Clara. "I don't suppose my Paul Wiley book is in yet?"

She straightened her face and walked behind the counter. "Not yet, I'm afraid. We did get a good sci-fi thriller in that you might like. It's a new author, but from what I've heard, he's destined for great things."

John's frown deepened. "What's it about? Have you read it?"

"I haven't, but I can tell you what it's about."

She looked up as Rick headed for the door. "Thanks for coming in."

He gave her a mock salute. "See you later."

The door closed behind him, and John shook his head. "If I were him, I wouldn't leave that new assistant of his alone in that shop."

Clara looked at him in surprise. "Why not? Rick seems happy enough with him."

"Rick doesn't know the family the way I do." John gazed up at the ceiling. "The Whittaker boys have been in trouble ever since they learned to walk." He looked back at her. "Lost their father when they were little. Fishing accident. Mother married again, but he and the boys never got along."

"Oh, that's sad. That must be hard for them all."

"I once caught Ryan, the oldest, stealing candy from my store. He was only about eight or nine. I let it go, although I did threaten to have him arrested if he ever did it again."

Clara felt a jolt of surprise. Somehow she'd never envisioned John Halloran as being that tolerant. "That was nice of you. I hope he appreciated it."

John shrugged. "Didn't do him any good. He got arrested a few years later. Him and his brother. They broke into a church and stole cash and a few other things. Tyler was underage, and they said he was under the influence of his brother. He got off with a few weeks of community service. Ryan went to jail for a couple of years."

Clara wondered if Rick knew his assistant's past history. If so, he should be commended for giving the kid a chance to prove himself. "Where is Ryan now?"

"He's still in town. I see him now and then. I think he's working up on the bluff at that construction site."

Clara smiled. Apparently, Rick wasn't the only one willing to give someone a second chance. "I hope he's staying out of trouble."

"Well, you know what they say." John's brown eyes gleamed behind the lenses of his glasses. "Once a thief, always a thief."

"There's always the exception."

"Maybe, but the Whittaker boys?" He shook his head. "I don't know. That Ryan's got a mean streak a mile wide." He looked up at the clock on the wall behind her. "Now, what's this new book all about?"

Clara stared at him, the memory of her vision still fresh in her mind. *A mean streak a mile wide.* Mean enough, perhaps, to have pushed his foreman off the scaffolding? No, now she was jumping to conclusions. Unless Ryan Whittaker had a strong motive to kill Scott, he couldn't be on her suspect list just because he'd been in jail and had a bad temper.

Aware of the curiosity in John's expression, she turned to the computer. "I'll pull it up for you. You can see the description for yourself." She spun the monitor around so he could read the reviews of the book.

Somehow she and Stephanie would have to get on that site and talk to some of the workers. Someone could have seen something that might lead to whoever was on that scaffolding after dark, in the rain, with the body of Scott Delwyn.

"Sounds okay," John said, disrupting her thoughts. "I'll take it."

"I'll get it for you." She glanced at her watch on the way down the aisle. Another hour or so to go before she could close up the shop. She could hardly wait until she could talk to Stephanie and figure out how and when they were going to question the construction workers.

After John left she had two more customers, and then at last it was time to close. The wind tore at her hair as she sped down the hill to the parking lot. She could just see the harbor below her in the swiftly gathering dusk. A dark gray ocean heaved choppy waves to the shore, and a few anchored fishing boats bobbed on the water.

In the summer months, the bay was full of activity, with numerous yachts dipping their colorful sails across the horizon. Clara could hardly wait for the warm sunshine and balmy breezes from a calm sea. Right now, her nose felt as if it had been jammed into an icebox.

She was almost home before the car finally warmed up. Letting herself into the house, she welcomed the blast of warm air that greeted her. Tatters was nowhere to be seen, which meant he was either closeted in the living room with her mother, or had behaved badly and was imprisoned in the utility room.

She opened the living room door carefully, prepared for the onslaught of a furry body. A soft whine warned her, and she put a hand through the opening. "Here, boy. Take it easy."

"Tatters, *sit*." Her mother's firm voice was answered with another whine.

Clara grinned. Jessie had worked her magic with the dog again. Clara opened the door all the way and received a wet lick on her hand.

Tatters sat on his haunches, tail thrashing the floor. His entire body quivered with the urge to leap up and bestow soggy kisses all over her face. Clara patted his head, murmuring, "Good boy." Her mother's uncanny talent for doggy discipline never ceased to amaze her.

"I've got a roast in the oven," Jessie said, folding up her knitting. "Dinner should be ready in a half hour."

"Great. I have a couple of things to take care of on the computer. I won't be long." Clara hurried down the hallway to her room, with Tatters trotting close behind.

Sinking onto her bed, she kicked off her shoes and pulled out her cell phone from her pocket.

Stephanie sounded out of breath when she answered, which was nothing new. "Clara? How were things in the store today? Were you busy?"

"Actually, it was kind of slow. I did manage to sell that new thriller you liked to John Halloran."

"I suppose he was complaining about waiting for his Paul Wiley book."

"Not really. He was too interested in telling me about the lurid past of Rick's new assistant."

Stephanie's voice rose with interest. "Tyler has a lurid past?"

"Kind of." Clara hesitated then decided it was okay to repeat gossip to her cousin. She told Stephanie everything that John Halloran had said about the Whittakers.

"Hmm," Stephanie murmured, when Clara came to the end of her saga. "Ryan Whittaker has a record, according to John he has a lousy temper and he works up at the construction site. Do you think he could be a murder suspect?"

"Anyone can be a murder suspect. Unless he's got a motive, though, we don't have any reason to think it's him. He's not the only one with a bad temper and connections to the construction site. Remember Lionel Clapham? Or even Josh Millstone's protestors. Any one of them could have lost their temper and struck out at Scott."

Stephanie's sigh seemed to hang on the line between them. "This isn't going to be easy, is it?"

"It never is, which is why I really wish there was some way I could convince Dan to investigate the death."

"Like we said before, the only way is to find some evidence that could make him suspicious."

"Which is why we need to get on the site and talk to some of the workers. Maybe someone there saw something."

"Okay. When do you want to go?"

Clara leaned back against the pillows. "They start back to work tomorrow. That might be the best time to talk to them, while their minds are still fresh from the night Scott died."

"I can't go tomorrow. It's Molly's day off. Someone has to open in the morning. We already lost sales on Saturday afternoon. I'm hoping we'll make up for that tomorrow."

"Okay, then. I'll go on my own before I start work."

Stephanie's cry of protest sounded urgent. "You can't go on your own. It's not safe."

Clara laughed. "What could possibly happen to me in broad daylight with dozens of construction workers skulking around?"

"You never know. I don't trust any of them up there. You said there were two people up on that scaffolding. What if it's two of the workers and they get spooked because you're asking questions and decide to get rid of you?"

"Don't worry, I'll be careful," Clara promised, sounding more confident than she felt. "I'll tell them I'm writing an article for the newspaper to put people's mind at ease about the project."

"Oh, good thinking!" Her voice pulled away from the phone. "*What? You're kidding. Oh crap.*" She spoke in Clara's ear again. "I have to go. Michael's got his head stuck in the banister again. You think he'd have learned a lesson from the last time. Talk to you later and be careful."

She was gone before Clara could answer.

———

Clara slept badly that night, disturbed by dreams that she couldn't remember when her alarm buzzed. Daylight filled the spaces between the slats of the window blinds. Tatters lay at her feet, twitching and uttering soft little whines as he chased something in his sleep.

She slipped out of bed and opened up the blinds to find sunlight warming the glass. The frost had already disappeared from the roofs and the lawn, though a part of the pathway that lay in shadow still had a glint of white.

A hot shower and a cup of coffee later, she felt ready to face the day. She'd dressed in a warm, fluffy white sweater to go with her black pants, anticipating a cold morning standing around the construction site talking to workmen. Pulling on her beige overcoat, she looked down at Tatters, who sat at her feet with a look of sorrow on his furry face.

"I'm sorry, Tatters." She wound a white wool scarf around her neck and turned up the collar of her coat, trapping her shoulder-length hair inside. "I know I'm leaving you sooner than usual but I have errands to run. Jessie will be home early this afternoon and I'll take you for a walk this evening. Meanwhile, you have to be good and not make a mess so that Jessie won't send you to the pound." She smiled, envisioning her mother's face if she heard her daughter refer to her by her first name.

She and whose army?

Clara's smile vanished. "Okay, that's enough. Be a good boy and go lie down. I'll see you tonight." She closed the door of her room and hurried down the hallway. Maybe it was her fault she kept reading Tatters' mind. After all, she talked to him like he was a human being and could understand what she said.

The unsettling thing was, she was pretty sure he did understand everything she said. And that was even more spooky.

7

The drive along the coast road lifted Clara's spirits. Even in the depths of winter, the scenery could take her breath away. The blue smudge of mountains rising against a brighter blue sky, the rocky shoreline with its cozy houses nestled among the trees and the sweep of the bay as she rounded the bend—so very different from the busy streets of New York but in its way, just as exciting and memorable.

She was getting used to being home again, and the realization gave her a warm feeling that stayed with her as she parked the car and made her way over to the construction site.

The entire area had been fenced off, and a small wooden shack stood just inside the gates. As she paused in front of them, a guy wearing a baseball cap and sunglasses appeared in the doorway.

She smiled at him, blinking in the sunlight and wishing she'd brought her own shades. "Hi," she called out. "I'm writing an article on the construction of the new resort and I was hoping I could talk to some of the guys out here."

The man stepped out of the shack and walked over to her. "You have a press pass?"

She shook her head. "I'm freelancing. I'm hoping to sell the article to a magazine." She widened her smile. "I promise I won't be long or disrupt anything."

He looked her up and down in a way that made her uncomfortable. "Lady, you'd be a distraction just walking in here."

Her smile faltered. "Are you going to let me in or not?"

"Not." He stuck both hands in the pockets of his windcheater. "Not without permission from the boss." He poked his face up close to the gate. "Written permission, that is."

She huffed out her disappointment. "Okay, who's the boss? How do I get in touch with him?"

The guy nodded at a sign hanging on the fence. "Call that number. They'll tell you who to talk to." He turned away and sauntered back into the shack.

Frustrated, Clara glared at his back then took out her cell phone. The sign read, "Hastings Corporation, Contractors." She quickly thumbed the number into the directory of her cell phone and slipped it into her pocket.

A quick glance at the shack assured her the guy with

the bad attitude was nowhere to be seen. She might not be allowed into the site, but there was no law preventing her from walking around outside it.

Just to be sure, she skirted around the back of the shack and walked along the fence that divided the site from the road. She could see the workmen walking around, both on the ground and up on the scaffolding, but she was too far away to attract their attention.

She reached the end of the fence and turned the corner, only to be brought to a standstill. Right in front of her the ground fell away, down a steep rocky slope and into a narrow gully. The only way she could access the far side of the site was back the way she'd come, past the gates and around the other side.

She couldn't see what lay on the other side from there, but a good guess would be the ocean. It seemed that if she wanted to speak to any of the workers, she would have to get past Prince Charming at the gates.

Since that wasn't going to happen without the boss's written permission, she reluctantly retraced her steps and made her way back to her car. Sitting behind the wheel, she stared moodily at the framework of beams and slats sketched against the sky.

There had to be another way. Tomorrow was her day off. She could wait until the workers were leaving and talk to them as they came out the gate. That might not be too practical. They'd be in a hurry to get home and would probably brush her off. Still, it was better than nothing. Maybe she could get Stephanie to come along. If there were two of them, the men might be more willing to talk.

With that hope in her mind, she pulled out onto the coast road and headed back to town.

With still an hour or so to go before she had to start work, Clara decided to pay a visit to Rick's hardware store. It would give her an opportunity to talk to Tyler. She wasn't sure exactly what the young man could tell her, but one thing she'd learned from past experience was never to leave a stone unturned.

Convincing herself that was the sole reason for her visit, Clara pushed the door open and walked inside.

A faint smell of fertilizer hung in the air as she approached the counter. Rick had to be somewhere in the back of the store, and the guy standing with his back to her had to be his new assistant. He was fiddling with something on the wall, and when he turned, she saw that it was a calendar, the familiar skyline of New York taking up half the page.

Today was the first day of March. February, it seemed, had left without her realizing it. She stared at the picture, torn between nostalgia for the places she missed, and memories she wished would vanish forever.

"Can I help you?"

Realizing she'd been staring way too long, she jerked her gaze back to the face of the young man in front of her.

Tyler Whittaker wore his dark hair too long, and looked as if he needed a shave. Thick, shaggy eyebrows dominated an attractive face, shadowing his navy blue eyes. He looked bored, yet fidgeted back and forth with a barely controlled energy—the kind of guy her mother would label "dangerous."

For a fleeting moment Clara wondered if Molly had met Tyler. He was the young woman's type, judging from the brief glimpse she'd had of Jason back in the Laurel Street Tavern.

"Is something wrong?"

He sounded edgy, and she dragged her thoughts back to the reason she was there. "I'm sorry. We haven't met." She thrust out her hand. "I'm Clara Quinn. I work in my cousin's bookstore across the street."

Tyler looked surprised, but took her fingers and gave them a quick squeeze. "Hi. Tyler Whittaker."

"Yes, Rick told me you were working for him." She glanced toward the back of the store but saw no sign of Rick. "How do you like working here?"

Tyler shrugged. "It's okay, I guess."

Something in his tone sharpened her interest. "But you'd rather be doing something else?"

"Yeah. How'd you know?"

"I don't know. Instinct, I guess." She smiled. "So what would you rather be doing?"

He looked as if he didn't want to answer that, but after a moment's hesitation, he muttered, "I would rather be in the navy."

It was the last thing she expected him to say. She recovered her surprise, saying, "Really? So why aren't you?"

The look of pain that crossed his face cut right to her heart. "They're not interested."

"I'm sorry." Guessing that it had something to with his past, she sought to change the subject. Anything to take that awful look away. "I hear you have a brother working up at the construction site."

His expression changed to one of suspicion. "Yeah, so what about it?"

"Oh, nothing." She began to feel she was treading out of her depth. "I'm just fascinated by the new resort. I can't wait to see it finished. I've seen the scaffolding. It's pretty high. It's going to be so fantastic when it's done. Does your brother mind working so high up? I'd be scared to death."

She was talking too fast and saying too much, she thought, as she watched conflicting emotions crossing Tyler's face. She waited, uncertain as to what she was waiting for, and hoping she hadn't scared him off altogether.

"Do you have the hots for my brother?" Tyler asked, sounding incredulous.

She almost laughed. Her cheeks burned as she shook her head. "No, no, of course not. He's not . . . I mean . . . I've never met him."

To her utter dismay, Rick's voice spoke from right behind her. "That's a relief."

She spun around, confusion making her voice come out in a high squeak. "Rick! I didn't see you there. I was just talking to your new assistant." She glanced at her watch. "Goodness, look at the time. I'd better get going. Stephanie will wonder where I am."

She turned back to find Rick's assistant looking at her as if she'd grown horns. "Nice to meet you, Tyler." She spun back and smiled weakly at Rick as she rushed past him. "See you later!" Feeling like an utter fool, she dashed out into the street.

She was sure that the gazes of both men were burning into her back as she stood poised on the curb, waiting for a car to pass so she could hurtle across to the bookstore.

Stephanie was at the counter when Clara rushed in the door. She glanced up at the clock murmuring, "What's your hurry? You're early."

"Am I?" Clara took a deep breath. "I thought I was late."

Stephanie gave her a sharp look. "What happened at the site?"

"Nothing." Thankful for the diversion, Clara slung her purse on the shelf behind the counter and shrugged out of her coat. "There was a security guy at the gates and he wouldn't let me in without written permission from the contractors."

"You couldn't talk to the men through the fence?"

"Nope. They were too far away."

"Bummer. What do we do now?"

"We could go over there tomorrow evening and catch the guys as they're leaving the site."

Stephanie sighed. "All right. But that'll be right around dinnertime. I'll think of something to tell George." She picked up a sheaf of invoices and slipped them into a drawer. "I don't think he'd appreciate me abandoning him and the kids at mealtime to go talk to a bunch of construction workers."

"I know." Clara felt a stab of guilt. "Look, I can do this on my own. You don't have to lie to George again. I know it's tough trying to get out of the house when you've got a family to worry about."

"Normally it's not a problem. George is the most understanding man in the world. It's just . . ."

She hesitated, and Clara stared at her. "Something wrong?"

"No, not really. At least, I don't think so. It's just that George seemed a bit distant last night. Like he had a lot on his mind. Stuff he didn't want to talk about. Usually he tells me if something's bothering him. Now I'm kind of worried about him."

"I'm sure it's nothing. If it were serious, he'd tell you. Why don't you ask him?"

"I did. He said I was imagining things."

"Well, maybe you are. Look, if you'd rather not go with me tomorrow, it's okay. Like I said, I can do this on my own."

Stephanie shook her head. "No, I don't want you going on your own. Especially at night in the dark. I'll figure something out."

"Well, don't worry if you can't make it. I'll be fine." She combed her fingers through her wind-tossed hair. "I'd better do something with this mess. I'll be right back."

Stephanie looked hopeful. "I don't suppose the Sense is telling you anything?"

Clara rolled her eyes. "If it were, you'd be the first to know."

"Okay. Just thought I'd ask."

Shaking her head, Clara headed for the bathroom.

It was the middle of the afternoon, long after Stephanie left for the day, when Clara heard the news.

The moment she saw Roberta Prince prance through the door, Clara knew something big had happened.

Roberta looked elegant as always, in a violet sweater and black pants beneath a gorgeous white fur jacket. She'd covered her ears with purple earmuffs, and her pale blue eyes looked huge beneath curly false eyelashes.

Clara avoided the woman as much as possible. There was something about Roberta Prince that caused her hackles to rise. It had nothing to do with the fact, of course, that Roberta was dying to get her hooks into Rick Sanders.

"Did you hear the news?" Roberta strutted up to the counter in her ridiculously high heels and leaned both hands on the surface for support. "The bank at the bottom of the hill has been robbed!" Her face looked pale under her makeup, and the crow's-feet at the corners of her eyes were more pronounced than usual.

Clara's jaw dropped. "The bank? Was anyone hurt?"

Roberta clutched her throat. "I don't think so, though Janice, you know, that pudgy clerk with the gray frizzy hair? Well, she was held up at gunpoint. Poor thing. She's scared to death." She shuddered. "I was late getting there to make my deposit. Just think, if I'd been on time, I'd have been in the bank when it happened. Oh, my God! I could have been shot!"

No such luck, Clara thought, then immediately felt ashamed of herself. "Who robbed it? Do they know? Did he get away?"

Roberta pulled off her earmuffs and laid them on the counter. "I don't know. Dan and Tim are still down there, interviewing everyone. I'm shaking so hard . . ." She dabbed at her eye with the back of her forefinger. "I can't cry. It will make my mascara run."

In spite of her dislike of the woman, Clara could tell Roberta was genuinely upset. Her compassion won. "Let's go down to the Nook. I've got coffee and aspirin there." She wasn't sure how much help that would be, but it sounded sympathetic, at least.

Roberta seemed to agree, since she headed off down the aisle to the Reader's Nook.

Clara followed, thinking about the teller who'd been held at gunpoint. Janice Phillips was in her mid-fifties, a dumpy, quiet-spoken woman who always seemed fearful of being reprimanded for talking to the customers. Definitely not the kind of person who could deal with a gun being waved in her face. She had to be badly shaken and Clara felt sorry for her. Something like that could haunt the poor woman for years.

She reached the Nook, and as she was about to turn the corner to go in, without warning a cold wind blasted across her face.

She was no longer in the bookstore. She could hear the wail of a police siren in the distance, and the roar of the ocean as waves crashed onto the beach just a few yards away. There was the bank, sunlight glinting on the windows. The street was empty except for one man, standing alone in front of the doors, peering inside.

She flinched as a woman screamed somewhere inside the bank. The man turned his head, then twisted around to look at her. Her stomach heaved when she saw his face. It was Scott Delwyn, his skin colorless, his eyes wide and staring.

He took a step toward her, then turned back to look at the bank. She could hear shouting now from inside—a man's voice, harsh with anger.

"Whatever's the matter with you?"

Clara blinked as the ocean, the bank and Scott Delwyn vanished. Roberta was peering at her around the end of the aisle, her face taut with concern.

Inwardly cursing the Quinn Sense, Clara rubbed a hand across her stomach. "Sorry. Indigestion. Must be the bologna sandwich I had for lunch."

Roberta made a face. "Ugh. How do you eat that stuff?"

Clara followed her into the Nook, still disoriented from the sudden transformation of her surroundings. Walking over to the table that held the coffeepot, she opened the small drawer and took out a bottle of aspirin.

"Do you want to take this with coffee, or would you rather have water?"

"Coffee's fine, thanks." Roberta took the bottle from her and shook three pills out into her hand. "I don't usually take this stuff but I can't seem to stop shaking."

Clara knew exactly how she felt. Her own hand shook as she poured coffee into two mugs. She'd never seen a ghost before. At least, not one she recognized. There was no doubt in her mind that Scott Delwyn was trying to tell her something.

Was the robbery connected to his death? If so, how? This was something that Dan should know about, and soon. But she had no idea how she could convey that information without a whole lot of awkward questions.

She carried the coffee over to Roberta and sat down. "Tell me more about the robbery. Did you talk to Janice? Did she know who he was?"

Roberta shuddered. "I couldn't talk to Janice. She was talking to Dan when I went in there. Talking and crying at the same time." She took a sip of her coffee. "You can't imagine how awful it was in there. No one was speaking. Everyone looked sick to their stomachs. I got out of there as quickly as I could." She shuddered again. "I'll have nightmares for weeks."

Clara leaned back, her mug in her hand. "I guess it will be on the news tonight. We might know more then."

Roberta sat up, her thin eyebrows arched high. "On the news? Of course! Why didn't I think of that? I should have hung around. I could have been interviewed."

Clara resisted the impulse to roll her eyes. "I should think they'd only interview the people who were there when the robbery took place."

"You think so?" Roberta looked disappointed. "I suppose you're right. I guess it's not worth going back there now. The reporters have probably left, anyway." She took another sip of coffee. "I think I will have that water, thanks. The coffee's too hot to swallow pills."

Clara got up and went over to the sink. She could still see Scott Delwyn in her mind, his face devoid of expression and his vacant eyes staring at her. What was he trying to tell her? Damn the Quinn Sense. If it was going to whisk her away and drop her in the middle of a crime scene, the very least it could do was leave her there long enough to figure out exactly what she was looking at and why.

She was relieved when Roberta finally decided she was well enough to leave.

True to form, however, she couldn't resist a parting shot. "I ran into Rick last night," she said, pausing to pick up her earmuffs from the counter. "He was entertaining the ladies down at the bowling alley."

Clara smiled. "I didn't know you bowled."

"Oh, I don't." She headed for the door. "I saw his truck in the parking lot as I drove past." She disappeared outside, leaving Clara frowning after her.

How the heck, she fumed, as she walked behind the counter, could Roberta know he was talking to women if she wasn't in the bowling alley? What difference did it make to her if he was, anyway? He was a big boy. He could talk to whomever he wanted.

Having settled that in her mind, she logged onto the computer and started entering the receipts for the day. She'd hardly begun when her cell phone buzzed in her pocket. Guessing it was her cousin calling, she pulled it out and flipped it open.

Stephanie's voice was shrill with excitement. "Guess what! There was a bank robbery here this afternoon."

"I know. The bank at the bottom of the hill. Roberta told me."

"Oh." Stephanie sounded disappointed. "Well, he got away with a large sum of cash, according to the news."

"Thank goodness no one was hurt."

"What's wrong? You sound weird."

Clara sighed. She might have known she couldn't keep anything from her cousin. Although she was alone in the store, she walked out to look down the aisles, just in case.

"Clara?" Stephanie's voice rose in alarm. "Are you all right?"

"I'm fine." Having satisfied herself that no one was there to overhear her, she added, "I had another vision."

Stephanie gasped. "You did? What was it?"

"I saw Scott Delwyn. He was standing outside the bank."

Another gasp. "You saw his *ghost*?"

"Yes. I think he was trying to tell me something."

"Ugh! Did he look creepy?"

Clara sighed. "That's not the point. I think his death and the robbery are connected somehow."

"No way! Scott wouldn't rob a bank."

"I don't mean he was actually involved with the robbery."

"Then what do you mean?"

"I don't know. I just know he wanted to tell me something *about* the robbery."

Stephanie was silent for a long moment before she said quietly, "Sometimes the Sense doesn't make sense at all."

"You're telling me," Clara said grimly. "Just try living with it for a while."

"I wish I could."

"I wish you could, too."

"So what are you going to do? Tell Dan?"

"I guess." Clara stared out the window. It was getting dark and the lights were bright inside the hardware store across the street. She could see someone moving around inside, but couldn't tell if it was Rick or a customer. "I talked to Tyler Whittaker this morning."

"You did? Why didn't you tell me? What did he say?"

"Not much. I tried to ask him about his brother, but he thought I was asking because I was interested in him."

Stephanie chuckled. "I bet that was awkward. Was Rick there?"

Clara briefly closed her eyes. "He came in and interrupted me so I didn't get much out of Tyler."

"Too bad."

"Did you think of an excuse to tell George about tomorrow night?"

"Not yet. I will." She paused, then added in a rush,

"I gotta go. The kids are much too quiet. We'll talk tomorrow."

Clara closed the phone and moved over to the window. As she reached it, she saw the front door of the hardware store swing open and a figure stepped outside. Recognizing Tyler, she watched as he paused for a moment on the sidewalk, then he pulled on a red wool hat, turned up his collar and loped off down the hill.

Tomorrow, she told herself, she'd try to meet Tyler's brother and talk to him. She didn't know why, but it seemed important that she question him.

That night, she dreamed she was on the beach with Tatters when farther along the shore a man who looked vaguely familiar started waving at her. At first she ignored him, but then he began running toward her, flailing his arms and shouting something she couldn't understand.

Tatters started barking and she struggled to keep him quiet, anxious to hear what the man had to say. He was almost close enough when a huge wave rushed onto the sands, cutting him off.

He stood for a moment watching her, before he pulled a red wool hat from his pocket, tugged it on and walked off in the opposite direction.

Frustrated, she called out after him, "Wait! Wait! What did you want to tell me?"

Tatters growled, and she opened her eyes to find the dog's nose close to hers, his breath warm on her face.

"It's all right, boy," she murmured, and patted his furry head. "Lay down and go back to sleep."

He grunted, pawed around for a moment, then flopped down with a *thud* that shook the bed.

She lay still, staring at the faint light creeping through the blinds. It seemed that Scott wasn't the only one anxious to tell her something. The stranger in her dream had looked enough like Tyler Whittaker to be his brother, and the red hat seemed to confirm it. She was more anxious than ever to talk to Ryan Whittaker.

8

Stephanie loved her husband more than anything else in the world—next to her kids, anyway—which is why she tried so hard to spare him the worry that she was sure he'd feel if he knew she was helping Clara track down a killer.

Sometimes she wondered if it wouldn't be better if she just told him in the hope that he'd have enough faith in her to know she'd be careful and not get into too much trouble.

The problem with that was that he'd probably try to talk her out of it, by pointing out that he and the children needed her, and if anything bad happened, they'd be lost without her. Not that she didn't already know that, and agonize over it at times, but as long as it wasn't out there in front of her, spoken in so many words, she could put it out of her mind long enough to get the job done.

Then again, she suspected that George knew all along what she and Clara were up to, which was probably why he'd been so preoccupied lately. He most likely figured she'd go ahead and do it anyway whether he objected or not, and it was probably better not to get in a fight about it. Since she thoroughly agreed with that, it was better that she didn't tell him.

Having won that argument with herself once more, she left a note for George on the table, telling him that she was going over to Clara's house and would order pizza when she got back.

After dropping the kids off at her mother's house, Stephanie convinced herself that she'd be gone no more than the hour—or so she'd promised everyone—and headed out to meet her cousin.

Clara, meanwhile, had spent most of the day trying to catch up on chores while entertaining Tatters. Jessie arrived home just in time to meet Clara on her way out the door.

"Where are you going?" Jessie demanded as Clara passed her on the step. "I thought you'd be home for dinner."

"I will be." Clara started down the path. "I'll be back in a couple of hours."

"But we always eat together on your day off."

"Sorry, Mom." Clara spotted Stephanie's car heading toward her. "I'm going out with Stephanie for a while. I won't be late." She hurried down the path before Jessie could ask any more questions.

Stephanie pulled up at the curb and waited for her to climb in and get settled. "What did you tell Aunt Jessie?" she asked as Clara fastened her seat belt.

"Just that we were going out for a while." Clara glanced at her cousin. "What did you tell George?"

"Same thing." Stephanie slid the gear lever into drive. "He wasn't home so I left him a note."

"You have a very tolerant husband."

"I know." Stephanie sighed. "Sometimes I feel bad about not telling him what we're doing."

"I know." Clara patted her arm. "But he'd only worry if you did."

"He'd want me to stop."

"Do *you* want to stop?"

Stephanie gave her a startled look. "Of course not! We're in this together. We always have been and we always will be."

Clara smiled. "Spoken like a true cousin and soul mate."

Ahead of them, the road wound around the shore line, and already pinpricks of light from the next town were popping up across the bay. As always, Clara felt uneasy about questioning strangers about a murder. Especially when all she had to go on was her unpredictable, unreliable Quinn Sense.

"I had a dream last night," she said as the car swept around the rocky slopes of the hills.

"You did?" Stephanie sounded surprised. "Why didn't you tell me before? What was it about?"

"I don't know if it meant anything. I dreamed a man in a red wool hat was trying to tell me something."

"Who was he?"

"I'm not sure, but I think it was Ryan Whittaker."

"Tyler's brother?" Stephanie laughed. "You're not getting interested in him, are you?"

"I've never met him."

"So what did he say in the dream?"

"That's just it. He was too far away for me to hear what he said. But I think we need to talk to him."

"You think he might have killed Scott?"

Clara sighed. "I don't know what to think. Let's just hope that someone says something soon that will help us, or we might never know the truth about Scott's death."

"That would be a shame."

"Yes, it would." She fell silent, going over in her mind the vision she had of Scott standing outside the bank as it was robbed and her gut feeling that somehow the two incidents were connected.

"There's the construction site up ahead," Stephanie said, sounding a little tense. "I hope we're in time."

"It said on the news that Scott was killed around five thirty, shortly after the shift ended." Clara glanced at her watch. "It's five twenty, so they should start coming out soon."

"Okay, just to get our story straight: we're doing an article about the new resort, putting a positive slant on it in the hopes of pacifying the protestors so the construction workers can get on with their job."

"Right. We—" Clara broke off. "I don't believe it."

"What?" Stephanie peered through the windshield. "What's the matter? Oh, crap."

She had apparently seen what Clara had seen—a large group of people, some of them carrying placards, surrounding the gates of the construction site.

"We're never going to get through that lot." Clara sunk back on her seat. "Just our luck the protestors picked tonight to hold a rally."

Stephanie pulled onto the gravel clearing that served as a parking lot and cut the engine. They could hear the chanting of the crowd, though it was too garbled to make out what they said. It was obvious, however, from the angry tone of the voices that the protestors were fired up about the project and were doing their best to shut it down.

A white van with the local television station's call letters on it shot past them, coming to a halt just short of the crowd. Two men jumped out, one with a spot light, the other a camera, and began shooting the scene.

"Let's get out of here," Stephanie muttered. "I don't want to end up on the evening news."

"Right." Clara sat up. "We'll just have to come back another night."

"Maybe Molly will fill in for you and we can try again tomorrow."

"Good idea. I'll ask her." Clara frowned. "I'll have to think of some way to repay her."

Stephanie grinned. "Don't you mean bribe her?"

"Okay, smart mouth. This is for a good cause, remember?"

"I know." She was silent for a while, and then added quietly, "I just hope the Quinn Sense is right about this."

"So do I," Clara muttered. "Believe me, so do I."

———

Clara's head felt clear for a change when she joined her mother in the kitchen the following morning.

Jessie greeted her with a smile, and leaned forward to scratch Tatters' ears. "You're up early. Sleep okay?"

"Like a baby. Did you?"

"I usually do. You're the one always having the nightmares. You talk so loud in your sleep sometimes, I'd swear there's someone in the bedroom with you."

Dismayed to discover her mother could hear her at night, Clara tried to shrug it off. "Only Tatters. You probably hear me talking to him."

Her mother gave her a knowing look. "You were talking in your sleep long before that dog got here. I do wish you wouldn't let him sleep with you. It's not healthy."

The change of subject was a relief and Clara jumped on it. "I like having him there. He keeps me warm."

"It's a wonder he doesn't smother you with all that hair in your face." Jessie shook out the newspaper. "I see that Dan hasn't had any luck catching that bank robber. What nerve that man has—holding up a bank in broad daylight. Though, of course, this is such a dinky little town. No one here ever expects something as dramatic as a bank robbery so the police aren't prepared for it. Not like a big city that's crawling with cops." She peered up at Clara. "I suppose you were used to bank robberies in New York."

Clara's back stiffened, and she made an effort to relax as she poured coffee into her mug. "Not really. If fact, this is the closest I've ever been to something like this."

Jessie grunted. "Well, I certainly hope Dan catches the thief. With everything else going on, the last thing we need is a criminal running around robbing people. What if he came into the library and pointed a gun at me? I'd faint dead away. I think Dan should have extra police patrolling the town until they catch that thug."

Clara carried her mug over to the table and sat down. "I doubt that a robber would expect to find much cash in the library, or the bookstore, for that matter."

"You never know." Jessie rattled the newspaper. "In this economy, people get desperate and they'll go after anything."

Clara thought about her mother's comment on the way to work. The bank job certainly seemed to have been an act of desperation—a lone robber hitting the bank in broad daylight. What had driven a man to such great lengths he had risked everything to get his hands on that money?

She was still thinking about it when she walked into the Raven's Nest. A couple of customers stood in one of the aisles, browsing the shelves. Molly waved at her from behind the counter, where she was setting up a display of bookmarks. Stephanie was probably in the stockroom sorting out the new deliveries.

With a wave back at Molly, Clara headed down the aisle, smiling a greeting at the customers as she passed. As predicted, Stephanie was in the stockroom surrounded by half-emptied boxes.

"I've been waiting for you to get here," she said as Clara closed the door behind her. "I talked to Molly this morning."

Clara tugged her arms out of her coat sleeves and hung it up on the hook. "Did you ask her about tonight?"

"We don't have to go tonight." Stephanie grunted as she lifted an armful of books from the box in front of her. "Molly had a great idea. She said that some of the construction workers usually go down to the tavern for happy hour on Fridays. If we want to talk to them that would be the best place to do it."

Clara rolled her eyes. "Don't tell me. The Laurel Street Tavern again, right?"

"Wrong. It's that bar out on the coast road. Not everyone lives in Finn's Harbor. Some of the guys live in Mittleford, so they go to the Blue Bayou near the construction site."

Clara took the books from her cousin's arms. "Well, I hope they serve better beer there than on Laurel Street. Or at least some decent wine."

Stephanie grinned. "I take it we're going to make Happy Hour at the Blue Bayou on Friday night?"

"I guess so. Is Molly coming?"

"I'm sure she'd love to." Stephanie looked at her watch. "Uh-oh. I have to run. I have a hair appointment in a half hour and I have to go home first. Put those cookbooks out on the table for me, please?"

"Sure." Clara followed her out into the store. "Talk to you later."

She was talking to thin air as her cousin flew down the aisle, shouted something to Molly and disappeared out the door.

Molly was only too happy to talk about the Blue Bayou when Clara asked her about it later. "It's a lot nicer than the tavern on Laurel Street," she said as she poured herself a cup of coffee in the Nook. "Not as noisy, better music, smells a lot sweeter and the women don't have muscles and tattoos." She grinned. "Well, they probably do, but they're a lot more discreet."

"Stephanie said the construction workers go there on Fridays." Clara took her mug of coffee over to a chair and sat down.

"Yeah, I've seen them in there a couple of times. When Stephanie said you planned on trying to talk to them as they were leaving the site, I figured the bar would be a better place to do it."

"So, do you want to come with us on Friday?"

Molly's eyes lit up. "Really? Cool! You know how I enjoy helping you guys do detective work."

"Well, we have to be careful what we say there. As I said before, we don't really know for sure what happened to Scott."

"Right. I'll remember. I—" She paused. "Was that the front doorbell?"

"I think so." Clara put down her coffee. "I'll go. You can clean up here and then it'll be time for you to go home."

Heading up the aisle, she felt a jolt of apprehension when she saw Dan Petersen standing at the counter. She hurried forward, hoping someone hadn't complained about her hanging around the construction site.

She greeted the police chief with a smile. "What can I do for you?"

His sharp gaze seemed to penetrate her brain when he looked at her. "It's my granddaughter's birthday. She's into all that vampire stuff that the kids are crazy about, for some reason I'll never understand."

Clara smiled. "You want me to pick out a book for her?"

"Yeah, a couple, if you can find them."

"Come with me." She beckoned him to follow her and led him down an aisle. "Do you know what she's already read?"

"Nope. Not a clue." He looked worried. "Can she exchange them if I get her something she's read already?"

"Sure she can. Just make sure you give her the receipt so she can bring it in."

He still looked doubtful. "Maybe I should just get her a gift certificate." He shook his head. "That seems like such a cop-out, as if I couldn't be bothered to think of something."

"Well, here." Clara pulled a book from the shelf and handed it to him. "This one just came in today. It's the first in a new series, and I think your granddaughter might like it. It's kind of like the Twilight books but with a different twist."

He took the book from her and turned it over in his hands. "Since I have no idea what the Twilight books are about, I'll take your word for it. Any more like this?"

She found a similar book for him and walked with him back to the counter. Ever since the moment she'd seen him in the store, she'd been bursting to ask him about the bank robbery. Now was her opportunity and she wasn't about to let it slip through her fingers.

Waiting for him to find his credit card, she asked casually, "So, any news on what happened at the bank?"

He flicked her a glance. "No more than what you've heard on TV."

"So you still don't know who did it?"

"Not yet, but we will." He swiped the card with an impatient flick of his wrist that warned her he didn't want to talk about it.

"You don't have any clues at all?"

His look gave her another quiver of apprehension. "If I did, I wouldn't be telling you about it."

She managed a weak smile. "I was just wondering if you . . . er . . . thought about the chance that the robbery might have something to do with Scott Delwyn's death. I mean, it's quite a coincidence, don't you think? Two big incidents like that, following . . . each . . . other. . . ." She let her voice trail off as Dan's face darkened.

For a long moment, the silence between them was as thick as a fog bank, then Dan said quietly, "I'm only going to tell you this once more. There's no reason to think that Scott's death was anything but an accident. There's no evidence to suggest it had anything remotely to do with the bank robbery. I sincerely hope you and your cousin don't take it into your heads to try and make out of this something it isn't. I'd really hate to have to charge you both with obstruction of justice."

Clara swallowed. "I'd hate that, too."

"Good. Then we have an understanding."

He held out his hand for the books and she hastily dropped them into a bag, slipped his receipt inside and handed it to him. "Thank you, Chief," she said, hoping her smile would help erase the resentment from his face. "I hope you find your robber soon."

"You and me both," he muttered and strode to the door.

She let out her breath as the door closed behind him. Well, that settled one question. There was no way Dan was going to listen to her about her suspicions.

She and Stephanie were on their own.

———

Two days later, she watched the clock all day until she could finally close up and join her cousin and Molly out at the Blue Bayou.

Molly had been right about the bar. It was decently

lit and there were actually curtains on the windows. The tables looked clean and the volume of the country music was low enough to have a decent conversation without yelling.

She found Stephanie alone in a booth, close to an enormous brick fireplace in which logs spat and crackled, sending sparks flying up the wide chimney. Clara could feel the warmth from it on the back of her legs as she pulled out a chair and sat down.

The smell of smoke and burning wood was far more pleasant than the beery body odors at the Laurel Street Tavern. In fact, Clara thought, as she checked out the old-fashioned wall lamps and the paneled walls of the booth, the Blue Bayou was a palace compared to its counterpart.

"Molly's over there," Stephanie said, nodding at the opposite side of the room. "She saw someone she knew and went over to talk to him. I thought it would be better if I stayed here."

Clara followed her gaze and caught sight of Molly's red hair. She was half hidden by a guy standing behind her, but Clara could see her talking to a young man seated at a table.

"Who is he? Did she say?"

"One of the construction workers. That's all I know. They seem to know each other really well, though."

Watching Molly's head lean closer to her companion's, Clara had to agree. The two of them were laughing and talking like old friends.

Turning back to Stephanie, she looked at the glass sitting in front of her cousin. "How's the wine?"

"Pretty good. They have chardonnay."

"My kind of place." Clara caught the eye of the young woman circling the tables and ordered a glass. "How long have you been here?"

"About an hour. We ordered nachos. They were good. Want some?"

"Maybe later. Though I usually have something waiting for me in the fridge when I get home."

Stephanie wrinkled her brow. "You're lucky to have a mom to cook for you."

"I guess. Sometimes I wonder if it's worth it."

"Still having problems with Aunt Jessie?"

"Now and then. I have to admit, it hasn't been as bad since we got Tatters. She spends her time scolding him now instead of me."

Stephanie laughed. "He's made himself useful, then. You'd better hope that Rick doesn't take him back."

"He'd have a fight on his hands if he tried."

"You're getting that fond of the dog?"

"Not just me. Jessie is having too much fun wielding her authority to let that dog go now. At least Tatters listens to her, which is more than I ever did."

"You've got that right."

The server brought Clara's wine just as Molly danced back to the table, holding a glass in her hand. She plunked herself down on a chair and gave the cousins a triumphant grin. "I found out something."

"You did?"

"What is it?"

Both women had spoken at once and Molly laughed. "What do you think of my informant?"

"We can't see much of him from here." Clara peered across the room but the table was now hidden from sight behind a group of people. "What's his name?"

"Brad Fielding. He works on the construction site. Guess what." She leaned forward and lowered her voice. "He was with Scott right before he died."

Clara put her glass down too quickly and slopped wine over the side. "What did he tell you?"

"Well, apparently Scott left his lunch box up on the scaffolding that night. His youngest daughter had given it to him for his birthday, and he knew she'd be upset if he went home without it, so he went back to get it." Molly paused, then added quietly, "Brad said that it was raining hard that night and getting dark. The scaffolding was slippery. Scott must have lost his footing and fell."

Clara frowned. It all sounded so feasible. She would never have questioned it either, if she hadn't seen that vision of Scott being shoved off the scaffolding. She couldn't tell Molly that, however, and she could hardly blame the woman for looking at her with doubt all over her face.

Stephanie cleared her throat. "Did he say anything else?"

Molly nodded. "One more thing. He thinks Scott might have been distracted by a text message. Earlier that day,

Brad saw him open up his cell phone and look at it as if he was reading bad news. He seemed upset and Brad asked him if he was okay. He didn't answer, just shoved the phone back in his pocket and walked away."

Clara exchanged a glance with her cousin. "Well, it's not much to go on. I wonder if anyone else there knew what he was upset about."

"Maybe Karen would know," Stephanie said. "She could have been the one who sent him the text message."

"There's one way to find out." Clara picked up her glass again. "I think it's time we paid the widow a visit. How about tomorrow morning?"

Stephanie nodded. "Sure. That is, Molly, if you don't mind holding down the fort again for an hour or so?"

"Of course I don't mind." Molly looked at Clara. "I can't help feeling, though, that you could be wrong about Scott's accident being murder."

"I know it seems that way. I just have to ask you to trust me. Thanks for talking to the guys over there. You've been a big help so far."

"Really?" Molly beamed. "Well, call on me any time. This is fun!"

Clara wasn't sure how much fun it was going to be talking to Scott's widow, but she held up her wine and touched glasses with Molly. "Here's to finding out the truth, even if we do seem to be spending most of our time in bars."

Stephanie lifted her glass. "I'll drink to that."

"And here's to finding out Scott's death was an accident, after all," Molly added. "Then we won't have to worry about a killer lurking about in Finn's Harbor."

There was little hope of that, Clara thought, as she met Stephanie's gaze. There was no doubt in her mind that Scott had been murdered. Proving it, however, was turning out to be even more difficult than she'd imagined.

9

"Now, what about Ryan Whittaker?" Stephanie asked, putting down her empty glass. "Aren't we supposed to be talking to him?"

"You are?" Molly's eyes widened. "What does he have to do with Scott's death?"

"Nothing, as far as we know," Clara said hastily. "We're just hoping he might know something that could help."

"Well, he's over there with Brad if you want to talk to him." Molly glanced over at the far table. "In fact, he just got up and went over to the bar."

Clara followed her gaze. "Which one is he?"

"You don't know him?"

Clara shook her head. "I know his brother works for Rick."

Still looking puzzled, Molly got up. "Come on, I'll introduce you."

Clara looked at Stephanie. "You coming?"

"I guess." With obvious reluctance, Stephanie took another sip of wine and got to her feet. "Let's do this."

Molly led the way over to the bar and tapped the shoulder of a tall, dark-haired guy in a leather jacket. "Hey, Ryan, I have a couple of friends who want to meet you."

Clara seemed to lose the use of her tongue as she looked into dark eyes that were blatantly checking her out from head to toe. She managed to mumble a greeting while Stephanie edged closer behind her.

Ryan Whittaker looked nothing like the man on the beach in her dream, which unsettled her. She'd been so sure the dream was a message, but now it seemed it was just a dream and nothing more. Ryan was even better looking than his brother, and had danger written all over him. Jessie would have a field day with this one. Clara was just a tad shorter than him and she instinctively stretched her back to try and reach his height.

He finally focused on her face and gave her a slow smile that must have taken years to perfect. "Hi, gorgeous. What's your name?"

"Clara." She felt behind her and found Stephanie's arm. Dragging her cousin forward, she added, "This is my cousin, Stephanie. She owns the Raven's Nest bookstore that's right across the street from where your brother works."

"Hi," Stephanie said, sounding breathless. "I'm married."

Clara gave her a startled look, while Ryan continued to stare into Clara's face. "You don't say," he murmured.

Clara cleared her throat. "I met Tyler the other day," she said, wishing she sounded a bit more confident. "He's a very nice young man."

Ryan's smile was beginning to slip. "So?"

"I . . . er . . . we . . . were friends with Scott Delwyn. We were just wondering if you were there the night he died."

The smile disappeared altogether and hostility crept into the black eyes. "What if I was?"

This was not going well. She should have rehearsed what she wanted to say. Anything she said now would sound like an accusation. She had misinterpreted her dream and it was obvious this man was not going to tell her anything.

She looked at Stephanie for help, but just then Molly stepped forward. "We're thinking of setting up a memorial fund for Karen," she said, "and we're trying to find out who were Scott's friends on the construction site."

Clara let out her breath as Ryan turned to look at her. "I've got no idea. I wasn't one of them." He frowned. "Why don't you ask Brad?"

Molly beamed. "Good idea. I will."

Clara added weakly, "Thank you, anyway."

The seductive gleam was back in his eyes as he murmured, "Anytime, gorgeous."

She could feel his gaze on her all the way back to the table.

"Wow," Stephanie said, sinking onto her chair. "That one is just too hot to handle."

Clara looked at her cousin. "What was all that about you being married?"

Stephanie shrugged. "I didn't want him looking at me the way he was looking at you."

Molly laughed. "It's all talk. He's no different than any of the other guys. He just puts on a better show."

"You could have fooled me." Stephanie eyed Clara with a sly grin. "He sure did a number on you."

Clara could feel her cheeks growing warm. "Oh, quit it. I was scared he was going to get mad at us for suggesting he had anything to do with Scott's death." She turned to Molly. "That was quick thinking, Molly. Good job."

Molly grinned. "Thanks, but I still don't know why you thought he was involved."

"Just a stupid hunch, that's all."

"Well, it turned out okay and that's all that matters." Stephanie gathered up her purse. "I have to run." She got to her feet. "Are you coming?"

"I think I'm going to stick around for a while longer," Clara murmured. "I haven't finished my wine yet."

"Me, too." Molly leaned back on her chair.

"Okay, see you tomorrow." Stephanie took off, rushing out the door without a backward look.

"Do you think she's upset with us for staying?" Molly asked anxiously.

Clara laughed. "She's probably upset she had to leave. Stephanie doesn't like being left out of anything."

"You know her really well."

"We've been close almost from the day we were born." Clara picked up her glass and took a sip of wine. "We grew up together. More like sisters, I guess."

"It must be nice, having a cousin who's also your best friend." Molly sighed. "I would have loved to have a sister. Or even a cousin to hang around with."

"You don't have cousins?"

Molly shook her head. "My mother was an only child, and my father grew up in foster homes. I have one brother, but he lives on the West Coast."

Clara nodded. "I'm an only child and so is Stephanie. I guess that's why we spent so much time together. We were always at one another's house, sleeping over most of the time."

"That's nice."

Molly looked sad and Clara sought to change the subject. "How did you meet Brad?"

"I met him in Mittleford last week." Molly smiled. "I'd been shopping and was loaded down with bags. I tried to open my car door and dropped a couple of them on the ground. Brad was getting out of his car in the next parking spot. He helped me load everything into the car and he was like, real friendly and cute, and we got to talking and he told me he worked at the resort project and mentioned this place. He said if I came down here, he'd buy me a drink."

"Ah, so when you heard that Stephanie and I wanted to talk to the construction guys . . ."

"I suggested we come here tonight so I could see Brad again."

"Devious. Sounds like something I would do."

Molly grinned. "I did get some information for you, though. Right?"

"Right." She wasn't exactly sure if it was going to be much help, but maybe their visit to Karen in the morning would turn up something. Catching sight of Molly staring across the room, she added, "Look, if you want to go and talk to Brad, go ahead. I have to get back home, anyway, and walk my dog. Just let me know if he tells you anything else about Scott."

Molly jumped to her feet. "You're sure? Cool! I'll see you tomorrow, then."

She was gone before Clara had time to answer.

Walking to the door, Clara felt a stab of envy when she saw Molly sit down next to the rugged guy at the far table. Her friend's face was flushed with excitement, and judging from the smile on the young man's face, he was just as thrilled to be talking to her.

It had been a long time since she'd felt that way, Clara thought, as she opened her car door and climbed inside. Though she had to admit, she'd come close a time or two when she'd been with Rick.

Thinking of Rick stirred up all her insecurities. It had taken her a long time to come to terms with how she felt about him. She'd been burned once, badly, and even now she wasn't sure she could completely trust her heart to someone else.

If only she knew how he really felt about her. Maybe then she could let go of all the doubts and just enjoy being with him.

She arrived home a short time later to find Tatters alone in the utility room and a note from her mother telling her not to wait up. Tatters, as usual, was ecstatic to see her, and without Jessie's stern voice telling him to heel, leapt up to smother Clara's face with his furry kisses.

She managed to calm him down enough to get a leash on him and then braved the cold once more. Their walk took them down to the harbor, but the wind cut through her coat like blades of ice and she gave up the idea of walking on the beach.

Even Tatters seemed content to trot along the seafront, and she returned to the house, grateful for the warmth of the living room. There was a casserole sitting in the oven and after heating it up she ate at the kitchen table, too tired to be bothered listening to the TV.

She fell asleep before Jessie returned home, and woke up to the sound of the wind rattling tree branches outside her window.

Jessie was in the kitchen, dressed for work and finishing up her usual mug of coffee. She gave Clara a searching look when she walked in, but said nothing until Clara had poured herself some coffee and sat down at the table.

"You look a bit peaky. Are you not sleeping well?"

Clara looked up with a start. "What? Yes, I'm sleeping okay."

"Well, you don't have any color in your cheeks."

"It's the middle of winter. No one has any color in their cheeks."

"You know what I mean." Jessie got up and walked over to the sink, carrying her mug. "I think it's that dog keeping you awake. He should be sleeping in the utility room."

Having heard that comment more times than she cared to remember, Clara didn't answer.

"Or is there something else keeping you awake?"

Clara sighed. "No, Mother, there's nothing going on. I'm sleeping perfectly fine, thank you."

Jessie came back to the table and sat down. "Are you happy, Clara?"

Taken aback, Clara stared at her mother. "Of course I am. Why wouldn't I be?"

"I don't know. You don't seem to have any friends— except for Stephanie, of course. Then again, she's your cousin. You have to be friends with her."

Clara decided to let that one go.

"What about that nice man at the hardware store? I thought you two were getting into something interesting."

Clara raised her eyebrows. "Whatever that means."

"You know perfectly well what I mean." Jessie sighed and got up. "There's just no talking to you these days.

You've changed, Clara, and I'm not at all sure it's for the better." She walked over to the door and looked back. "You have to live life to the fullest. You never know when it might end. I'll see you tonight."

Clara buried her face in her hands until she heard the front door close behind her mother. Jessie meant well, she reminded herself. Her mother worried about her. She wished she wouldn't.

Still, Jessie's last words remained with Clara as she showered and dressed. *You never know when it might end.* It had ended for Scott Delwyn far too soon. She frowned, thinking about the comments Molly's friend had made the night before.

Scott had received some kind of text message that had apparently upset him. A few short hours later he was dead. Coincidence? It seemed there were too many coincidences concerning his death,.

She stared at her image in the mirror. *Come on, Quinn Sense. Where are you when I need you?* Her hair could use a trim, she decided. It was almost to her shoulders. She brushed a handful of it back from her face. She'd often wondered what she'd look like with short, blonde hair instead of her heavy, dark brown mane. Thinking of blonde hair made her think of Roberta Prince, and thinking of Roberta made her think of Rick. Why did everything always bring her back to Rick Sanders?

Inpatient with herself, she dragged a brush through her hair, dashed on some lipstick and eyeliner and headed for the bedroom. After settling Tatters down on her bed, she was about to leave when it occurred to her she ought to call Karen Delwyn to ask if she and Stephanie could stop by.

She had to call Stephanie at the store first to get the number from the customer list, and promised to pick her up in fifteen minutes.

Karen's phone rang four times before she answered. Clara was on the point of hanging up when she heard the other woman's tired voice. She seemed pleased when Clara told her she and her cousin were thinking of paying her a visit.

"Come on over," she said, sounding brighter. "I made chocolate chip cookies for the girls this morning. If there's any left over by the time you get here, you can have some."

Clara felt guilty as she closed her phone. Karen had sounded so desperate for company, and here they were going over there to ask questions about her dead husband. She'd make a point of visiting her again, Clara promised herself as she walked down the path to her car. When she had more time to sit and talk.

Stephanie had her coat on when Clara got to the Raven's Nest. "We're just starting to get busy," she said as she scrambled into Clara's car. "We can't stay long at Karen's."

Clara felt the stab of guilt again. "We have to at least stay and eat some of the cookies she baked."

"Cookies?" Stephanie sat up. "What kind of cookies?"

"Chocolate chip."

"Well, maybe we can spare an hour or so." Stephanie settled back on her seat with a look of gleeful anticipation.

Karen greeted them at the door, looking a little more at ease than when they'd last seen her. She showed them into the living room and left them there while she went to get the cookies.

Clara's stomach took a nosedive when she saw a photo of Scott, Karen and the two girls on the mantel above the fireplace. They looked so happy and carefree, never dreaming that in such a short time their lives would be shattered.

The anger rose up in her again, and with it the vow to find out who was responsible for taking the life of this man.

Karen came back with a tray of cookies and three cups of steaming-hot tea. Putting the tray down on the coffee table, she said, "I've had so many people stop by this week. I didn't realize we had so many friends." Her voice wobbled and she quickly placed a cup and saucer in front of Clara. "Help yourself to the cookies."

Stephanie leaned forward and took one. "Thanks. These look good."

"They're the girls' favorites." Karen glanced at the photo on the mantel. "Scott loved them, too. I always put a couple in his lunch box when I made them."

Clara looked at Stephanie, who gave her a slight nod.

"He must have really loved that lunch box to go back for it that night," she said, smiling at Karen.

The widow looked puzzled. "His lunch box?"

"Yes." Now that she'd started the conversation, she wished she didn't have to finish it. Apparently Karen hadn't heard why her husband had gone back to the scaffolding on the night he died. "I . . . er . . . we heard that your daughter had given Scott a lunch box and he went back for it because he knew she'd be upset if he came home without it."

Karen was looking at her as if she'd gone out of her mind. "My daughter never gave her father a lunch box. Scott bought one for himself from Rick's hardware store when he got the job at the resort project."

Stephanie made an odd sound, her mouth full of cookie. Clara sent her a warning look and loudly cleared her throat. "Someone must have got it wrong," she said, reaching for her tea. "You know how these rumors start. Someone says something and someone else hears it differently. Like that telephone game we played when we were kids." Uncomfortable with the pained expression on Karen's face, she swallowed her tea too fast and choked. Somehow she managed to put the cup down without spilling anything.

"I'm so sorry," Stephanie said, having apparently emptied her mouth. "Scott was such a nice man. He didn't deserve to die in such a stupid accident."

Karen looked as if she were about to cry. "I haven't said anything about this before, but I'm getting to the point that if I don't tell someone soon I'll go totally out of my mind." She looked at both cousins in turn. "I hope I can trust you not to repeat anything I tell you."

"Of course you can."

"Absolutely."

They'd both spoken at once, and Karen seemed satisfied with that. "The truth is, Scott was acting really weird the last couple of days before he died. I think he was struggling with some kind of problem." She picked up her tea, her hand shaking enough to rattle the cup in the saucer. "It must have been huge for him not to tell me what it was. I kept asking him, but he wouldn't admit he was worried. He said I was imagining things."

Clara frowned. "Do you think it was about money?"

"That was my first thought, but I don't think so." Karen sipped her tea and put down the cup and saucer. "I checked our bank balance and we're not rich, by any means, but there's more than enough to pay the bills." She sighed. "Unless there's a bill I don't know about. I can't find anything in the house, though, so unless he hid it really well, I don't think this was about money. Whatever it was, it was driving him crazy." She gulped, and her eyes were full of tears when she looked at Clara. "I hate to say this, but I think my husband might have killed himself."

Clara opened her mouth to answer, but before she could form the words she was jolted out of her chair. The walls of the room disappeared, to be replaced by a tree-lined street with a row of shops. It was cold, so cold she dragged her scarf from her neck and covered her hair with it.

Little bits of ice bounced off the pavement at her feet as the hail pummeled her head. Farther down the street, a man stood outside the bank. He didn't have to turn around for her to know he was Scott Delwyn.

As she watched, he stepped closer to the bank, holding out his hands as if begging someone for something. Then he spun around and stared at her, still with his hands outstretched. She tried to call out to him, but the wind whipped the words from her mouth.

"Indigestion," someone said, in Stephanie's voice.

Clara blinked. She was back in Karen's living room, and both women were staring at her. Karen looked concerned, but Stephanie's face was alight with suppressed excitement.

"Are you all right?" Karen got up from her chair. "Can I get you something? Water? Antacid?"

"Thank you, I'm fine." Clara picked up her tea again. "A sip of this should take care of it." She was careful to drink more slowly this time, and smiled at her hostess as she set down the cup and saucer. "Please, sit down, Karen. I'm okay."

Her face still creased in doubt, Karen sat down. "Well, as I was saying, I think it's entirely possible that Scott jumped off that scaffolding. I would give anything to know what it was that drove him to do it."

"Well, I hope for your peace of mind you find out eventually," Clara said, "but if what you say is true, maybe Scott sacrificed his life so you wouldn't find out."

Karen stared at her for a moment, then her face crumpled. "You're right, Clara. Thank you. I'm so glad I told you now. Scott wouldn't want me digging around trying to find out what he didn't want me to know. I guess I'm always going to wonder about it, though." She fished in her pants pocket and pulled out a tissue. After blowing her nose, she looked at Stephanie. "So tell me, how are the kids doing? I don't know about you, but I worry about mine all the time they're in school. I know I should be enjoying the break but it never works out that way."

Clara sat back and tried to relax as her cousin and Karen exchanged horror stories about their kids' school lives. She kept seeing Scott's tormented face in her mind and frustration had her gritting her teeth. If only she knew what he was trying to tell her.

She was still turning it over in her mind when Stephanie got to her feet. "I really hate to break this up," she said, buttoning her coat, "but I should get back to the bookstore. Molly's there alone and Saturdays are always busy."

"Of course." Karen got up as Clara jumped to her feet. "It was so nice of you both to come over. I feel so much better after our little chat."

"We'll be back," Clara promised, still feeling guilty for the purpose of their visit.

She was hardly in the car before Stephanie flung herself into the passenger seat, exclaiming, "Where did you go back there? I know the Quinn Sense took you somewhere."

Concentrating on backing out of Karen's driveway,

Clara murmured, "I didn't go far." She told Stephanie what she'd seen in the vision. "I'm more convinced than ever that the bank robbery is somehow connected to Scott's death."

"It sure looks like it. I wish we could tell Dan that."

"I tried." Clara paused while she made a left turn. "He threatened to charge us with obstruction of justice."

"What?" Stephanie sat up. "You didn't tell me that! He can't do that! Can he?"

Clara shrugged. "I don't know, but I don't think we should test him enough to find out. From now on, we'll have to be pretty discreet about who we talk to about this."

"You're absolutely certain that Scott was thrown off that scaffolding by someone?"

"Positive."

"Then we'll just have to risk it with Dan." Stephanie settled down again. "I couldn't bear to see the pain in Karen's eyes when she talked about her husband committing suicide. We have to find out the truth, even if it's just to set her mind at rest."

"Not to mention punishing whoever was responsible."

"Yeah, well . . . that, too. What about the lunchbox thing? Do you think Brad lied about that?" She gasped, a hand over her mouth. "What if Brad is the killer!"

Clara wrestled with the thought for a while, then shook her head. "No, I don't think so. I think if Scott lied to his wife, he probably lied to Brad, too. I think he made up the story to cover up where he was really going that night."

Trouble Vision

•

Stephanie was quiet for a moment, "Whatever it takes, Clara. We're in this together, remember?"

Clara shot her a smile. If there was one person she could rely on, it was her cousin, and something told her they would have to rely on each other a great deal before this was over.

10

"We've been going about this all wrong," Clara said as she sat down on her bed that evening with her cell phone pressed against her ear.

At the end of the line, Stephanie sounded tired. "What does that mean?"

Clara shoved Tatters over and swung her bare feet up on the bed. Leaning against the headboard, she patted the dog's head. "We've been wasting our time trying to find out what happened at the construction site. What we need to do is look into the bank robbery. Maybe we can find the connection if we know more about it."

"Good idea. What do you think we should do next?"

Clara sighed. "I don't know. I'd love to ask Dan about the police report, but that would be pretty stupid. He'd probably throw me in jail."

"Well, I know how you can find out more."

"And what's that?" Clara asked cautiously. No doubt Stephanie was about to come up with another of her harebrained plans. Though she had to admit, once in a while, by some miracle, her cousin's ideas actually produced the desired result.

"Well, Dan isn't the only one who gets to see the police report."

"So?"

"So, you get Tim to ask you out on a date. Then you can casually ask him how the investigation is going. He's Dan's chief deputy, I bet he knows everything there is to know about the robbery."

Clara sighed. "I am not going on a date with Tim Rossi."

Stephanie's voice rose in exasperation. "Why *not?* You know he'd jump at the chance to go out with you. He can't take his eyes off you when he's in the store."

"For one thing, I'm not interested in dating Tim."

"But if it's to find out about the robbery—"

"For another thing, it's not fair to let a guy think you're interested in him when you're not."

"But—"

"For a third thing, if Dan found out, he'd bust us both."

"You're just making excuses."

"And why would I do that?"

"I dunno. Maybe you're afraid of upsetting Rick Sanders."

"That's ridiculous. It has nothing to do with Rick. He's just a friend, and I'm certainly not going to let him dictate my social life."

"Oh, yeah? I see you when he comes in the bookstore. You look at him the way Tim looks at you. You get all twittery."

Clara puffed out her breath. "Now you're just being juvenile."

"Has he kissed you yet?"

Clara winced at her cousin's sly tone. "No, he hasn't. Nor do I expect him to, so quit the interrogation. There's a simple way to find out more about the bank robbery."

To her relief, Stephanie jumped on the change of subject. "What? Tell me! What is it?"

"I can talk to Janice at the bank. She was there when the robbery happened. She can tell me everything I need to know."

"Now why didn't I think of that?" Stephanie paused, then spoke away from the phone. "Olivia! Put Jasper down this minute. *No!* He will not fit into your dollhouse so quit trying to stuff him in there." She sighed into the phone. "I'd better go and rescue the poor cat. I'll talk to you tomorrow."

Clara was about to wish her cousin good-night when Stephanie added, "Do you want me to come with you to the bank?"

"No, thanks. I'll go on Monday morning on the way

to work. It's Molly's day off, so you'll need to be in the bookstore."

Stephanie sounded relieved. "Okay, but if you need me, just holler. I still think you should date Tim Rossi. He'd be a lot more exciting than Rick Sanders. If you'd spent as much time with Tim as you have with Rick, Tim would have kissed you plenty of times by now."

She hung up before the retort left Clara's lips.

Lying back on the pillows, Clara closed the phone. Damn her cousin. She had a way of pushing all the wrong buttons.

Clara tried to concentrate on something else, but Stephanie's words kept coming back to her. *Has he kissed you yet?* No, he hadn't. He hadn't even come close. Some of the things he said made her think he would like to take their relationship further, yet he hadn't made any moves toward that.

Was he waiting for her to make the first move? She hoped not. It wasn't in her nature to be that aggressive. Now, if it were Roberta Prince, that would be a whole new ball game. Roberta wouldn't waste time dancing around. She'd be all over Rick at the first opportunity.

That thought didn't sit well with Clara. Much as Rick claimed he wasn't the least bit interested in Roberta, he was a red-blooded American male, and Roberta was, well . . . Roberta. Glamorous, sophisticated, and once she made up her mind she wanted something, the devil himself couldn't stop her.

Disgusted at the path her thoughts had taken her down,

Clara fastened Tatters' leash about his neck and took him out for a long walk.

Alone in the bookstore the next day, she had plenty of time to dwell on her thoughts. She did her best to keep busy, but every time the doorbell jingled, she prayed it wouldn't be Roberta, or conversely, that it would be Rick.

It seemed ages since she'd seen him. The longing to talk to him was so strong she was tempted to cross the street to his store. If she hadn't been alone in the store, she might have done just that, but even a visit with Rick wasn't enough to make her abandon the Raven's Nest while it was in her charge.

About an hour before closing time, just as she was thinking of taking a break in the Nook, she heard the doorbell ring and Dan's chief deputy strolled in. Tim had a habit of ducking his head when he came through the door, as if he was afraid of bumping it. It always made her smile, since he wasn't that much taller than her, and there was plenty of room to pass through the doorway.

She was still smiling when he approached the counter.

He smiled back, dark eyes twinkling at her. "I wasn't sure you'd still be open."

"We close at five on Sundays." She glanced at the clock. "You've got forty-five minutes to find what you want."

"Well, I was kind of hoping you'd find it for me." He glanced around the store as if making sure they were alone. "Dan told me you helped him find books for his granddaughter."

"Yes, I did." She was beginning to feel as uncomfortable as he looked. Stephanie's words came back to her in sharp focus. *You know he'd jump at the chance to go out with you. He can't take his eyes off you when he's in the store.* Surely Stephanie hadn't sent him here suggesting that he ask her for a date?

Tim cleared his throat and stretched his neck as if his collar was too tight. "Well, it's my mother's birthday and she likes to read, but I'm not sure what she likes." He cleared his throat again. "I think she reads . . . ah. . . . those love stories, but I don't know. . . ."

His voice trailed off as his face turned red. Relieved, Clara finally understood. "Your mother likes to read romances?"

Tim nodded. "Do you have anything like that here?"

"Well, we stock mostly fantasy, sci-fi and other paranormal stuff, but I think I can find you something your mother might like. Some of our fantasy books have great romances in them."

Tim coughed and Clara hid another smile as she led him down the aisle. Stephanie was wrong about the deputy being a mover and shaker. This man had his shy side.

She found the book she was looking for and put it into his hands. "There, I think she'll enjoy that one. We'll get her turned on to a whole new genre!"

Tim looked doubtful, but he took the book, muttering his thanks.

Stephanie's words popped into her head again. *Then you can casually ask him how the investigation is going.* Maybe her cousin had something there. On impulse, she said quickly, "I was just going to grab some coffee in the Nook. Would you like a cup?"

Tim looked surprised, then pleased. "Well, I don't normally drink coffee this late in the day but I'm not going to refuse an offer like that. Thanks!"

Feeling somewhat guilty again, Clara ushered him into the Nook and toward a chair. He looked around as he sat down, saying, "I've never been in this part of the store. It looks comfortable and cozy. No wonder it's always crowded in here in the mornings."

"I think it's more the coffee and donuts that bring in the crowds, but thanks, anyway." She put the coffee down in front of him. "So, how's the investigation going with the bank robbery?"

Tim, it seemed, much to her relief, had none of Dan's reluctance to talk about the crime. "Not too well, right now. We got shots of the robber on the security cameras, but he was wearing a ski mask and cap and all we have is a general height and weight description."

"Do you think it was a local man?"

Tim shrugged and stretched out a hand to pick up his coffee. "There's no way of telling. There was no getaway car—nothing to identify him. He didn't even speak. Just shoved a note at Janice and waved a gun at her. He had it all well planned. He was out the back door and over the fence before we even got there. Dan took a dog out to track him, but it was in the middle of that hailstorm we had, and the dog lost the scent. That guy thought of everything."

Clara hesitated, then decided she had nothing to lose. "Is there anything at all that might suggest that the robbery is connected to Scott Delwyn's death?"

Wariness crept across Tim's face. He put down the mug and stood up. "Dan told me you were asking him about that. Take a tip from me, Clara, Dan's got a short fuse when it comes to things like murder. Scott's death was an accident, and having you go around talking like it was something else is just going to stir up trouble. You don't want Dan mad at you. Take my word for it."

"He already is mad at me." She cradled her mug in her hands, feeling utterly defeated. "I'm not trying to make trouble, Tim, really I'm not, but I think that Scott didn't fall off that scaffolding without some help."

"What gives you that idea?"

She was so tempted to tell him, knowing all the same she couldn't. Even if she did, he'd never believe a word of it. "I don't know. Just a hunch."

He smiled.

"It's a strong hunch."

"Dan doesn't believe in hunches. He only believes in evidence. Unless you have some of that to back up your theory, he's not going to listen. We did a thorough investigation, and nothing turned up to suggest it was anything but an accident."

"I know." Clara looked up at him. "I just wish I had

that evidence. I know what I think, and I feel so utterly helpless to do anything about it. Dan is threatening to charge me with obstruction of justice if I don't stay out of it."

Tim stepped forward and wound an arm around her shoulders. "Cheer up, sunshine. Dan's just trying to protect you, that's all. He doesn't mean half of what he says."

Taken by surprise, Clara gave him a weak smile.

"Sorry, am I interrupting something?"

The voice had come from behind her, but she didn't need to turn around to know to whom it belonged.

"Hi, Rick." Tim dropped his arm and moved away from Clara. "I was just about to take off." He picked up the book Clara had given him and held it up. "Guess I'd better pay for this before I leave."

Still with her back to Rick, Clara nodded then braced herself to turn around.

Rick winked at her, his grin spreading across his face. "Caught in the act, huh?"

She raised her chin. "I haven't the faintest idea what you're talking about. Excuse me." She brushed past him and rushed up the aisle, followed more slowly by Tim.

After ringing up the charge, she dropped the book in a bag and thrust it at the deputy. "That'll be eight ninety-nine."

Tim took his time drawing a card from his wallet and swiping it, while Clara wondered what the heck Rick was doing down there in the Nook and what he was thinking.

"Thanks for the help," Tim said as he headed for the

door. "And don't worry about Dan. His bark is a lot worse than his bite."

The door closed behind him with a *snap*.

"What was all that about Dan?"

Clara jumped. She hadn't seen Rick come up the aisle. She avoided his gaze, trying to make a big deal out of recording the transaction, then tidying up the counter. "Oh, he just got annoyed with me because I was asking too many questions about the bank robbery."

"Still playing sleuth, huh?"

"Something like that." She finally looked at him, but he was staring at the door, as if deep in thought about something. "So, did you come to look at the new cookbooks?"

"No." He turned back to her. "I closed up early and thought I'd stop by and see how the monster is doing."

"Tatters?" Just saying his name made her smile. "He's doing just fine, though he's not too happy about taking walks in this weather. He can't wait for the warmer weather to get here."

Amusement lit up Rick's face. "He told you that?"

She wondered what he'd say if she told him she could read the dog's thoughts. "I know he finds it hard to leave a warm bed to go out in the cold."

"I know exactly how he feels." Rick glanced at the window. "I haven't seen him a while. Mind if I tag along on one of your walks?"

"Of course not!" She tried not to sound too thrilled. "Tatters would love that."

"Okay. It's a date. Just let me know when." He walked over to the door and looked back at her. "See you later, then."

She smiled and nodded. "Later."

The door closed, and her smile faded. He hadn't seemed in the least disturbed by seeing her in another man's arms, even if it was just a casual hug. In fact, he'd joked about it. Not that she knew exactly what she'd expected him to say, but complete indifference wasn't too encouraging.

Why couldn't she ever tell what he was thinking, much less read his mind? Why was it that whenever she needed the Quinn Sense the most, that was the precise moment it always let her down?

Angry at everything, she slammed the cash drawer shut and sat down at the computer. She needed something to take her mind off Rick Sanders and his infuriating attitude.

Minutes later, realizing she'd overreacted—something she tended to do when it concerned Rick—she closed down the computer and prepared to close up shop. Tomorrow was another day. Hopefully it would be a better one.

She locked the door and started walking briskly down the hill to her car, her mind still on Rick. He said he'd like to join her on her walk with Tatters. He didn't say when. Would he just forget about it, leaving her wondering when he was going to take up the offer? Or would he drop by and surprise her when she was unprepared, so she'd waste yet another opportunity to find out exactly how he felt about her?

Annoyed with herself, she opened the car door and climbed inside. What did it matter, anyway? She wasn't even certain how she felt about him. Oh, sure, she was attracted to him. After all, he was good to look at, fun to be with, kind and considerate—all the things that attracted her to a man.

Maybe that was the problem. Maybe she was still too afraid of getting hurt again. Maybe unconsciously she was putting up barriers. Then again, if he was really interested, wouldn't he make an effort to break those barriers down?

Driving down the hill, she growled under her breath in frustration. Why did everything have to be so complicated?

She had almost reached the bottom of the hill when a shadow stepped out into the middle of the road. Instinct jammed her foot down on the brake, and she swerved to avoid hitting the idiot with an apparent death wish.

She hit the curb hard and the car fishtailed for a few yards, then came to a screeching halt. Trembling, she cut off the engine and swiveled around in her seat to stare at the road behind her. There was no one there.

She blinked, staring into the shadows cast by the store-fronts. It wasn't quite dark yet, and she could see the street clearly. There was no doubt in her mind that someone had stepped out in front of her, yet there was no sign of anyone on the sidewalks.

Whoever it was couldn't have disappeared that fast. She stared again, willing the mystery man or woman to make an appearance and prove she wasn't going out of her mind.

She was about to turn back and restart the engine, when a slight movement caught her eye. She saw someone moving along the storefronts, slowly, as if he were feeling his way. He reached the bank and put his hand on the door.

Finding it locked, he backed away, then turned so she could see his face. She recognized him at once. It was Scott Delwyn, or at least, his ghost, and his mouth was wide open, as if crying out for help.

Clara blinked, and the vision disappeared. The lights of a car appeared at the top of the hill, heading down toward her. She quickly restarted the engine and pulled away from the curb. Whatever Scott was trying to tell her, it was obviously becoming more urgent. Tomorrow she would talk to Janice, and do her best to find out what the connection was between his death and the bank robbery.

Walking Tatters that night, she kept looking over her shoulder, half expecting Rick to pop up somewhere and surprise her. When he didn't appear, she returned home disappointed and disgruntled.

Tatters kept looking up at her, as if trying to understand why she was in such a funk. She couldn't tell him, of course. She wasn't even sure herself. Everything seemed to be coming down on her head at once, leaving her confused and frustrated, and there seemed no end in sight.

———

The following morning, she got up early and left the house with plenty of time for her visit to the bank. There were two customers waiting in line when she walked in—an elderly man in jeans, a heavy jacket and a baseball cap, and a woman carrying a briefcase and an umbrella.

Janice took the man's deposit, while Alison, the other teller, waited on the woman. Clara was relieved when the man left first, giving her the opportunity to talk to Janice.

The bank teller, however, wasn't a lot of help. "I don't remember too much," she said, when Clara asked her what happened. "I was too scared. I'd never seen a gun in someone's hand before—except on TV, anyway. It was like my eyes were glued to it. I just took the money out of the drawer and handed it over. Besides, Dan told me the robber was wearing a ski mask. It was on the security cameras. Even if I had looked, I couldn't have seen his face."

"You didn't recognize anything about him? His voice? The way he walked? Something about his hand when he took the money?"

Janice shook her head. "I never looked up that far. Like I said, I was staring at the gun, praying it wouldn't go off. As for his voice, he never spoke. He just held up the note asking for all the money in my drawer."

Clara let out her breath in frustration. "What happened to the note?"

"He took it with him." Janice nodded. "He was a sly one. He didn't leave any clues behind."

Clara thanked her and headed for the door. Not that she'd really expected to find out anything new. Still, she'd hoped that Janice would say something that might give her a hint at a connection between the robbery and Scott's death.

She reached the door and stepped outside, shivering as a cold blast from the sea lifted her hair. She was about to cross the sidewalk to her car when a voice spoke softly behind her.

"Excuse me?"

Clara turned, surprised to see the woman customer from the bank. "Can I help you?"

"I think I can help you." The woman looked up and down the street, then added, "I couldn't help overhearing you asking that teller about the robbery."

Clara held her breath for a moment.

The woman glanced over her shoulder again. "It's obviously important to you, and there's something I didn't tell the police," she said, speaking so low Clara had trouble understanding her. "I don't want to get involved, so I have to ask you to promise not to tell anyone that I told you."

Excited now, Clara nodded. "I promise."

"I figure you must have a personal reason to want to know about the robbery, so that's why I'm telling you."

"You're right, and I'd really appreciate anything you can tell me."

"Well, when the robber came in, he made everyone lie

facedown on the floor." Again the woman looked over her shoulder. "I was closest to him when he walked over to the counter. I saw his shoes."

Clara frowned. "His shoes?"

The woman nodded. "That's all I saw of him, but he had sneakers on. You know, the kind that have those built-up soles? They were black, with three bright gold stars on the sides."

"Ah." Now Clara understood. "They were distinctive."

"Very." The woman looked worried. "I know I should have mentioned it to the police, but like I said, I really don't want to get involved. So, if they do find out about it, please don't tell them I told you."

"Don't worry." Clara smiled. "I don't know your name or where you live or anything about you. I couldn't tell them who you are even if I wanted to, which I don't."

Relief shone in the woman's face. "Thank you. I hope you find that dreadful man. I just thank the good Lord he didn't hurt or kill anyone. Good luck to you."

She hurried off, leaving Clara to stare after her. Black shoes with gold stars. Maybe she could ask at the shoe store if they remember someone buying shoes like that. Unless the robber had bought them online. Then she'd be out of luck. Which wouldn't surprise her, since every move she'd made in this investigation had ended up a dead end.

11

Arriving at the bookstore later that morning, Clara was relieved to find Stephanie there on her own with no customers to wait on. It gave her a chance to tell her cousin what she'd found out at the bank.

"We should tell Dan," Stephanie said, when Clara was finished. "It could help him catch the robber."

"Well, let's see how popular the sneakers are." Clara walked behind the counter and sat down at the computer. A few clicks later and she had a page of footwear pictures in front of her. "Here we go."

Stephanie joined her at the computer. "I see black shoes with one gold star. Can't see any with three, though."

"Okay, let's try again." After clicking around the web a few times, Clara leaned back. "Well, if they're out there, they're not that popular."

"Okay, then!" Stephanie reached for her purse. "We start staring at men's feet from now on."

"Sounds like a plan."

Stephanie headed for the aisles, calling out over her shoulder, "You know, even if Dan catches the robber, that doesn't mean he had anything to do with Scott's death. Even if he did kill Scott, he's not going to confess. So unless you have had second thoughts about there being a link there, we still have to find that connection."

"I know." Clara got up from the chair. "And I haven't had second thoughts. I saw Scott again last night."

Stephanie had disappeared between the shelves, but seconds later she popped her head out again. "What did you say?"

"I saw Scott again. He was at the bank and he was crying for help."

"Did he say anything?"

"No." Clara picked up a box of pens and started stacking them in a display holder. "But I've got a strong feeling that he's getting desperate, like he's running out of time."

Stephanie raised her eyebrows. "I'd say he's already run out of time."

"You know what I mean. I think he wants us to find out who killed him before something happens."

"Like what?"

Clara shrugged. "I don't know."

Stephanie shook her head. "I don't think we'll ever get to the truth of this one."

"Don't say that." Clara shoved the last pen in place. "We can't give up. Let's just keep looking for those shoes."

"All right, but I really wish the Quinn Sense would be more helpful."

Just as the words were out of her mouth, the door opened and Molly danced in, a large shopping bag swinging in her hand. "Hi, you guys!"

Stephanie stared at her in amazement. "What are you doing here on your day off?"

Molly grinned. "I was shopping for a new outfit and thought I'd stop by for a free cup of coffee and a donut." She looked around the store. "Wow, where is everyone? You're not exactly rushed off your feet."

"Don't remind me." Looking grim, Stephanie headed for the door. "If this keeps up, I'll go broke by the end of the year."

"It's a temporary lull," Clara said, shaking her head at Molly. Knowing how her cousin worried about keeping up sales, she added, "We've had them before and we always make up for them later."

"We've got a long way to go before the summer tourists get here." Stephanie looked back at her. "I hope we can hold on that long."

"We'll have to come up with a promotion of some kind." Clara looked at Molly. "There's something you can help us with—come up with a great idea to promote the bookstore."

"Sounds like fun!" Molly wandered over to the aisles.

"I'll think about it while I'm drinking my coffee." She disappeared in the direction of the Nook.

"See you later." Stephanie gave her a cousin a wave and stepped out into the street.

Left alone at the counter, Clara tried to concentrate on ideas for a promotion. When nothing came to her, she decided a cup of coffee might jog her brain, too.

Molly was munching on a donut when Clara joined her in the Nook. "These are good," she said as Clara poured coffee into a mug. "Chocolate frosting is my favorite."

"Mine, too." Clara carried her mug over to the couch and sat down. "The problem is that all that sugar and fat sticks to my hips."

Molly laughed. "You're lucky. You're so tall you don't have to worry about looking fat."

Clara winced. "Trust me, it still shows if I let it get out of hand."

"Well, you look great." Molly took another bite of her donut, swallowed, then added, "Seen Rick lately?"

Clara eyed her warily. "He comes in now and then."

"No, I mean, have you *seen* him? Outside of work."

"Not for a while." Anxious to change the subject, Clara added, "What about you? Are you seeing that nice young man from the construction site?"

"You mean Brad?" Molly grinned. "No, but we'll be hanging out soon. I got a text message from him this morning. He asked me out on a date." She nodded at the shopping bag at her feet. "He's the reason I went shopping. To get a new outfit. Wanna see it?"

Without waiting for a reply, she dived into the bag and pulled out a red velvet top and black skirt. "What do you think?"

Clara nodded her approval. "Love it. That should get his attention."

"I'm counting on it." Molly stuffed the clothes in the bag and jumped to her feet. "Gotta run. See you on Wednesday."

Clara called out to her departing friend, "Enjoy your date." Leaning back on the couch, she sipped her coffee. She remembered when she used to rush off like that, excited about meeting a guy she liked. It seemed a long time ago now.

Since New York she had dated no one, unless she could call the occasional dinner with Rick a date. Even then, he had made it sound like a thank you for taking care of Tatters, rather than an opportunity to spend time with her.

At first she'd been relieved about that, but lately she'd been feeling sort of let down, disappointed even. It seemed that she was finally getting over her breakup with Matt, and was ready to move on. Now if only she knew exactly where she stood with Rick, things would be a lot less complicated.

She envied Molly, so secure and confident, that a simple text message could make her day.

Clara put her mug down. *Text message*. Brad had said

that Scott received a text message that apparently had upset him the day he died. She'd meant to ask Karen about it, but the suggestion that Scott may have killed himself had driven all thoughts from her mind.

There was something else she had forgotten. If Scott had received a text message from someone, the message should still be on his cell phone.

Excited now, she pulled out her own cell phone and thumbed Stephanie's speed dial number.

Her cousin answered on the third ring. "Hold on a minute," she said, then added offstage, "I've told you before, Olivia. Cats do not like wearing clothes. Take that T-shirt off Jasper and leave him alone."

Olivia's voice could be heard in the distance. Then Stephanie again. "I don't care what Michael said. Jasper has a fur coat to keep him warm. Are you still there?"

This last was spoken into the phone.

Clara sighed. "I'm still here. That's if you're talking to me."

"Sorry, but you know how it is. I'm constantly on watch here."

"I know. I won't keep you. I just wanted to tell you that I'm going to see Karen again tomorrow."

"You are?" Stephanie sounded worried. "Has something happened?"

"No, not really. I just got to thinking about that text message that Scott saw on the day he died. We forgot to ask Karen if she sent it."

"Oh, crap, we did. So you're going to ask her about it?"

"Yes, I am. And if she didn't send it, it should still be on his phone, so we can find out who did."

"That's right! We should have thought about that."

"It could give us a lead."

"It could." Stephanie paused. "Do you want me to go with you?"

"No, it'll be better if I go alone. I'll stop by the store afterward and tell you if I find out anything."

"Okay." Again the pause. "You spoke to Janice without me and now Karen."

"I have more time than you do. I don't have a husband and three kids. Besides, tomorrow is my day off."

"I know. It's just that we've always done this stuff together and . . ."

"You're feeling left out."

"Sort of, I guess."

Clara smiled. "I'm just going to run over and have a quick word with Karen. I promise if I do any serious sleuthing, I'll expect you to be there."

"Oh, I will! Just say the word."

Clara hung up, still smiling. She and Stephanie had grown up practically joined at the hip. She'd missed her cousin when she'd first moved to New York, so much so that she'd considered moving back to Finn's Harbor the first few weeks she was away. Then her new life had taken over and the cousins had gradually spent less time on the phone, sent fewer e-mails and spent little time together during Clara's brief visits home.

All that was behind her now, and it was good to have

back that close relationship with her cousin. As for her mother, she still had to work on that one.

Hearing the doorbell, Clara left her chair and headed for the front of the store. She was surprised to see Tim at the counter and hurried over to him, wondering if he had some news for her about the robbery.

Her hopes were dashed when he greeted her. "I just stopped in to thank you for the great book you picked out for my mother. She loves it, and told me she's going to look for that author's next book."

Clara smiled. "I'm so glad she likes it. I thought she might."

Tim stuck his hands in his pockets. "Not too busy in here today?"

"It's a Monday. They're always quiet." She walked behind the counter. "Just as well, since I'm holding down the fort on my own."

He nodded. "Pretty cool job here. No stress."

"Not like yours." She did her best to sound indifferent. "How's the investigation into the bank robbery going?"

Tim shrugged. "Going nowhere, if you want the truth. Looks like that one got away."

She was starting to feel guilty, wondering if she should mention the shoes. Then she remembered that frightened customer's face who'd begged her not to tell anyone. "I'm sorry," she murmured. "That must be so frustrating."

"It is. Finn Harbor's first bank robbery in living memory and we can't catch the guy. It makes it look bad for the chief. For all of us, I guess."

She decided to take a chance. "What about the security cameras? Didn't they give you any clues?"

"Nothing. The guy was wearing a heavy jacket and a ski mask. Could have been anyone."

"What about his feet?"

Tim blinked. "His feet?"

"I was just wondering if the cameras showed his whole body or just his head."

"Ah." Tim still looked somewhat confused. "I don't really remember. I'm sure we would have noticed though, if there'd been anything unusual."

Clara let out her breath. She'd done all she could. For now. If she or Stephanie spotted someone wearing black shoes with gold stars, however, she would have to tell Dan and Tim what she knew.

"Well, I'd better get going." Tim seemed reluctant to leave as he turned for the door. "See you later."

Clara felt a cold draft as he closed the door behind him. Tim was a nice man. She wondered why he hadn't hooked up with someone by now. Or maybe he had and was keeping it quiet. She wandered to the window and looked out. Tim had already disappeared down the hill.

Across the street, the lights gleamed behind the windows of the hardware store. A fog was creeping in from the ocean, blotting out the sun. A truck rumbled past, probably on its way to the construction site.

Clara wondered where Brad would take Molly for their date. Feeling that pang of envy again, she turned her back on the window. Time to get the shelves straightened up. It would help keep her mind off things.

Later that evening, she set off down the street with Tatters eagerly trotting along in front of her. The fog was thicker now, spinning moist webs around the streetlamps. As she approached the beach, she could hear the roar of the ocean as it pounded the sand with cold fury.

"It's too cold to go out there," she told Tatters as he jerked on the leash, anxious to run on the sand.

The truth was, the sands looked forbidding in the murky darkness. She was already unnerved by visions she'd had of the late Scott Delwyn, and she was in no mood to venture onto that stretch of lonely beach.

Tatters trudged along at her side as she retraced her steps, obviously disappointed by the short walk. As she opened the front door to let him in the house, he looked up at her.

Roll on, summer.

"Amen. And quit that."

She followed him into the hallway just as her mother emerged from the kitchen.

"Who were you talking to?" Jessie said, as Clara closed the door.

"Myself." Clara leaned down to undo Tatters' collar. "I was wishing it was summer. That fog is miserably cold and wet."

"Oh, I thought maybe you had company on your walk." Jessie looked down at the floor. "One of these days, Tatters, I'll teach you how to wipe your feet before you come in."

Good luck with that.

Clara coughed. "I'm going to get a cup of coffee. Want some?"

"No, I think I'm going to bed. I have to get an early start in the morning. We're setting up an exhibit at the library and it has to be finished before we open."

Jessica set off for her room, leaving Clara to enjoy her coffee alone.

The following morning, Clara called Karen to see if she would be home. The widow seemed happy to hear from her and an hour later Clara was ringing her doorbell.

After bringing in coffee and a plate of banana bread, Karen sat down with Clara in her tastefully furnished living room. "I'm glad you stopped by," she said as Clara helped herself to a slice of the bread. "I wanted to talk to you. I'm going back to work next week. They've offered me a full-time job at Harley's department store in Mittleford. I was working there part-time, but now I'm going to need the money. Scott had life insurance, but that won't go far with two girls to raise."

Clara swallowed her mouthful of bread. "That's a great store. It might be good for you to get back to work. It will help take your mind off things."

"Oh, I'm sure it will." Karen picked up her coffee.

"About the insurance, though. The insurance company won't pay on the policy if the death is a suicide. So I hope you won't take what I said too seriously about Scott killing himself. I was upset and not thinking straight."

Clara hurried to reassure her. "Of course not! I never did think he killed himself, anyway."

Karen gave her an intent look. "You didn't?"

Realizing she'd probably said too much, Clara cleared her throat. "No . . . ah . . . I mean . . . from what you've said about him, Scott didn't seem like the kind of guy who would do that. I mean, he had everything to live for. You, the girls, his job . . ."

Karen shrugged. "I still think something was worrying him, but maybe you're right. It's hard to believe that he was in so much trouble he couldn't bear to tell me about it."

Clara reached for her coffee. "Did you, by any chance, send him a text message the day he died?"

Karen looked startled. "A text message?"

"Yes. Someone mentioned that Scott received a text message that day and that it seemed to upset him."

Now Karen looked frightened. "I knew he was into something bad. I wonder who it was."

"Well, there's one way to find out. The message should still be on his cell phone."

Karen's eyes grew wide. "That's weird. His cell phone wasn't with the rest of his stuff they gave to me. I didn't realize that until now. He never went anywhere without that phone. I wonder where it went."

Clara was wondering the same thing. "I'll be talking

to Dan later on today," she said casually. "I'll ask him for you."

"Thanks." Karen was still frowning. "Though now I'm not sure I want to know what's on it."

"You can always delete everything without reading it."

"You know I can't do that."

"Well, let's see first if Dan has the phone. I'll call you after I've talked to him."

"Thanks." Karen sighed. "I should be calling him myself, but I just can't seem to face talking about what happened yet."

"I know. I'm sorry, Karen. This must be so hard for you."

"Having friends like you helps." Karen gave her a weak smile then frowned as her doorbell rang. "Who can that be?" She glanced at the clock and rose to her feet. "Sorry, Clara. I won't be a minute."

She headed for the front door, and Clara grabbed the opportunity to take another slice of the banana bread. Karen was wasting her talents in a department store, she thought, as she munched on the tangy, sweet bread. She should open up a bakery.

She heard Karen's voice at the door. "It's nice to see you, Thelma. Come on in."

The voice that answered was vaguely familiar. Then Clara remembered: Karen's next-door neighbor. She'd met her at the funeral.

Karen appeared in the doorway and ushered in the chubby woman. "Thelma, this is Clara Quinn. She works in the Raven's Nest bookstore."

"Of course! I remember!" Her face wreathed in smiles, Thelma toddled toward Clara, holding out her hand. "How are you, honey? We met at Scott's funeral, remember? Super to see you again!"

Clara shook the thick fingers and let go, murmuring, "Nice to see you, too."

"Sorry if I'm interrupting," Thelma said, eyeing the banana bread with unabashed enthusiasm. "I just stopped in to give you my news."

"You're not interrupting anything," Karen said, picking up the plate of bread. "Sit down and have a slice of bread. Clara and I were just . . . ah . . . talking."

"About books," Clara said, seeing the uncomfortable look on her friend's face.

"Oh, I don't have time to read books." Thelma took a slice of the bread with a nod of thanks. "Especially now that I'm packing up."

Karen raised her eyebrows. "Packing up?"

Her mouth too full of bread to speak, Thelma nodded, waving her hand while chewing furiously until she finally swallowed. "We're moving. Ray's been offered a job in Portland. At last he'll be working again. I must say, it's a huge relief. No more scrimping and saving just so I can keep him fed." She laughed, patted her chest and burped. "Things have been tough since my old man left."

Catching the flash of light from the large diamond on Thelma's finger, Clara wondered what had happened to the woman's husband.

"Good thing we don't own the house," Thelma added,

bringing the rest of the bread up to her mouth. "That's the nice thing about renting, you can just pick up and leave when you want." She took another huge bite of the bread, leaving a tiny piece in her fingers.

"You're right." Karen sighed. "I've thought about moving since Scott . . . passed away. This house has so many memories, it's hard to live with them here. But the thought of having to sell right now gives me nightmares."

Thelma nodded. "Know what you mean. When I got divorced, the first thing I did was put the house up for sale. Not that I got much for it, but I couldn't afford the mortgage on the pittance Ralph got away with for alimony."

Deciding she'd heard enough, Clara got up. "Sorry to eat and run, but I really should get going. I have to be at the store soon."

"Oh, of course." Karen shot up while Thelma settled back on her chair, obviously planning to stay for the long haul.

Feeling sorry for her friend, Clara said good-bye to the chatty woman and headed for the front door.

"Thanks for coming over," Karen said as Clara stepped outside.

Blinking in the glare of sunlight, Clara smiled. "Good luck with the job. Let us know if you need anything. I truly mean that."

"I know you do." Karen looked sad. "I'll be fine . . . eventually."

Clara's heart ached for the young widow as she crossed

the sidewalk to her car. How awful it must be to lose a husband and to be left alone to raise two daughters. Karen seemed to be holding up all right publicly, but inside she must be going through agony.

Angry all over again at the people who had caused such tragedy, Clara silently renewed her vow to hunt down the killers and see them punished for their horrible crime.

She was fired up now, and ready to tackle Dan. At least this time she had a legitimate reason to call on him.

12

The police chief seemed less than pleased to see her when he answered her knock on his office door. "Don't tell me," he said, as she sat down in front of his desk. "You know who robbed the bank and you've got him tied up somewhere waiting for me to arrest him."

She raised her chin. "Sarcasm will get you nowhere. You should be grateful that at least two of your citizens care enough about law and order they're willing to do something to help."

Dan laid down his pen. "What I'd like," he said, folding his hands together on the desk in front of him, "is for those two citizens to allow me to do my job, instead of taking matters in their own hands."

She leaned forward. "Those two citizens helped solve two murders, if my memory is correct."

"You lucked out, that's all." Dan's face softened. "Look, don't think I'm not grateful for what you and Stephanie did in the past. Stupid, maybe, but you did help close some cases for us and I'm thankful for that. But you've gotta realize the chances you two are taking messing with the bad guys. You've been lucky so far. That might not be the case the next time. Just butt out in the future, okay?"

She squirmed on her chair. "I hear what you're saying."

He looked unimpressed. "I hope you take it to heart. So, why are you here, then?"

She took a deep breath. "I've just come from Karen's house. She said that Scott's cell phone wasn't among his personal belongings that you gave back to her. She was wondering what happened to it."

Dan shrugged. "She got back everything we had. There was no need to keep anything. If the phone wasn't there, then he didn't have it with him when he died."

"Karen said he never went anywhere without it."

"Then I reckon it fell out of his pocket on the way down and got lost in all the rubble down there." He frowned. "It's probably not working now, anyway."

"Maybe not, but there could be information on there that's important to Karen."

His frown grew deeper. "Like what?"

"Like who it was who texted him on the day he died. A message that apparently upset him."

"And you know this, how?"

Again she squirmed. "Someone who was with him that day told us."

"So you've been asking around about this."

"Sort of. I guess."

He groaned—a sound that came from deep in his belly. "Do I have to lock you two up before you come to your senses? On second thought, that might be a good idea."

Deciding she'd reached the point of no return, Clara got up from her chair. "It might be a good idea if you searched for Scott's cell phone. Just in case there's something important on it."

"And it might be a good idea if you scooted out of here before I slap cuffs on you. I hope you haven't been filling that poor widow's mind with your crazy ideas. She's been through enough. For God's sake, let it lie."

Clara answered with a hasty wave and beat it out of the station.

Remembering her promise to her cousin to stop by the bookstore after seeing Karen, she drove to the parking lot and left the car to walk up the hill. Even the sunlight couldn't ward off the freezing wind from the ocean. Clara hunched her shoulders and dug her hands deep in the pockets of her coat.

Many of the souvenir shops were closed for the winter, and would stay closed until Memorial Day weekend, the start of the tourist season. Then the striped awnings would come out, the windows would have fresh displays and people would crowd the sidewalks.

Clara wondered what summer would be like in Finn's Harbor once the new resort and golf club opened. It was bound to change the little town, but would it be for good or bad? There were so many mixed emotions among the residents. It was no wonder some of that anxiety and frustration spilled over to end up in brawls and fistfights.

Was Scott's death part of that? A fight that had spiraled out of control until a man lay dead on the ground? Or was it something deeper? Something connected to the bank robbery? So many questions, and no answers. If only Karen had been given Scott's phone, they might have had at least one clue by now.

Turning into the store, she was relieved to see only two customers browsing the aisles. She wanted a few minutes to talk to Stephanie before she left. Molly was at the counter, and waved to her as she walked in. Stephanie was nowhere to be seen, and Clara headed for the stock-room.

Her cousin was standing in the middle of the room when Clara opened the door. She was talking to Angela, her sales rep—a thin woman with orange-framed glasses that almost matched the color of her hair.

Clara returned Angela's greeting, then took her time taking off her coat before hovering around in the background until the sales rep left.

"I just came from the police station," she said when Stephanie handed her some catalogs.

Stephanie raised her eyebrows. "You didn't get arrested, did you?"

"Do I look like I got arrested?"

"I don't know." Stephanie tilted her head to one side. "You don't look too happy."

"I'm frustrated." Clara quickly recited the events of the morning.

"Seems like Dan was ready to lock you up," Stephanie said when Clara was finished.

Clara sighed. "What is it with you and being arrested? Do you want to see me behind bars or something?"

Stephanie looked offended. "No, of course not. I just don't want you to do anything that could get you into trouble. So, what do you think happened to Scott's phone?"

"I don't know." Clara sorted through the catalogs in her hand without really looking at them. "I suggested Dan look for it, but he wasn't too thrilled with my request."

"You're not saying we should dig through that stuff, are you?" Stephanie pushed her hair back from her face with both hands. "In the first place, we'd have to get onto the site, and it would have to be when everyone is gone, and if we're caught, we'd be in a ton of trouble—"

"I know." Clara patted her shoulder. "Calm down, Steffie. I wouldn't know where to begin looking anyway. We'll just have to think of something else."

"That reminds me. I almost forgot. Molly has something to tell you."

"What is it?"

"I don't know. I told her you were planning on dropping in this morning. She wanted to wait until you got here before she said anything."

As if reading her mind, the door opened and Molly appeared in the doorway. "Oh, there you are." She beamed. "I thought you two might be in here."

"Are the customers gone?" Stephanie peered past her.

"All gone." Molly looked excited as she closed the door. "I've got something to tell you both."

"What is it?"

"Okay, so shoot."

The cousins had spoken together and Molly looked from one to the other. "I went on a date with Brad last night."

Disappointed, Clara tried to sound interested. "Oh, yeah. How was it? Did he like your new outfit?"

"Yes, he did." Molly grinned. "We had the best time. Brad was pumped because he's been offered a new job. Lionel Chatham's renovating his inn. Brad says he's spending a ton of money on it. He offered Brad almost twice what he's earning on the construction site. Apparently Lionel's been hitting up most of the workers up there. Brad says he's trying to get ahead of the competition."

"Really." Clara stared at Molly. "I wonder where Lionel got the money to do all that."

Stephanie uttered a soft gasp. "Don't tell me you think it was Lionel who robbed the bank?"

"I don't know what to think. It is quite a coincidence, though—him coming up with all this money a week after the bank is robbed?"

"He just doesn't seem the type to do something that rash."

"Well," Molly said, butting in, "that's not what I wanted to talk to you about. We were at the bowling alley and we bumped into Stacey Warren."

Clara shook her head. "Do I know her?"

"She's Eddie Hatchett's girlfriend. The one who drove him to the hospital the night Scott Delwyn died?"

"Oh, okay." Sensing something important was coming, Clara waited.

"Remember Eddie said that he hurt his wrist when he fell off his bike and Stacey drove him to the ER in Mittleford?"

Both cousins nodded.

"Well . . ." Molly looked really pleased with herself. "Stacey did drive him to the hospital that night."

Clara let out her breath. "Oh, I thought—"

"Wait." Molly held up her hand. "It wasn't five thirty when he called Stacey. It was more than two hours later."

Stephanie looked puzzled, but Clara jumped on it. "So he doesn't have an alibi for the time of Scott's death."

"No, he doesn't." Molly was almost leaping up and down with excitement. "What's more, he lied about it. That means he has something to hide."

"You're right." Clara looked at Stephanie. "We need to talk to Eddie Hatchett."

"I'll do it, if you like." Molly grabbed Clara's arm. "We could go back to the Laurel Street Tavern on Friday and—"

"No, thank you." Clara smiled at her to soften her words. "It's going to take wild horses and a herd of elephants before I set foot in that place again." She turned back to Stephanie. "What are you doing around five thirty this evening?"

Stephanie grinned. "Guess we're going to talk to Eddie Hatchett."

Molly groaned. "You guys have all the fun."

Stephanie put an arm around her shoulders. "Sorry, Molly, but someone has to take care of the Raven's Nest. Look on the bright side: you'll be nice and cozy in a warm bookstore while we'll be. . . ." She broke off and looked at Clara. "Where exactly will we be?"

"I don't know, but I'm going to find out where Eddie's working today." Clara moved toward the door. "We'll catch him on his way home and talk to him."

Stephanie visibly shuddered. "That's another good reason why you should stay here, Molly. This could get dangerous."

Molly frowned. "Don't you think maybe we should talk to Dan?"

"I don't think that's going to do any good at this point." Clara glanced at her cousin. "Aren't you supposed to be somewhere?"

"Oh, crap. Is that the time?" Stephanie grabbed her coat from the hook. "Gotta run. See you tonight. Are you driving or shall I?"

"I'll pick you up at five."

Stephanie waved as she rushed through the door. "Another pizza night. George will divorce me." She disappeared up the aisle, and a moment later the doorbell jingled, followed by the door slamming shut.

"I've got errands to run," Clara said as Molly followed her to the counter. "Could you put these catalogs back in the drawer for me?"

"Sure." Molly took them from her. "You will be careful, won't you? Tonight, I mean."

"Of course. We're always careful. Besides, I'm taking Tatters with me. He'll take care of us."

"I'd feel a lot better if you were taking Dan with you. I wouldn't trust Eddie Hatchett if he was locked up in a cage."

"Don't worry. He won't be able to do much if we talk to him on the street with people around. We'll be fine."

"I hope so." Molly hesitated. "Will you call me after you've talked to him? I don't think I'll sleep tonight unless I know you're both okay."

Clara laughed, though it sounded forced, even to her. "I will. Now quit worrying, and I'll see you tomorrow."

Stepping outside, she glanced across the street. Tyler was outside the hardware store with a broom, sweeping off the step. They must not be too busy over there. She hesitated just for a second or two, then charged across the road.

Tyler barely glanced at her when she said hello, and she headed into the store, wondering if Ryan had mentioned her awkward encounter with him. Catching sight of Rick in the back of the store, she walked toward him, belatedly trying to think of an excuse why she was there.

Rick looked up as she approached, and gave her one of his lazy smiles. "Hi there. What brings you into this bastion of male dominance?"

She laughed. "Are you telling me you don't have women customers? I thought most men hated shopping and sent their wives to do it."

"Clothes, maybe. Food, absolutely. But power tools?" He shook his head. "Definitely a man's job."

"I stand corrected." She picked up a gadget that looked like a distorted question mark with a clip. "What's this?"

"It's a carabiner. Used for tightening and holding ropes."

"Oh, like in rock climbing?"

"Well, not this one." He took it from her and turned the card over so she could read the back. "This is called a Figure Nine and is used for heavy loads. It's not recommended for climbing." He put the tool back on the shelf. "You like rock climbing?"

She shuddered. "No. I have no head for heights. I can't go up a ladder without getting dizzy. How about you?"

"I tried it a couple of times, but the first time I fell I figured it wasn't my thing."

"You fell? Were you hurt?"

"Just my pride, though it was a few weeks before I could kneel without wincing."

"Ouch." She wandered along the shelves, pretending to be interested in the array of tools.

"Are you looking for anything in particular?"

"What?" Deciding to give up the pretense, she blurted out, "I was wondering if you'd like to join Tatters and me this evening on our walk. I'm sure he'd love to see you."

She wasn't looking at his face, but his voice sounded a little weird when he answered, "Sure. What time and where?"

"Come by the house. Whatever time you can make it."

"Okay. I'll grab something quick to eat and I'll be there around nine."

"Sounds good." From the front of the store came the sound of the door slamming shut. "Guess you've got a customer. I'll see you tonight, then."

She almost ran up the aisle, racing past Tyler who was on his way to the counter. Without stopping, she shot out the door and started down the hill. She'd done it. She'd actually invited him over to her house.

She stopped short with a little moan. What had she done? Jessie would be there and would insist on meeting him and she'd ask him all kinds of awkward questions. Clara had been an absolute idiot to invite him over.

Walking again, she tried to calm down. She'd wait outside for him. That way, Jessie wouldn't have a chance for an inquisition. Would he think it strange if she didn't invite him in? After all, she'd been in his house. Well, too bad. It was better than being embarrassed by her mother's prying into stuff that was none of her business.

Reaching home, she let an exuberant Tatters out into the backyard, then turned on her computer. The Hatchetts didn't have a website, but Bob Hatchett was listed under local electricians. After dialing the number on her cell phone, Clara waited for someone to answer.

On the third ring, a female voice cheerfully announced, "Hatchett's Electricians. Can I help you?"

Clara sent up a silent prayer. "I'd like to speak to Eddie Hatchett, please."

"Eddie's not here," the voice assured her. "Can I take a message?"

"Actually, I'm an old friend. I'd like to surprise him. Can you tell me where I can find him?"

The voice cooled considerably. "Eddie is working on the hotel project on the coast road."

Clara felt a jolt of surprise. "Really? I thought he . . . er . . . left there."

"The new foreman is a friend of Eddie's father. He gave Eddie his job back." The voice sounded suspicious now. "Bob Hatchett is here, though. May I tell him who's calling?"

"That won't be necessary. Thanks." Clara closed her phone. So Eddie had gotten his job back at the construction site. That was interesting. Could that be a motive for murder? It seemed a bit extreme—to kill a guy just to get a job back. Then again, people had killed for less.

She spent the rest of the afternoon wrestling with worries over what she would say to Eddie when she caught up with him and wondering how her meeting with Rick would go later that evening.

By the time she was ready to pick up Stephanie, Clara was wishing she'd never invited Rick along on her walk with Tatters. She looked forward to her nightly jaunt with the dog. It was relaxing, giving her time to sort out her tangled thoughts. What's more, she didn't have to worry about her reaction when Tatters spoke in her head.

With Rick along, it would be anything but relaxing. She'd be weighing everything she said, and she'd have to be careful not to respond to Tatters if he transmitted his thoughts again.

Stephanie was waiting for her at the front gate, hugging herself to keep warm. "I was just about to go inside again," she said as she opened the car door and slid onto the seat. "I swear it's getting colder."

"Don't say that." Clara drove away from the curb, one eye on the rearview mirror. "I keep hoping spring is just around the corner."

"I wish it was." Stephanie leaned forward to turn up the heat. "I'm so sick of this weather. I don't know how you go out every night with that dog."

A soft growl answered her from the backseat and she swung around. "Don't tell me you brought him along?"

Clara glanced in the rearview mirror again and saw Tatters' eyes staring back at her. "I thought we might need him for protection."

"What about my allergies?"

"You don't have allergies to dogs."

"My kids do."

"Then make sure you brush the hairs from your clothes before you go home."

Stephanie looked back at the dog. "It's going to take a mean dog to intimidate Eddie Hatchett. Are you up to the task, Tatters?"

Watch me.

Clara cleared her throat. "He can look intimidating when he wants to."

"Well, let's hope he wants to." Stephanie turned back to stare out the windshield. "So, where are we going?"

"Out to the construction site."

"What? I thought Eddie was fired from there."

"He was. The new foreman hired him back. I guess he's a friend of Eddie's father."

"Hmm." Stephanie kept her gaze on the road ahead. "That was a little convenient."

"Exactly what I thought."

"So we're going out to the construction site. Well, at least it's not snowing."

"Good thing it's not. This road can be treacherous in the snow." Clara glanced out over the ocean as they swept around the curve. The black horizon signaled the oncoming night, and she shivered, in spite of the warmth in the car. Tonight she'd be walking with Rick, in the dark. She wasn't sure if the shivers were from apprehension or excitement.

"Do you know what you're going to say to Eddie, if we see him?"

Her thoughts shattered, Clara jumped. "What? Yes. No. I don't know. I guess I'll ask him point-blank about his trip to the hospital."

"What if he lies again?"

"Then I'll tell him that his girlfriend told Molly the truth."

"Won't that cause trouble for his girlfriend?"

"I hope not. After all, she probably didn't know he'd lied about it."

"Well, I guess we'll find out soon enough." Stephanie nodded at the windshield. "We're coming up on the site now."

Clara squinted at the shadowed road ahead. She could just see the outline of the scaffolding rising against a rapidly darkening sky. "Let's hope we see Eddie before everyone leaves," she muttered.

"I'm sure Tatters will protect us," Stephanie said, sounding not at all sure. "Won't you, boy?"

Tatters whined in response. He didn't sound too confident, either.

Clara's fingers tightened on the wheel. Maybe she should have told Dan what they knew, after all. It was too late now. She'd reached the gravel parking lot, her tires crunching on the stones as she coasted into a space between a truck and a motorbike.

"Okay," she said, doing her best to sound positive, "let's see what we can find out."

Stephanie scrambled out and walked around the car as Clara opened the back door to let Tatters out.

Fastening his leash, she said quietly, "You're just here for support, so don't do anything rash."

Unless someone makes a wrong move.

"Unless I give you an order." Clara looked him in the eye. "I hope we're clear."

Stephanie uttered a nervous giggle. "Do you think he understood that?"

Clara shrugged. "Guess we'll find out."

"Maybe we should have put a muzzle on him."

Give me a break.

Clara gave him a sharp tug on the leash. "He'll be fine," she said, hoping Tatters understood the warning in her voice.

The workmen were moving about beyond the closed gates, but so far it didn't look as if anyone had left yet. Clara could see a light in the guardhouse just inside, and wondered if the same guy was on duty.

"Isn't that Eddie over there?" Stephanie tugged on Clara's arm. "The guy standing by the cement mixer."

Clara squinted again, trying to see the man's face. "It's hard to tell from here. Guess we'll have to wait until they come out."

Before she could stop her, Stephanie stepped forward and put her mouth up to the fence. "Hey, Eddie!"

Clara seized Stephanie's arm. "Wait!"

The burly guy had turned, and was staring at the gates.

Just then, the door to the guardhouse opened and a familiar figure stepped out.

Clara groaned. It was the same guy she'd spoken to the last time she was there.

He walked up to the gate and stared at Stephanie. "Okay, what's all the fuss about?"

"We just wanted to speak to a friend of ours." She smiled up at him. "Eddie Hatchett. Do you know him?"

The guy didn't answer. Instead he looked at Tatters. "So what's with the dog?"

"We were just taking him for a walk," Clara said, hoping he wouldn't recognize her.

The hope was short-lived. The guy scowled. "Oh, it's you. What do you want this time? A blow-by-blow description of how to dig a hole? What the heck are you snooping around here for, anyway? What are you up to?"

Clara raised her chin. "We're not snooping, we just—"

"Did somebody call my name?"

The harsh voice had come from behind the guard. He turned, and Eddie Hatchett stepped up next to him.

Staring from one cousin to the other, he demanded, "Do I know you?"

"You know a good friend of ours," Clara said hastily. "Molly Owens."

Just then a bell started ringing from inside the site. "Time to open up," the guard said, looking at his watch. "You can talk outside. No dogs allowed in here. No visitors, either, unless you got a pass." He trudged back to the shack and disappeared inside. A moment later, the gates slid open and clicked into place.

Eddie's face was a mask of suspicion as he walked toward the cousins.

Clara swallowed. Once more, she'd put herself in the line of fire without a clue how to proceed. All she could hope was that Eddie didn't fly off the handle and cause a scene, because heaven knew what Tatters would do if provoked. She could be in big trouble in more ways than one.

13

The first thing Clara noticed was that Eddie wore heavy boots. So much for her hope that he'd be wearing the incriminating sneakers. "We were wondering if we could have a word with you," she said, trying to sound confident. It wasn't going to help matters if Eddie realized her heart was pounding way too fast and her palms were sweaty.

"What about?" Eddie glanced at the gold watch on his wrist. "Make it quick. I've got a date."

Clara opened her mouth, then shut it again. It was as if every word in the English dictionary had vanished from her mind. She felt Stephanie give her a sharp nudge in the side and opened her mouth again. "It's about the night you hurt your wrist."

Eddie held up his bandaged wrist and stared at it. "What about it?"

"Well, you told Molly that your girlfriend took you to the hospital around five thirty."

A group of guys strolled past them, one of them calling out to Eddie, "That your fan club, Hatchett?"

The rest of the guys laughed, but Eddie wasn't laughing. In fact, he looked as if he might explode any moment.

He took a step toward Clara, then halted as Tatters bared his teeth in a soft, warning growl.

Clara tugged lightly on the leash. "I was just wondering why your girlfriend told Molly that she took you to the hospital two hours later than you say she did."

"Oh yeah?" Eddie folded his arms, and glared at Tatters. "What's it to you?"

"Scott Delwyn was a friend of ours. We're trying to find out the truth about the night he died. When someone lies about what happened that night, it looks kind of suspicious, don't you think? I wonder what the police chief would think about that."

Eddie's tough expression faded to a worried frown. "There's no need to bring the cops into this. So I lied. When I heard that Delwyn had fallen off the scaffolding, I got worried. Everyone in this place knows I threatened him when he fired me. I was afraid I'd be blamed for his death. So when Molly started asking questions about that night, I decided it was safer to say I wasn't around. I was figuring on them at the hospital not mentioning what time I got there if anyone checked."

Clara gave him a hard stare. "Are you saying you think

someone killed Scott Delwyn? That his death wasn't an accident?"

The defiant look returned to Eddie's face. "All I'm saying is that Scott may have been an s.o.b., but he was careful. He'd never take chances up there. I just can't see him falling off, that's all. One thing I do know, I didn't kill him. Now quit bugging me about it and get out of my way."

Again Tatters uttered a low growl.

"It's all right, boy." Clara tightened her hold on the leash. "Just one more question." Ignoring Eddie's scowl, she continued, "Do you have any idea who might have wanted to hurt Scott?"

"Nope, I don't. What's more, I don't care. I'm sorry he's dead, but I didn't like the bastard, and I'm sure I wasn't the only one." Eddie hunched his shoulders and shoved his hands into the pockets of his jacket. "Now, I'm leaving. You'd better keep a tight hold on that dog of yours, or something bad might happen to him, too."

Bring it on, soldier.

Clara felt Tatters straining on the leash and tugged it. "Thank you, Eddie. Good-night."

Eddie looked from her to Stephanie, grunted and marched off toward the parking lot.

Tatters stared after him, the hair on the back of his neck forming a stiff ridge.

"Whew," Stephanie said, fanning her face with her glove. "I'm sure glad that's over."

"Yeah, except we're no closer to finding out who killed

Scott." Clara watched Eddie climb into his truck. "Interesting though that he thought someone had pushed Scott off that scaffolding. Guess we're not the only ones who think it's murder."

"Unless Karen was right and Scott killed himself."

"Not according to the Quinn Sense."

Stephanie started walking toward the parking lot. "I don't know how we're going to prove anything when no one knows anything."

Tugging on Tatters' leash, Clara followed her. "Well someone knows something. Whoever killed him knows what happened. Sooner or later, that person's going to slip up. I just hope we're around when he does."

"Well, do me a favor," Stephanie said when Clara joined her inside the car. "Next time we go talk to someone, let's make it either earlier or later. I'm sure George is getting tired of feeding the kids dinner."

"I know. I'm sorry. It's just the way things have worked out." Clara slid the car into gear and pulled out of the parking lot. "Does he know where you are and what you're doing?"

"He thinks I'm planning a special event at the store." She sighed. "Sooner or later, I'll have to think of something."

"When is Edgar Allen Poe's birthday? We could celebrate that."

"Can't. It's already gone. It was January nineteenth." She brightened. "We could celebrate it next year, though. That's a great idea!"

"It doesn't help us much now, though."

"Oh, don't worry. I'll think of something. Besides, once this is over, I'll tell George the truth. Like I always do."

"That's if he doesn't find out first. Like he always does."

"Okay, okay. Thank heavens he's such a sweetheart. No one else would put up with me."

Clara glanced at her. "You're a great wife and mother, Steffie. I'm the one who's always dragging you away from your family."

"You don't have to drag me. I come willingly. We're in this together, remember? Just like the old days."

"Yeah, and look how many times the old days got us into deep doo-doo."

"That's what makes life interesting." Stephanie patted her cousin's arm. "I wouldn't have it any other way. Though I must say, this case is more than frustrating. So many dead ends. We don't have any real suspects. Just a lot of possibilities."

"I know. Unless we get really lucky, or the Sense lets me see faces, we might have to give up on this one."

"Never!" Stephanie struck a pose. "The fighting Quinns never give up. Didn't your dad ever say that to you? Mine says it all the time."

Clara laughed. "Mine said it all the time, too." Her smile faded. "He had to give up in the end, though."

"I'm sorry. I know how much you miss him. I shouldn't have said all that."

"It's okay. It's good to talk about him now and then.

Jessie rarely mentions him anymore. I think she's moving on."

"Isn't that what he would have wanted?"

"I guess so." Clara glanced at the clock on the dashboard. "Well, you should be home in time for dinner tonight." She pulled up at the curb. "See you tomorrow." She hesitated, wondering if she should say something about meeting Rick later, then decided to wait until tomorrow to tell Stephanie. That's if there was anything to tell. After all, they were just going for a walk.

Stephanie turned around to pat Tatters. "You were a good boy," she told him. "You scared that nasty man. Good dog!"

Tatters whined and wagged his tail.

She climbed out of the car, saying, "That dog does come in handy at times. See you!"

Clara waited for Tatters' comment, but the dog was silent. Feeling slightly let down, she took off down the street.

Jessie was walking out the front door as Clara walked up the path. "I was hoping you'd get home before I left," she said, as Tatters ran up to her. Leaning down to pet the dog, she added, "I have an appointment. I've left supper in the fridge for you."

"Thanks, Mom, but you know I'm quite capable of fixing my own dinner. I did it all the time in New York."

Jessie looked up at her. "Well, you're not in New York now, and I have more time than you. Besides, I like to cook, and it's no fun cooking for yourself."

"I have to agree with that." Clara stepped into the hallway. "Thanks again. Have a good time."

"I intend to." Jessie gave Tatters a final pat and hurried down the path.

Watching her mother trotting along in her fashionable pantsuit and high heels, Clara wondered if the "appointment" was her mother's way of saying she had a date.

Jessie was always vague when she talked about her evenings out, and Clara preferred not to visualize her mother with another man. Especially if that man was Tony Manetas, the owner of the Pizza Parlor. He'd made no secret of the fact that he was interested in Jessie. Then again, he didn't bother to hide his affection for most of his female customers, which made Clara wonder what her mother saw in him.

The next two hours passed slowly. After heating up the meat loaf and eating some of it, feeding Tatters and watching the news, Clara wandered into her bedroom and turned on her computer. According to the news anchor, there'd been no further developments in the bank robbery case. Nor was there anything online.

Clara answered a couple of e-mails and then turned off the computer. The moment she stood, Tatters was at the door, wagging his tail. It was time to get ready for their walk.

She took longer than usual to fix her hair, put on comfortable shoes and pull on her coat. All the while, Tatters paced back and forth between the bedroom and the front door. She kept waiting for his thoughts to enter her mind, and when he remained silent, she wondered if perhaps the line of communication between them had for some reason been broken. Moments later, she was outside on the dark street, with Tatters straining on the leash as usual.

"We're waiting for someone," she told him just as Rick's truck turned the corner and coasted toward them.

He pulled up at the curb with a slight squeak from the brakes, and parked under the streetlamp.

Tatters stood watching the truck, his entire body quivering with excitement. The moment Rick appeared from behind the vehicle, the dog uttered a sharp bark and leapt forward, dragging Clara with him.

Rearing up on his hind legs, Tatters plunked two massive paws on Rick's stomach.

Rick's breath came out in a strangled, "Oof!"

"Sorry," Clara muttered, dragging on the leash. "Sometimes he gets away from me."

"It's okay." Grinning, Rick massaged the dog's shaggy neck, then gently pushed him back on all fours. "Ready for a walk, mutt?"

Tatters barked, bounding around like a spring lamb.

"Guess that's a yes." Rick took the leash from Clara, adding, "Let me give you a break."

Happy to give up the boisterous animal, Clara fell into step beside him. "He likes to go to the beach. Are you up for it?"

"Sure." Rick tucked his free hand in his jacket pocket. "There's nothing like a brisk walk on the beach in the middle of winter."

Clara laughed. "It doesn't seem to bother Tatters."

"Why should it? He's got a thick fur coat to protect him."

"Maybe I should invest in a fur coat."

"I thought fur coats were considered unethical in this environmental age."

"Fake fur, then."

"I can think of better ways to keep warm."

She sent him a sideway glance, unsure how to take that. He was looking straight ahead, and she couldn't tell from his expression if he was teasing or not. She decided to ignore it, and launched into a conversation about the new hotel project.

After discussing the pros and cons for several minutes, they both agreed that only time would tell if the new resort would be good for the town.

"I must admit," Rick said, as they crossed the street to the sea wall, "it will be nice to have a golf course close by."

"Do you play?" Clara paused at the wall, her gaze on the breakers cresting offshore. The full moon laid a silver path across the ocean, and in the distance, tiny dots of lights gleamed in the darkness from across the bay.

"Not as much as I used to." Tatters whined and Rick looked down at him. "I guess you want to run on the sand." He looked back at Clara. "How about it?"

Remembering her vision, Clara shivered. The last thing she needed was to have another one with Rick at her side.

Seeing her hesitation, Rick was quick to respond. "I know

the beach isn't exactly hospitable in this weather. Why don't we let Tatters off the leash down there and we watch him from the wall?"

"Sounds like a good idea. As long as we don't lose him."

"He won't go far." Rick started for the steps that led down to the sand. "How about it, Tatters? You'll come back when I whistle, right?"

The dog barked, and leapt ahead to the top of the steps.

Leaning down, Rick unclipped the leash. "Okay, mutt. Enjoy your freedom for a little while."

Tatters wasted no time tearing down the steps. Once his paws hit the sand, he was off, leaping and bounding toward the ocean.

Clara sat on the wall, watching the big dog trot along the water's edge. "He's not going in the sea," she said as Rick sat beside her. "He must know the water's cold."

"He's not stupid, that dog." Rick tucked the leash in his pocket. "In fact, there were times when I could swear he knew every word I spoke."

Clara smiled. "I know what you mean."

Rick was silent for a long moment, while Clara wondered what he was thinking. When he finally spoke, he took her completely off-guard. "Mind if I ask you a question?"

The fact that he'd asked first suggested it was going to be an awkward question. Bracing herself, she said warily, "Sure. What is it?"

He hunched his shoulders as if he were cold. "I was just wondering if you and Tim Rossi . . . I mean, I don't want to butt into your personal life, but when I saw you two the other day, I started wondering . . . you know."

Her rush of relief made her sound breathless when she answered. "There's nothing going on between Tim and me. We're just friends, that's all. I was upset over something Dan said to me and Tim was trying to make me feel better. He's a nice guy, but I'm not interested in him in that way."

She looked up to find him gazing at her, with a look in his eyes that made her pulse speed up.

"Good," he said softly. "Because I have to tell you, I got worried."

She was having trouble breathing. "You did?"

"Yes, ma'am. I did."

He leaned toward her, and then she was in his arms, with his mouth firmly on hers.

After a really satisfying moment or two, he let her go. "I've wanted to do that for so long," he said, keeping one arm around her shoulders.

She smiled up at him. "Then why didn't you?"

He didn't answer at once, and she felt a trickle of concern.

After a moment or two, he said quietly, "From some of the things you've said, I know that you had some kind of bad experience when you were in New York. I got the impression that's why you came back to Finn's Harbor to live. Whatever happened back there must have hit hard, because you've had a fence built around you covered with warning signs to keep out. Much as I wanted to get closer to you, I figured it would be better if I waited until you were ready to take down those signs. I didn't want to scare you off before I'd even had a chance to show you what a terrific catch I am."

The tension broken, she burst out laughing. "Modest, too, I see."

Looking into his eyes, her heart skipped at what she saw there. Sobering, she looked away, pretending to search for Tatters. He was just a few yards off, sniffing at something in the sand.

She wanted to tell Rick about Matt and her broken heart, but couldn't find the words to begin. When she'd stayed silent for too long, she forced out words. "I was going to marry him."

Rick took a while to answer. "You don't have to tell me. What happened back then has nothing to do with us now."

"I want to tell you. It's just . . ."

"I know."

She tried again. "I didn't tell anyone I was getting married. Not even my mother. I guess deep down I must have sensed something could go wrong." *Where had the Quinn Sense been then? Why hadn't she listened to her instincts?*

She took a deep breath. "I found out the night before the wedding that he'd left town with someone else. He didn't even have the guts to tell me himself."

She hadn't noticed the tears in her eyes until one trickled down her cheek.

"Not all men are jerks." Rick turned her to face him. "I know it's hard to trust again. I thought I'd found the love of my life, too. I guess we married too young. She missed the single life—the parties, the dates, all the excitement. I wanted kids, she didn't. She kept saying she was too young to mess up her figure. One day, she just left, saying she was going back to her old life. I guess we just wanted different things."

Clara dashed at her cheek with the back of her hand. "I'm sorry."

"Me, too. But life goes on and we have to move on with it." He lifted her chin with the tips of his fingers. "I can't think of anyone I'd rather move on with than you."

His kiss lasted longer this time. Clara closed her eyes and gave herself up to the moment. Until a voice spoke in her head.

It's about time.

She pulled away from Rick, and saw Tatters sitting just a few feet away, his tongue hanging out of his mouth and his ears twitching.

"I think he approves," Rick said, following her gaze.

"You might be right." She stood up. "I guess it's time I took him home."

"Too bad." Rick got slowly to his feet. "Things were just getting interesting."

Clara smiled. She felt light-headed, as if she'd drunk a little too much wine. The ache that had lurked in her heart for so long was no longer there. Rick was right. It was time to move on and she was more than ready.

She watched him bend down to clip the leash to Tatters' collar. He was a good man. An honest man. Learning to trust again was hard, but with Rick she felt reasonably sure she could get there. Right now, that was enough for her.

———

On her way to work the next morning, Clara was almost at the parking lot on the hill when she saw the car. It was cruising toward her—a gleaming red beast on dazzling silver wheels. Sleek and low to the ground, it shouted speed and excitement, with more than a hint of danger. The sort of car a hunk would drive.

Curious to see the man behind the wheel, she eased her foot on the brake. As the car drew level with her, she threw a glance sideways. What she saw disappointed her. The driver was kind of scruffy looking, wearing a fur-lined jacket and a baseball cap pulled low over his eyes.

She could see a shadowy figure sitting in the backseat, and as the car flashed past her, she caught a glimpse of his face. He looked a lot like Scott Delwyn.

She dismissed that immediately, figuring that the dead man was on her mind so much she was imagining things.

The driver, however, had also looked vaguely familiar, and as Clara pulled into the parking lot, her mind worked furiously to remember where she'd seen the man before. Had he been one of the protestors? She tried to remember what Josh's followers looked like, but no one stood out.

Walking up the hill, she mentally went over everything

she'd done and every place she'd been since she'd first heard that Scott Delwyn had died. Still nothing came to mind. She must have been frowning as she walked into the Raven's Nest, since Stephanie looked at her with concern in her eyes.

"Are you okay? Has something happened?"

"No . . . yes . . . I don't know."

Molly was busy with a customer, and Stephanie beckoned to Clara to follow her down the aisle to the storage room. "We just got a new shipment of books," she said, waving her hand at the pile of cartons in the middle of the room. "I'm anxious to see what's here." She pulled a box cutter from her pocket and carefully slit open the top carton.

"Did you happen to see that red car go past here a few minutes ago?" Clara walked over to her and started taking books out of the carton.

"What red car?"

Clara shook her head. "I guess you didn't see it, or you would have known what I was talking about. It's the kind of car you usually only see in a dealer's window."

Stephanie pulled out a book and read the cover. "It probably belongs to one of the bigwigs who own the resort project." She turned the book over. "This looks interesting. It's a debut time-travel series about a newly discovered kingdom that no one knew existed."

"Sounds good." Still thinking about the car, the memory of her meeting with Karen popped into Clara's head. What would Scott's widow have to do with a luxury sports car? Was it because the passenger in it had looked like Karen's dead husband? Or was it the Quinn Sense trying to tell her something?

Stephanie said something else, and Clara murmured, "Uh-huh." Somehow she couldn't get rid of the idea that the car and Karen were connected. She tried to remember their conversation. It was about the cell phone. No, that wasn't it. Something later. What had they been talking about when Thelma rang the doorbell and interrupted them?

Thelma. It had something to do with Thelma.

"Are you okay? Are you having another vision or something?" Stephanie sounded excited. "Where are you?"

Clara shook her head. "I'm right here. I just can't— Oh!"

Stephanie stared at her. "What? What? Tell me!"

Clara let out her breath. "The guy driving that fancy car down the hill. I remember now where I've seen him before. It was Thelma's son. I can't remember his name, but I do remember his face." She clutched her cousin's arm. "Where do you think an out-of-work guy would get a fancy car like that?"

"Maybe he stole it."

"Or maybe," Clara said slowly, "he robbed a bank."

14

Stephanie dropped the book she was holding back into the box. "You mean we have another suspect."

"Yes, I think we do." Clara slipped out of her coat and hung it on the hook. "What's more, Thelma told Karen they were moving. If her son is the bank robber, we have to move fast, or they'll be gone and we'll never find out if he's the one who killed Scott."

"Oh, I keep forgetting you think it's all connected." Stephanie frowned. "But if Scott is connected to the bank robbery, doesn't that make him a criminal, too?"

"I don't know." Clara hung her scarf over the hook on top of her coat. "All I know is that I saw two people shove Scott off the scaffolding. I wish I did know more than that. This whole case is so confusing. I wish the Sense

-223-

would either give me something to point me in the right direction or stay out of my mind altogether."

"Well, maybe Dan will see that guy driving around in a fancy car and figure out there's something fishy."

"Maybe, but even Dan can't do anything without evidence, and there seems to be a shortage of that around."

"We could just be jumping to conclusions about this. After all, we've suspected just about everybody remotely connected to Scott."

"I know. I can't help feeling we're just grasping at straws and that we're missing something important."

"I'm sorry, Clara. I wish there was something I could do to help. Right now, though, I have to go clean the house before my kids get out of school. Once they come home, nothing gets done."

Clara gave her a little push. "Go ahead. I'll figure it out."

"Okay. Meanwhile, if you could get some of those books out on the shelves . . ."

"Sure." Clara waved her off, then turned back to the cartons. She needed something to do to keep her mind off things. All this effort of trying to figure things out was giving her a headache.

A half hour later, she had the books out on the shelves. She was helping Molly rearrange the window display when the phone rang. It was Stephanie, and she sounded excited.

"I saw that red car," she said, "outside the diner on the waterfront. Your friend must be having lunch there. That's some car."

Clara glanced at the clock. "I wonder if he's still there."

"You're not going to accuse him or anything, are you?"

"No, I have a better idea."

"What is it?"

"I'll tell you if it works out."

Hanging up the phone, Clara called out to Molly. "Can you hold down the fort for a few minutes? I've got an errand to run."

"Sure." Molly waved a hand at the aisles. "We're not exactly swept off our feet here."

Clara wasted no time in dashing back to the stockroom for her coat and scarf. "I'll be back as soon as I can," she called out as she tore out the door.

She was looking back as she said it, and didn't see the woman on the steps until she smacked right into her.

Momentarily out of breath, she flinched when Roberta Prince snapped, "Why don't you look where you're going?"

"I'm sorry." Clara edged around her. "I'm in a hurry and—"

"I can see that." Roberta brushed her sleeve as if getting rid of a distasteful bug. "You nearly knocked me off my feet." She switched her purse to the other hand. "If you're going to see Rick, I can save you the trouble. He's not in the shop."

"I'm not going to see Rick, if you must know." Clara started down the steps. "Not that it's any of your business."

"Oh, my, we are touchy about it, aren't we? Did you two have a disagreement, then?"

Clara was so tempted to turn around and tell Roberta about the kiss she'd enjoyed last night, then thought better of it. She hadn't even told her cousin yet. It was something she wanted to keep to herself for a while.

To her relief, she heard the door to the bookstore slam shut. *Let Molly deal with the witch*, she thought, as she hurried down the hill to her car. She had bigger fish to fry.

It only took a few minutes to drive down to the waterfront and park in the diner's cramped lot. The red car was still at the curb, where Stephanie had seen it. Thelma's son had apparently decided not to park it with the other cars.

She couldn't really blame him. The car was beautiful— a gleaming mass of shiny red metal and chrome. It still had the sales sticker in the window, and temporary plates. He must have just bought it.

Before she got out of her own car she flipped open her phone and dialed Karen's number. The widow answered right away.

"One quick question," Clara said, after asking how Karen was doing. "What was Scott's cell phone number?"

Karen gave her the number, and Clara keyed it into her address page. "Thanks," she said when she was done. "I can't talk now but I'll get back to you." She hung up before Karen could ask any questions.

Minutes later, she was seated in the diner with a cup of coffee and a donut in front of her. At the opposite end of the room, Thelma's son sat talking to a man dressed in a poorly fitting suit and no tie.

It could have been the man she saw in the back of the car, except he looked nothing like Scott Delwyn. In fact, Clara was now convinced that she'd seen Scott's ghost again, and that he was still trying to tell her something.

She took a sip of coffee, then pulled a tissue from her pocket. She let it float to the floor and bent down to pick it up. Both men's feet were hidden from sight, and frustrated, she sat up. She'd have to get closer if she wanted to take a look at their shoes.

After taking her cell phone out of her pocket, she dialed the number Karen had given her and waited. Seconds later, she saw the driver of the car dig in his pocket and come up with a cell phone. Holding it to his ear, he spoke into it.

His voice echoed in the phone at Clara's ear. She quickly closed her phone and slipped it back in her pocket. She didn't need to see his shoes now. Thelma's son had Scott's cell phone. Now she could go back to Dan.

———

Stephanie hummed as she pushed the vacuum cleaner around the living room carpet. Life was good. Business at the bookstore was slowly picking up after the post-Christmas lull, the kids were doing well in school, spring was just around the corner and she and Clara were in the middle of another adventure. What more could she ask for than that?

A couple of things, she amended. One, that they find out who killed Scott Delwyn, and two, that Clara find someone who could make her happy for the rest of her life.

Clara had never told her the full story about what had happened in New York. Stephanie knew it had to do with a guy who had apparently treated her cousin bad enough to send her running back to Finn's Harbor.

Not that Stephanie wasn't happy about her cousin's return, but she wished the circumstances had been better. Whatever had happened to Clara must have been unbearable, since she wouldn't talk about it to anyone.

Stephanie sighed. What Clara needed more than anything was a man like George. Dependable, kind, loving, reliable George.

The house phone rang, making her jump. It had to be a business call, since most of her personal calls came through her cell phone. Still thinking up adjectives to describe her beloved husband, she hurried over to the couch and picked up the receiver. "Hello!"

A soft, female voice answered her. "I'd like to speak to George, please."

"George isn't here. Can I take a message?"

There was a short pause on the line, then the voice spoke again, sounding flustered now. "Oh . . . er . . . isn't this where George works?"

Stephanie frowned. "No, this is his home. Who's this?"

"I'm sorry, I must have the numbers mixed up. Please excuse me."

"Wait—" The line clicked in her ear, and Stephanie

replaced the receiver. A knot was beginning to form in the middle of her stomach. *Stop it*, she told herself. It was nothing. She was overreacting. Her George would never look at another woman.

The caller ID number was staring at her from the message panel on the phone. After hesitating for several seconds, she snatched up the receiver and dialed the number. A recording answered her.

"This is Annabelle. Please leave a message."

Annabelle. Stephanie felt sick. George had been preoccupied lately, as if something was on his mind. Was it this Annabelle person? Abandoning the vacuum cleaner in the middle of the room, she walked slowly into the kitchen and opened the freezer. Reaching inside, she lifted out a carton of ice cream and carried it to the kitchen table. A glance at the clock told her she had at least an hour before Michael got home from school. After fetching a spoon, she sat down, opened the lid on the ice cream and began to eat.

Tim was in the front office when Clara walked into the police station. He lifted a hand in welcome when he saw her.

"Hi there! What can we do for you?"

"I need a word with Dan." Clara glanced down at the door to Dan's office. "Is he in?"

Tim got a weird look on his face. "He is, but I'm afraid he won't talk to you."

"Why not?"

Tim shrugged. "He said to tell you, if you came in again, that his office is off-limits."

Clara tightened her lips. "Really. Well, you can tell Dan that I have information about Scott Delwyn's death that will incriminate a suspect. If he wants to catch a killer, I suggest he listens to what I have to say."

Tim looked worried. "Scott's death was an accident, Clara."

"So everyone keeps saying. I happen to know that it was murder."

"Dan doesn't like it when you talk like that, remember?"

Clara leaned her hands on Tim's desk. "Listen to me. I have evidence now that will convince Dan that Scott was murdered. I need to talk to him."

"I don't know." Tim glanced around as if afraid of being overheard. "He said he'd have my badge if I let you bug him again."

Clara straightened. "What are you going to do? Arrest me?"

"Uh . . . well . . . I . . ." Tim ran a hand through his hair.

"I thought so. Sorry, Tim, but I have to talk to Dan."

Feeling the eyes of everyone in the place following her, she marched down to Dan's office and rapped on his door.

His sharp command to enter unnerved her for a moment, then she braced herself. Once he heard what she had to say, he'd be apologizing to her. Taking a deep breath, she opened the door.

Dan didn't even look up from the papers he was studying on his desk. "What is it?"

"I have something important to tell you."

At the sound of her voice he paused, then rubbed his fingers across his forehead. "Of course you do." He looked up at her, and his expression was enough to freeze a volcano. "How did you get past my deputy?"

"He understood the urgency of my visit."

"Did he, now?" Dan's voice was heavy with sarcasm.

Clara winced. "I found Scott Delwyn's cell phone. At least, I know where it is."

"And where is it?" His tone suggested she better have a good answer.

"It's in the hands of . . ." She hesitated.

"Yes?"

"I . . . er . . . don't remember his name."

"No kidding."

Clara was beginning to feel just a little desperate. "His mother is Thelma something or other. She lives next door to Karen Delwyn, Scott's widow."

Dan stared at her beneath his bushy eyebrows, blue eyes cutting into her mind. "You talking about Ray Hogan?"

"Hogan, that's it!" She slapped the desk. "Of course. Ray. I knew it was something short. Ray Hogan. Yes. He's the one who has Scott's cell phone."

"And you know this, how?"

Excited now, Clara sat down, earning another fierce frown from the man across from her. "I was in the diner with Ray Hogan. Well, I wasn't with him, exactly. He was at the other end of the diner and I was by the door, and—"

"Get to the point?"

"Oh, sorry. Yes, well, I called Scott's cell phone and Ray Hogan answered. He said hello. Right in my ear."

"You called Scott's cell phone."

"Yes. I got the number from Karen. There's more." She leaned forward. "Ray Hogan is driving a brand-new car—and a very expensive one at that. Since he's unemployed, I have to wonder where he got the money to spend on a fancy new sports car."

Dan kept looking at her so long she started to squirm. Finally he let out a long sigh. "All right, I'll have a word with Ray. Meanwhile, you are to stay far away from him. Understand?"

"Of course, yes."

"You haven't done a very good job of listening to me up to now."

"Sorry, but I had to find some evidence to make you . . . I mean . . . so that you'd realize Scott's death wasn't an accident."

"Hmm."

Clara got up. "So you'll talk to him?"

"I'll talk to him. This doesn't mean, however, that Ray had anything to do with Scott's death."

"Then why does he have Scott's cell phone?"

"That's what I'm going to find out. And you're going to butt out, right?"

"Right." She headed for the door, then turned to look back at him. "You will tell me what he said?"

"I'll think about it."

She had to be satisfied with that. For now. She sent Tim a triumphant wave as she passed by his desk. He answered her with a resigned shake of his head.

Heading back to the store, she replayed the conversation again in her head. Dan hadn't exactly apologized, but he had said he'd talk to Ray. That was something. It had to be incriminating evidence. How else would Ray have Scott's phone unless he was with him when he died?

She waited until she was parked in the lot before calling Stephanie. The phone rang three times, and Clara was about to hang up when her cousin answered. The minute she heard Stephanie's voice, Clara knew something was wrong.

"What's the matter? Are you sick?"

"No. Yes. Oh God, Clara, what am I going to do?"

Stephanie's voice had risen on a wail. Alarmed now, Clara said firmly, "Whatever it is, we'll deal with it. Did something happen to one of the kids?"

"No."

Stephanie was crying now, intensifying Clara's anxiety. "Is it George?"

Instead of answering, Stephanie dissolved into wrenching sobs.

"I'm coming over there."

Allison Kingsley

"No . . . the bookstore . . ."

"Molly can take care of the bookstore. I'll be right there."

Clara made a quick call to Molly, then tore out of the parking lot with little regard for anything that might be coming down the road.

Minutes later she was at Stephanie's door, one finger on the bell.

It seemed like forever until her cousin opened the door. Clara took one look at her and held out her arms.

Sobbing, Stephanie fell against her. "I . . . don't know . . . what to do!"

"Let's get inside." Clara pulled her into the house and shut the door. Still holding her arm, Clara led her cousin into the kitchen and made her sit down.

An empty carton of chocolate ice cream sat on the table with a spoon sticking out of it. Clara made a face. "You might have saved me some."

Stephanie only cried harder.

Clara spotted a box of tissues on the windowsill and carried it over to the table. "Here." She sat down opposite her cousin and folded her arms. "Now, tell me what's going on."

Stephanie grabbed a fistful of tissues and blew her nose. Dabbing at her eyes, she mumbled something Clara couldn't understand.

"What?" Clara leaned closer. "Take a deep breath, then tell me. Is George hurt? Where is he?"

Stephanie howled.

Clara felt as if a hand of ice had clutched her heart. "He's not . . . ?" No matter how she tried, she couldn't say the word.

Stephanie blew her nose again. "He's not dead, if that's what you were going to say."

"Thank God." Clara slumped back on her chair. "Then for pity's sake, tell me what's going on."

"I think he's . . . cheating on me." The tears started flowing again.

Clara stared at her, then burst out laughing.

Stephanie glared, her eyes puffy and red-rimmed. "It's not a laughing matter. I thought you, of all people, would understand what—"

"Steffie." Clara sat up, reached across the table and gripped her cousin's hand. "Listen to me. Can you honestly see George having an affair? I mean, this is *George* we're talking about. The father of your children."

Stephanie looked annoyed. "Are you saying that my husband is not attractive to women?"

"No, I'm saying he's not attracted *to* women. He adores you, Steffie. And his kids. He'd never risk losing all that."

"Then tell me who Annabelle is and why she's calling my husband."

Clara stared at her. "Annabelle?"

"Yes, she called this morning. She asked for George, then got all squiggly when I said he wasn't here. She thought she was calling his work number. She said she'd got the numbers mixed up. Why would a woman have George's work number and his home phone number?"

"Any number of reasons. Why didn't she call his cell if she wanted to talk to him privately?"

Stephanie's jaw dropped. "I never thought of that. Maybe he didn't want to give it to her in case she called him while he was here."

Clara shook her head. "You're determined to condemn him without giving him a chance to explain. Why don't you just ask him who Annabelle is?"

Tears ran down Stephanie's cheeks again. "I'm afraid he'll tell me he's . . . in love with . . . her and wants . . . a *divorce*! How can he *do* this to me? Less than a month away from our *anniversary*?" Once more, her voice soared to a wail.

Just then the back door opened and Michael walked in. Luckily he was in too much of a hurry to get to his room to notice his mother's puffy face and wobbly voice. After calling out a hasty "Hi!" he threw his coat on a chair and disappeared down the hallway.

Stephanie buried her face in a handful of tissues, sniffed a few times, then wiped her eyes. "I have to act as if nothing has happened. For the kids' sake."

"Nothing *has* happened yet." Clara leaned back. "I'm willing to bet everything I have that you're wrong about George."

"Then why has he been so distant lately? He's been acting like he's keeping a secret from me. I should have suspected something like this all along. I just never thought my George . . ." Her voice broke, and she cleared her throat. "It's my fault. I've been running around with you all over town, drinking in bars and stuff, while he's been at home looking after the kids. It's no wonder he's turned to another woman."

Clara tried not to feel offended. Stephanie was upset. She didn't realize what she was saying. "Do you have this woman's number?"

Stephanie nodded. "It's on the ID pad. I called her back. That's how I got her name. *She* didn't want to tell me who she was."

"What did she say when you talked to her?"

"I didn't talk to her. I got a recording. On the phone she'd just used to call me. It was obvious she didn't want to talk to me."

"Well, give me her number."

Stephanie gave her a suspicious look. "What for?"

"Well, obviously you can't go snooping around to find out who she is. But I can."

"Really?" Stephanie momentarily brightened. "Promise you'll tell me the truth when you find out, no matter how bad it is?"

Convinced that George was innocent, Clara had no trouble giving her promise. "I'd better get going. Molly's probably busy in the Nook by now."

Stephanie jumped up. "I'll get the number. Just don't tell George we suspect anything. I want to find out all I can about this Annabelle woman before I confront him with it. In the meantime, I can't go on any more escapades with you. I need to stay home and keep an eye on my husband."

Clara followed her into the living room. "Please don't say anything to George until I've checked this out."

"I won't." Stephanie read the number out to her while Clara entered it in her address page. "But it will be hard."

"Keep thinking positive." Clara gave her a hug. "I know this is going to turn out all right."

She left the house, worried about her cousin's state of mind. Stephanie was impulsive, apt to jump to conclusions and sometimes acted without thinking.

Much as Clara wanted to believe that George wasn't having an affair, she couldn't help thinking about her own heartache, not so long ago. She couldn't imagine Matt cheating on her, either, but he had. She prayed that her cousin was wrong about George. Stephanie would be devastated, and totally lost without him.

Anxious to clear up the mystery, she called the number while still parked in Stephanie's driveway. She got the same message her cousin had heard, and put her phone away, discouraged and worried.

There were two customers waiting at the counter when she got back to the Raven's Nest, and she dropped her coat behind it and apologized for the delay. After serving them, she walked down to the Nook, where Molly was cleaning up.

"We had a rush on coffee and pastries," she said when Clara hurried in to help her. "A whole bunch of people came in at the same time. I thought they were never going to leave."

"I'm sorry. I should have been here, but I was worried about Stephanie."

"No problem." Molly carried some mugs over to the sink. "Is she okay?"

"She's fine. Just a little family upset, that's all."

"I don't know how she does it. Taking care of a husband and three kids and working all week. It must be hard on her."

"It is, but she loves it." Clara stacked plates in a pile and took them over to the sink.

"Oh, I nearly forgot. Dan called. He wants you to call him."

Her stab of excitement almost made her drop the plates. "Did he say why?"

"Nope. Just to call him."

"I'll go do it now." Clara looked around. "Can you manage here?"

"Sure. I'm almost done, anyway."

Deciding that the stockroom gave her the most privacy, Clara closed the door and flipped open her phone.

Dan answered on the first ring. "I talked to Ray Hogan," he said in answer to her greeting.

Clara held her breath.

"He says he found the phone in a trash can. He figured someone had thrown it away and he fished it out."

"And you believed him?"

"I had no reason not to."

"What about the car, then?"

"I asked him about that. Seems that he borrowed it from a friend. He had an important appointment to keep and his own car wouldn't start."

"Yeah, right. He's lying. I know he is. I think he's the bank robber."

"I thought you suspected him of killing Scott Delwyn."

"I do. I keep telling you, Scott's death is connected to the robbery."

She could hear the impatience in his voice when he answered. "Well, Ray Hogan can't be the bank robber. He was in Mittleford at the time of the robbery, taking his mother shopping. Thelma confirmed it, as well as the shop assistant who served them. Look, I know you think you're helping Karen, but dragging all this up will only make things more miserable for her. Leave it be, Clara. We've got no reason at all to suspect Scott's death was anything other than an accident. As for the bank robber, we'll find him eventually. Let us do our job, and don't give me a reason to get tough with you."

Knowing when she was beaten, Clara hung up. She knew what Dan was thinking. Just because she and Stephanie had had some luck tracking down killers in the past, she was grasping at straws in the hopes of doing it again.

There didn't seem any way to convince him otherwise, so the best thing she could do was keep looking for something—anything—that would make Dan realize she was telling him the truth.

The biggest blow was finding out Ray Hogan had an alibi. She was certain she'd seen Scott's ghost in the back of the car Ray was driving and that Scott was trying to tell her that Ray was responsible for his death.

Then again, just because Ray hadn't robbed a bank, it didn't mean he hadn't killed Scott. Ray Hogan was involved in this mess somehow, she was certain of that. She just had to prove it.

15

That night, Clara took Tatters down to the waterfront again. She needed time to think, away from distractions, and gazing at the ocean always helped to clear her mind. Seated on the wall, however, she found it hard to concentrate on her problems. She kept remembering Rick's warm body next to her, and how it felt to be kissing him.

She still hadn't told Stephanie what had happened. For one thing, it didn't seem right to be sharing her big news when her cousin was so worried about her marriage. Not only that, it wasn't as easy to share those moments with her cousin as it had been in the past. Maybe she was scared that if she talked about it, something would go wrong. Right now her relationship with Rick was so new and fragile, she didn't want to take anything for granted.

She watched Tatters race along the edge of the waves,

kicking up wet sand with his hind legs. How she wished she could be that carefree. Tatters didn't need a lot to keep him happy. Just a warm bed and a full stomach. Next time around, she was coming back as a dog.

A gust of wind hit her in the back, and she hugged herself, wishing she'd worn a warmer jacket. She stood up and opened her mouth to yell for Tatters, but no sound came out. A familiar sensation swept over her, transporting her away from the ocean.

She was on Main Street, a little way down from the bank. It was spitting hailstones again, and they were bouncing off the sidewalk at her feet. A white mist swirled down the road and around the doors of the bank. Suddenly they opened, and a man ran out. A ski mask covered his face, and the collar of his jacket was pulled up at the back of his neck.

She looked down at his feet. He wore black sneakers, and three gold stars gleamed along the sides of them. As she watched, he started down the street toward a red sports car parked at the curb. He reached it and pulled off his mask. Just before he climbed into the car, he turned his head in her direction. She instantly recognized Ray Hogan.

Another man approached the red car from the opposite direction. He stood watching as Ray climbed into the car and drove away. Clara didn't need to see his face clearly to know that it was Scott Delwyn.

She called out, but her words were no more than a whisper. Dan was wrong. Ray had robbed the bank. But Dan had said that Ray was in Mittleford when the robbery occurred. Then again, if Eddie could lie about his alibi, then why couldn't Ray? But that would mean his mother and the shop assistant had lied, too.

She had to talk to Scott. Maybe he could tell her who killed him. As she started forward, the mist grew thicker, holding her back. She could feel rain now, hitting her face and dampening her hair. She heard a whine and looked around. Tatters? Where was he?

The dog whined again and the mist evaporated. She was still sitting on the wall, and Tatters sat in front of her, his head to one side as if trying to figure out what she was doing.

"Come here, boy." She held out her hand and he shoved his nose into her palm. She patted him for a moment, then fastened his leash around his neck. "Let's go home. I have some thinking to do."

He turned at once, and led her at a fast pace back to the house. Once inside, she went straight to her room, taking the dog with her. Moments later, Jessie tapped on the door. "Clara? Is everything all right?"

"Everything's fine, Mother. I'm just tired, that's all."

There was a long pause, then Jessie said quietly, "Well, all right. Have a good night's sleep."

Seated on her bed, Clara waited while seconds ticked by without any more sound from the door. Jessie must have given up and gone to bed.

Tatters made an odd noise and she looked at him. He was staring at her, with what she could swear was disapproval in his eyes. She raised her chin. "What are *you* looking at?"

As if you didn't know.

She sat up straighter. "I just didn't feel like talking to her, that's all."

Tatters went on staring at her.

"Oh, all right." She got off the bed. "But if she starts cross-examining me again, I'm going to blame you for putting me in a lousy mood."

With Tatters at her heels, she walked down the hallway to the living room.

Jessie was folding up the newspaper, and looked surprised when Clara walked in. "I thought you were going to sleep."

"I thought I'd have a glass of wine first. It will help relax me."

Jessie frowned at her. "Clara, what's going on? You're not in some sort of trouble, are you?"

Clara laughed. "No, Mother, I'm not in any trouble." She walked over to the kitchen, saying over her shoulder, "You want some wine?"

"I could use a glass. Thank you."

Clara poured two glasses and carried them back to the living room. She gave one to her mother and took the other one over to the couch. Sitting down with it, she balanced it on the arm. "How are things at the library?"

"Fine. How are things at the bookstore?"

"Fine." Clara took a sip of wine.

Jessie moved over to the couch and sat down next to her. "How are things with you and that nice hardware store man?"

Clara felt her nerves tensing and made an effort to relax. "Okay, I guess."

Tatters sneezed and she looked at him, expecting to hear some scathing comment. He just lay down, however, and rested his jaw on his paws.

"You seem unhappy." Jessie said, raising her glass to her lips.

"I'm not unhappy." She made herself smile at her mother. "I'm a little tired, that's all."

"Maybe you should get a check-up. You haven't had one since you got back from New York. Doctor Wills is a lovely doctor. I know you'd like her."

Clara simply nodded. How she wished she could tell Jessie what was really bothering her. That she knew a murder had been committed, and that she knew the identity of the bank robber, and that she couldn't do anything about it because everything she knew came from the Quinn Sense. That she was frustrated, and afraid that Ray Hogan was going to get away with everything.

Of course, Jessie would understand about the Quinn Sense. She'd known about it ever since she'd married Clara's father. He'd warned her that some members of the Quinn family had inherited the Sense and that there might be times when they could read her mind.

Jessie had been skeptical at first, until Clara's uncle— a confirmed bachelor with no intention of ever settling for one woman—told Jessie that that she was carrying a baby girl before Jessie had any idea she was pregnant.

He'd also told Jessie that her disapproval of his lifestyle

could backfire on her when her daughter grew up following in his footsteps. Clara had smiled at that when she'd first heard it, yet here she was, closing in on her thirty-second birthday with no marriage prospects in sight.

An image of Rick popped into her mind and she quickly suppressed it. It was far too early to be thinking along those lines.

The reason she had kept her inheritance of the family gift to herself was because it made her feel different. A freak of nature. She'd always hated that, and had vowed long ago that no one—except Stephanie, the only person in the world she could trust with her secret—would know.

Much as Jessie might understand and even sympathize, sooner or later she would feel compelled to tell someone, and then everyone would know. Even Rick. That was something she couldn't allow to happen.

"Are you going to tell me what you're thinking, or are you going to sit there in silence all night?"

Clara started and looked up to find Jessie staring at her, her forehead creased in a frown. Clara felt bad, knowing her mother was genuinely concerned about her. "I'm sorry. I guess I'm preoccupied."

"There's nothing wrong with Stephanie, is there?"

Clara's eyes widened. With everything going on, she'd totally forgotten her promise to her cousin. "Not that I know of." That was something else she couldn't tell her mother. All these secrets were beginning to wear her down. "I'm sorry, Mother. Really I am. I'll get some sleep and I'll be fine in the morning. I promise." She got up, went over to her mother and planted a swift kiss on her cheek. "Please don't worry about me. I swear to you, I'm okay."

Jessie caught her hand as she straightened. "You know I'm always willing to listen if you need to talk."

Clara smiled. "I know. I appreciate that." She looked down at Tatters, who appeared to be sleeping. "Come on, boy. Time for bed."

Tatters got up, stretched his legs one at a time then strolled over to the door.

Jessie shook her head. "I swear that dog knows every word we say."

"Of course he does." Clara laughed. "Good night, Mother."

"Good night, dear."

Clara put her empty wineglass in the sink and led the dog down the hallway to her room. Once inside, she closed the door and flipped open her cell phone. After dialing the number Stephanie had given her, she waited. The recorded female voice answered her.

Frowning, Clara laid the phone on her bedside table. Tomorrow, she promised herself, she would track down this Annabelle and find out why she was calling George. Meanwhile, there was still the problem of what to do about Ray Hogan.

She sat down on the bed, bouncing up and down as Tatters leapt up beside her. She couldn't come right out and accuse Ray of lying about shopping with his mother, and Thelma was obviously lying to protect her son. Then again, maybe Ray had given her some story about why he needed an alibi and she had no idea he'd robbed a bank.

Tatters pushed his nose into her palm and she patted his head. Maybe she could catch Thelma in her lie. The woman would surely be easier to deal with than her mean-looking son.

Reaching for the alarm clock, Clara set it two hours earlier than usual. She would pay Thelma an early visit before she started her shift at the bookstore. She picked up her cell phone and dialed Stephanie's number. Her cousin would have to take some time off in the morning. At least she wouldn't have to ask her to leave her family at dinnertime again.

Stephanie answered, and as she did so, the words she'd spoken that morning popped into Clara's head. *I need to stay home and keep an eye on my husband.*

"Clara! Is everything okay?"

Clara swallowed the words she was going to say. "Everything's fine. More than fine."

"So what's up?"

Unable to think of anything else, Clara said awkwardly, "I've got something to tell you." Maybe it wouldn't hurt to tell her cousin about Rick after all. It might even take Stephanie's mind off her own troubles. Taking the plunge, she gave her cousin a brief rundown on what had happened between her and Rick the night before.

"Well, it's about time," Stephanie said, sounding pleased. "So what now?"

"Er . . . I don't know. I haven't seen him since. I haven't really thought beyond that."

"Well, you need to think about it. This could be the beginning of a lifetime change for you both."

"I don't know if we're ready for that. We just want to take things slow and sort of see what happens."

"Well, don't wait too long. Remember, Roberta is waiting in the wings and she's a lot pushier than you are."

"You don't have to keep reminding me of that."

Stephanie paused, then lowered her voice. "I don't suppose you've found out who Annabelle is?"

Feeling guilty for neglecting her cousin's problem, Clara murmured, "Not so far, but I'm going all-out tomorrow."

"Just don't let her know that I suspect anything." Stephanie paused again then added tearfully, "I can't bear to think of George with another woman."

"I'm as certain as I can be that he's not having an affair."

"Is that the Quinn Sense talking?"

"No, it's my gut feeling. I promise, tomorrow I'll have some answers."

———

The next morning, Clara reached the waterfront and was dismayed to find Thelma's street blocked by a police car and several orange-and-white-striped pylons. Catching sight of Tim, she beckoned him over. "What's going on?"

Tim jerked a thumb over his shoulder. "One of the trucks headed for the construction site loaded with sand hit the curb while it was turning the corner. The jolt shook the flap open and the truck driver lost his load. It's gonna take a while to clear this lot up."

Clara glanced at her watch. "Wonderful. Guess I'll have to go around a different way."

Tim gave her a sly grin. "You could stay and talk to me while you're waiting."

She smiled back. "You know, normally I would, but I've got an important errand to take care of before I go to work. Rain check?"

"You got it." He lifted his hand, then took a step away from her car to let her back up.

She got the car turned around and made it onto the next street. It was one she hadn't used in years, and she drove slowly, marveling at the new stores that had sprung up in place of the houses that had once stood there.

Antiques stores, souvenirs and beach supplies, an ice cream parlor, a beauty parlor . . . Clara slammed on her brakes. Fortunately there was no one following behind her. Parking wasn't allowed at the curb, and she had to pull into a side street, park and then walk back.

She turned the corner and started walking back toward the beauty parlor. Looking up at the sign over the door, she was satisfied that she hadn't imagined things. The sign was decorated with red hearts and pink swirls around the name: "Annabelle."

Clara pushed open the door, and bells chimed a jaunty

tune until she closed it behind her. There were two customers seated in pink recliners, feet bare and hair wrapped
in rose-colored towels. Two assistants hovered over the
women, one bending over to examine fingernails while
the other attended to the toes.

The shop was heavily scented, and elevator music
played in the background. A woman with startling orange
hair standing up in spikes hurried forward, her bright red
lips split in a smile. "Welcome! Welcome to Annabelle's!
Are you here for the special? A full day of pampering,
complete with delicious snacks? Nails, hair, body, the
works?"

Having recognized the voice, Clara gulped. "Ah, not
exactly." Looking at Annabelle's painted face, she was
more certain than ever that George couldn't possibly be
having an affair. Not with this woman, at least. "I assume
you're Annabelle?"

The woman's smile slipped. "Ah, yes, I am. How may
I help you?"

"You know George Dowd?"

The smile returned. "Ah, George! Such a nice man.
Lucky woman, that wife of his. He adores her, you know.
Not many men would set foot in our pretty little parlor
to book a day's beauty treatment for his wife."

Clara was beginning to understand. "George booked
the special for Stephanie."

"Ah, yes, I believe that's her name." The woman's face
crinkled with concern. "You won't breathe a word to her,
will you? It's supposed to be a big, dark secret. It's for

their anniversary, you know. He has plans to take her out that night. Somewhere very special, he said, and he thought she'd enjoy getting gussied up for the occasion. He's arranging everything and he doesn't want her to know until that morning."

"So it was you who called the house the other day."

Annabelle gasped, one hand over her mouth. "Oh, goodness. Did I give everything away? I made such a silly mistake. George gave me two phone numbers and I called the wrong one. I'll never forgive myself if I've spoiled his surprise."

"You didn't spoil it," Clara assured her. "Stephanie has no idea."

"Oh, thank goodness." Annabelle fanned her face. "Whew!" She laughed. "So what can I do for you, then?"

"Oh!" Clara backed toward the door. "I just stopped by to make sure everything was set for the big day. I'm Stephanie's cousin."

"Oh, how lovely to meet you. Yes, rest assured we will take care of your cousin. Mrs. Dowd will look and feel like a new woman when she leaves here."

There was no way Clara would spend a day in that place with all that preening and fussing going on. Stephanie, on the other hand, would probably love every minute.

"Are you sure we can't do something for you?" Annabelle pranced forward. "That hair, for instance. A trim? Just a touch of color?"

"Thanks, but no thanks." Clara backed all the way out the door, then spun around and sped back to her car.

She could still smell the perfume on her clothes as she drove to Thelma's house and parked at the curb. The good thing was that she was sure Stephanie's husband wasn't cheating on her. The bad thing was that she couldn't tell her without spoiling the surprise.

She'd have to think of some way to calm Stephanie's fears without spilling the beans about George's anniversary gift. Meanwhile, she needed to concentrate on how to find out if Thelma had deliberately lied about going shopping with her son on the afternoon of the robbery.

Thelma answered the door, looking surprised to see her. "Of course I remember you. You're Karen's friend, right?" she said when Clara reminded her who she was.

"Right. I was there when you told Karen you were moving. I thought I'd stop by to see if you needed help with anything."

Thelma seemed ill at ease, and she stared at Clara as if trying to figure out the meaning behind her words.

A quiver of apprehension ran down Clara's back. Something—the Quinn Sense? Her own instincts?—was telling her this was a mistake

As if sensing her discomfort, Thelma's face cleared. "That's so sweet of you, hon, but I've got everything under control." She put a hand up to her hair, and the sun glinted on her diamond ring. "I've got time for coffee, though, if you want to join me?"

"I'd like that. Thanks."

Clara followed Thelma into the living room. A pile of boxes sat in a corner next to a table holding sheets of white wrapping paper, a box cutter and rolls of tape. Thelma moved an open box half full of books out of the way so that Clara could sit on an armchair.

"I hate packing," Clara said, looking around. Across the room, leaning against the wall, was a large box with a picture of a flat-screen TV on the front. Next to it was a box apparently holding a desktop computer.

Thelma must have seen her looking at them, as she waved a hand at the boxes. "My son took me shopping. He's a good man, my Ray. He knows how to take care of his mom."

He was certainly doing a great job of it, Clara thought, considering he was unemployed. So he had taken his mom shopping after all. Had Thelma had the days mixed up when she told Dan it was the day of the robbery? "I think I saw him," she said, smiling up at Thelma. "I think he was driving a brand-new red sports car. It looked expensive."

Thelma had that odd look back on her face. "Oh, that!" Her laugh sounded forced. "No, that's not Ray's. He borrowed it from a friend when his own car wouldn't start." She shook her head. "He's got to get that old clunker fixed, or buy a new one. It's always letting him down." She headed for a door on the other side of the room. "Make yourself comfortable. I'll make us some coffee, then you can tell me all about the bookstore."

Clara watched her leave, struggling with indecision. Did Thelma suspect that Ray had robbed a bank, or was she simply a mom closing her mind against the possibility that her son could be involved in a crime?

Whichever it was, it seemed unlikely that she would admit anything. Clara's only hope was to catch her out in a lie and right then she didn't have the faintest idea how to do that.

Staring at the boxes again, Clara remembered her vision. Ray running out of the bank, ski mask pulled over his face, wearing the distinctive black shoes with the gold stars. Shoes that he hadn't been wearing when she'd seen him in the diner.

What had he done with the shoes? Did he know that someone had seen them and would remember them? If so, he surely would have gotten rid of them. Or had he?

She felt a quiver of excitement. If she could find the shoes, she'd have the evidence she needed. Dan would have to believe her. She would have to tell Dan about the witness in the bank, but since she didn't know her name, she couldn't tell him who she was. Would it be enough? It was a chance worth taking to find out.

She got up from the chair and walked over to the kitchen door. Thelma was at the counter, pulling down mugs from a cabinet.

She looked up as Clara asked, "Could I use your bathroom?"

"Sure, hon. It's down the hallway, third door on the right."

"Thanks. I won't be a minute."

It took only a moment for her to figure out which bedroom was Ray's. His clothes were all over the floor. A quick glance told her the shoes weren't in plain sight.

Under the bed? She bent down to look. There were empty beer cans under there, one worn slipper and a half-full bag of potato chips, but no black sneakers.

Straightening, she headed for the closet. She had to rummage around in a pile of plastic bags, boxes and clothes before she found what she was looking for—one black sneaker with gold stars on the side.

With a little gasp of triumph, she picked up the shoe and backed out of the closet. Now all she had to do was get out of there with it.

Carefully she opened the bedroom door, then crept down to the bathroom and slipped inside. Trying not to think about where the shoe might have been, she stuck it in the waistband of her pants and pulled her sweater down over it.

Walking into the living room, she was surprised to find it empty. She'd expected to see Thelma sitting there waiting for her. She hesitated, wondering if she should wait for her to appear. It didn't seem right just to walk out on her, especially if the poor woman was about to find out her only son was a bank robber and probably a murderer as well.

She could hear no sound from the kitchen, and quickly made up her mind. Maybe, after Ray was arrested, she'd come back and tell Thelma how sorry she was, and offer her help to get her moved.

With that settled in her mind, she started for the door. She was halfway across the room when a male voice spoke from behind her.

"Where do you think you're going?"

She froze, afraid to turn around. "I just came by to see if your mother needed help getting packed up to move." She took a step toward the door. "She said she was okay so I'm leaving now. I have to go to work."

"You're not going anywhere, hon."

Clara stared in horror as the front door opened to reveal Thelma barring her way.

Thelma looked past her to the man behind Clara. "I told you she was snooping around asking too many questions."

"Well, now I have a question." Ray came up behind her and spun her around with two hands biting into her shoulders. "What were you doing in my bedroom?"

Clara's heart was beating so fast she could hardly breathe. "N-nothing. I mistook it for the bathroom, that's all."

"Oh, yeah? You think I keep the can in my closet?"

"No, I . . ."

She gasped as Thelma came up behind her and pulled up her sweater. "Well, what do we have here?" She tugged the shoe out of Clara's waistband. Glaring at her son she muttered, "I told you to get rid of these."

"Well, I like 'em. I'll be able to wear them when we get to Florida."

"We won't get to Florida if you don't get rid of her."

Clara barely recognized Thelma's hardened face. All vestiges of the friendly, motherly neighbor had vanished, leaving behind a threatening, dangerous criminal. It all became clear now. "You were the second person," she said, eying the distance between her and the door. If she made a dash for it, she might just make it outside. She was pretty sure she could outrun them both. "You helped your son throw Scott Delwyn off the scaffolding."

Ray uttered a grunt of surprise. "How'd you know that? How'd you know about the shoes? Where are you getting your information?"

As if reading Clara's mind, Thelma took hold of her arm, her grip surprisingly strong. "Never mind how she knows. It's enough that she does. That settles it. She's gotta go."

"But—" Ray began, but was silenced by a jerk of his mother's hand.

"No buts. Tonight. When it's dark. In the ocean."

Clara's spine froze. She tugged her arm, but Thelma's fingers bit into her flesh, making her wince. "You can't just murder me. You'll never get away with it. I—" She was going to tell them that Stephanie knew where she was, until she remembered that her cousin had no idea she was in Thelma's house. Besides, it probably wasn't a good idea to drag Stephanie into this. These two monsters could go after her, too.

Thelma grabbed Clara's other arm and twisted them behind her back, making her cry out. "Bring me that packaging tape over there," she said, "and be quick about it. Our landlord will be here any minute to inspect the house."

"What are we going to do with her until dark?" Ray asked as he crossed the room. "There's nowhere to hide her here."

"Put her in our storage unit." Thelma tightened her grip as Clara struggled to free herself.

Desperate now, Clara blurted out, "I told Dan I knew Ray had robbed the bank."

Pausing with the tape in his hand, Ray swore. "Why, you—"

"That's enough! If Dan had believed her, he would have been here by now. Get over here and wrap her wrists with the tape."

Terrified now, Clara fought as hard as she could, but she was helpless against the two of them. She was forced through the kitchen and out to the garage, where the red car sat in gleaming splendor. So much for the story about borrowing it.

Ray opened the back door of the car and Thelma shoved her prisoner inside. "Tape her ankles," she ordered as Clara struggled to sit up. "Don't give her any chance to escape."

"You won't get away with this—" Clara began, but Thelma thrust her face up close to hers.

"Of course we will. It will look like an accident. You went walking along the waterfront and fell in. Just like Scott Delwyn fell off the scaffolding." She laughed, and the ominous sound seemed to rattle around in Clara's head. "Without proof, hon, there's nothing Dan can do."

16

After binding Clara's ankles with the tape, Ray climbed into the driver's seat while Thelma stood holding the door.

"Aren't you coming with me?" he said as she started to close the door.

"I can't. I have to be here when the landlord comes to inspect the house. Just take her to the unit, lock her in and come back here. We'll deal with her later, together."

Ray didn't look too convinced. "I don't like this. How will I get her out of the car and into the unit?"

"She'll walk, won't you, hon?" Thelma leered at her. "Unless you'd like me to hit you over the head and have Ray carry you in there."

Clara gritted her teeth. Right then she'd give anything

to be able to punch that grinning face. "I'll walk," she muttered and leaned back on the seat.

"Make sure you tie her up to something when you get there," Thelma said, and slammed the door.

The car slid smoothly out of the garage and into the street.

Clara stared at the houses as they passed, praying she could catch someone's attention and signal that she was being kidnapped. It had started to snow, however, and no one was out in the cold wind.

How stupid she'd been not to tell Stephanie she was going to talk to Thelma. Then again, she had no idea Thelma was involved in the murder, and she just hadn't figured on Ray being at home.

If only she could call her cousin. Clara shifted to a more comfortable position. As she did so, she felt her cell phone in her pocket. Thank heavens for her habit of carrying it with her instead of leaving it in her purse, which still sat in Thelma's living room.

Catching sight of Ray's face in the rearview mirror, she shifted over as far as she could go so that he couldn't see her. Then she twisted her arms to one side and, after some concentrated probing, managed to hook the phone out of her pocket.

It fell on the seat, and she had to grope to find it again. It took a while to get it open, and then she had to feel the buttons to get the right ones. Praying she had it right, she jabbed out Stephanie's speed dial number.

A second later she started talking, loudly, to cover any sound that might come from the cell phone. "Where are you taking me? Why do you think you can get away with this? Your mother is so wrong and I'm surprised you even listen to her."

"Shut up," Ray snarled.

At the same time, from down by her hip, she heard the faint sound of her cousin's voice. Her spirits plummeted. It was Stephanie's voicemail. Clara coughed loudly as the beep sounded for her to begin recording. She started talking again, fast and with intense desperation.

"Where is this storage unit you're taking me to? You can't lock me up in a storage unit." She looked out the window. "Where are we? Isn't this Fernwood Avenue? Is the storage unit near here? Dan will know you and Thelma killed me. You'll never get away with it. Just because you got away with killing Scott Delwyn doesn't mean you can get away with killing me. Everyone will know that Ray Hogan and his mother are murderers, and locking me up in a storage unit isn't going to change that."

"Shut up before I shut your mouth for you," Ray yelled, just as the beep that ended the recording sounded on her phone. He swung the wheel, viciously, sending the car screeching around a corner so fast her phone shot off the seat and disappeared under the seat in front.

Exhausted, Clara slumped back. She'd done what she could. Now all she could hope was that Stephanie checked her cell phone before nightfall, and that somehow she would find the storage unit before the Hogans came back to kill her.

———

Stephanie grunted as she kicked open the back door with her foot. Loaded down with shopping bags, she staggered into the kitchen and dumped everything on the table. Grocery shopping was not one of her favorite things to do. She always ended up tired and grumpy.

Today had been even worse than usual, since she'd spent the morning worrying about George and a woman named Annabelle. Part of her agreed with Clara. Somehow she just couldn't imagine George cheating on her.

George was the worst liar she'd ever come across. He'd never be able to hide an affair from her. True, he'd been acting weird the last few days, but now that she really thought about it, when would he have had time to see another woman? Unless he'd taken off from work.

Maybe she should call the auto shop and find out if he'd been missing lately. No, she'd put the groceries away first, then call.

By the time she'd finished stacking everything in the cabinets and fridge, she'd changed her mind again. She'd call Clara. Maybe she'd have some news for her that would put all her fears to rest.

She looked around for her purse. It wasn't on the

chair where she usually dropped it when she came in. After a quick search of the living room, she decided she must have left her purse, with her cell phone inside, in the car.

Before she went to get it, she decided, she'd better change the bed sheets and do the laundry before the kids got home. Determined not to think about George and what he might be up to, she put on her favorite CD and filled the house with music while she worked.

She had just turned off the vacuum cleaner when she heard the phone ringing in the living room. Molly was on the line, sounding upset. "I called your cell phone," she said, "but you have it turned off."

"Oh, sorry, it's in my purse. I left it in the car." She frowned. "Is something wrong?"

"I'm slammed here," she said, "and Clara didn't come in today. I'm gonna be leaving in a half hour. What do you want me to do?"

Stephanie glanced at the clock. It was almost three thirty. *Where was Clara?* "It's not like her to just not show up. Have you called her cell?"

"Twice. She's not answering." Molly's voice rose. "I gotta go. I got people waiting."

"I'll be there as soon as I can." Stephanie hung up, then dialed Clara's cell phone. Her cousin's recorded voice answered her.

Frowning, Stephanie replaced the receiver. Something must have happened. She thought about calling her aunt

Jessie's cell, but the number was on her own cell phone and she couldn't remember it. She called her mother instead and asked her to pick up the kids, then called George.

He answered right away, and his voice did a lot to steady her nerves. "Don't worry," he said, when she told him Clara was missing. "I'm sure there's a perfectly reasonable explanation. She's probably got car trouble or something."

"Then why hasn't she called? She wouldn't just not turn up without letting me know."

"Maybe her phone battery's dead. Why don't you call Jessie and ask her."

"I don't want to worry her if she doesn't know where she is." Stephanie gripped the phone harder. "Something's wrong, George. I know it."

"Where's your cell phone? Why aren't you calling on that?"

"I left it in the car."

"Well, she probably called you on that and left you a message."

Stephanie closed her eyes. Of course. Why hadn't she thought of that? "I have to go the store. Molly's leaving at four. Mom's picking up the kids. Can you pick them up from her on your way home from work?"

"Sure. Don't worry, Steff. I'm sure Clara's just fine. Let me know if she left a message on your cell phone."

"Okay. I'll check it on my way to the store." She hung up, then hurried to the bedroom to change. Another night that she wouldn't be there to cook dinner for George and the kids. It would be a miracle if her marriage survived all this.

It was snowing steadily by the time she climbed into her car. The clock on her dashboard showed ten after four. Molly would be waiting for her to get there so she could leave. Deciding to check her phone once she was at the store, Stephanie pulled out of the garage and set off carefully down the street.

Seated on the concrete floor of the storage unit, Clara tried to shift into a more comfortable position. Her back hurt, her hands felt numb and her entire body felt like it was encased in ice.

She'd wriggled and struggled so hard in the hours since Ray had left here there that she was now exhausted. Too weak to do much more than cry out every now and then, her voice too muffled by the tape that covered it for anyone to hear her.

It would be starting to get dark before long. Where was Stephanie? Had she heard the message Clara had left on her cell phone? Surely the police must be looking for her by now. Maybe her directions had been too obscure. Maybe there was more than one storage center near Fernwood Avenue and they couldn't find the right one.

Even if they did find the right one, how long would it take them to check out every unit? Would she be able to make enough noise for them to hear her?

Fear and desperation swept over her, and tears started running down her face, soaking the tape over her mouth. It tasted horrible, and she worked her jaw back and forth and side to side, trying to work it loose.

It was then that she heard it. Faint, but unmistakable. A dog barking. A big dog barking. *Tatters!*

She could hear the anxiety in his voice, and her heart skipped with hope. Gathering the last of her strength, she drew in as much air as she could manage through her nose, and let it out on the loudest screech she'd ever uttered in her life.

It sounded pitifully weak through the tape, but a dog's ears could pick up sounds that humans couldn't hear. Tatters' barking grew louder, filled now with excitement. Now she could hear someone calling her name. Was it Dan? No, it couldn't be . . . Rick?

They were at the door of the unit now. She could hear the voices outside, almost drowned out by Tatters' frantic barking. Seconds later the door slid up, and blazing daylight momentarily blinded her.

She heard Stephanie's voice as she tugged the tape from her cousin's mouth. Tatters' frantic tongue licked her face and finally, Rick's arms pulled her to her feet and folded around her.

Another voice spoke. She looked over Rick's shoulder and saw Tim standing there, a worried frown on his face. "Clara? Are you okay?"

She couldn't seem to stop the tears sliding down her

cheeks. "I am now," she said, and buried her face in Rick's shoulder.

———

Seated on the couch in her mother's living room with Rick's arm around her, Clara finally began to feel safe again. Her cousin had given her a mug of hot milk laced with brandy, and she could feel the fiery liquid spreading warmth in her chest.

Tim sat across from them, a notebook on his knee, while Stephanie anxiously hovered over her.

Clara looked at them all in turn, still fighting the persistent tears. "Thank you," she said, squeezing Rick's hand. "I could have died in there tonight. They were going to kill me."

"We know," Stephanie said, gripping Clara's shoulder so hard it hurt. "We heard everything you said on the cell phone. I'm so sorry, Clara. If I'd gone back to the car to get my phone, you wouldn't have been stuck in that awful place for so long. You must have been terrified."

"I was scared you hadn't got my message, or that you wouldn't be able to find the unit."

"You helped by giving us a street," Rick said, pulling her closer. "Tatters did the rest. He must have heard you or something. He led us to the right unit." He shook his head. "You do have a way of landing yourself in hot water. I'll have to find a way to keep you occupied so you don't go off chasing crooks at the drop of a hat."

She glanced up at him. "Like what?"

"Give me time. I'll think of something."

Tatters, who was lying in front of the fire, raised his head. *He's right. Don't ever do that again.*

Clara smiled. "I won't."

Rick looked down at her. "You won't what?"

"I won't ever forget that you all rescued me." She glanced up at Stephanie. "What about the bookstore? Who's looking after it?"

"I closed the shop. I figured you were more important that a few customers."

Clara exchanged a special look with her cousin. "Thank you, Steffie."

"You're more than welcome."

"Which reminds me." Rick sat up. "I left Tyler in charge of the store. I'd better get over there and help him close up." He let her go and stood, looking down at her with concern in his eyes. "You'll be okay?"

"I'll be fine, now. Thanks."

"See you tomorrow?"

"Okay." She watched him leave, feeling a weird sense of emptiness now that he was gone.

"Guess I'll go, too." Tim folded his notebook, shoved it in his pocket and got to his feet. "Dan will probably want a word with you tomorrow."

She nodded. "What about Thelma and Ray?"

"Dan was on his way to pick them up when we went looking for you. They're probably in custody by now."

She shivered. "I hope so."

"And I have to go home and see to my kids," Stephanie said after Tim had left. "Will you be okay here until Aunt Jessie gets home?"

"Of course. Thank heavens it was her night to work late at the library."

Stephanie looked worried. "You are going to tell her, aren't you? I mean, she's bound to find out once the news breaks."

"I'll tell her when she gets home. I'm just relieved she wasn't here when we all walked in."

"Meaning Rick, I suppose."

Clara sighed. "You know how she can be. Jumping to conclusions, and all."

"I don't think she could be mistaken about Rick's feelings for you."

Clara pretended to be shocked. "What does that mean?"

"Oh, come on, Clara. Anyone can see he's crazy about you, and that you're lapping it up."

"I am?"

"Yes, you are."

"Well, now that we're alone, I have some good news for you."

Clara could see hope flaring in her cousin's eyes. "So tell me!"

"George isn't having an affair. He's planning a surprise for your anniversary, and that's all I can tell you so don't ask any questions."

"A surprise?" Stephanie looked confused. "So who's Annabelle?"

Clara hesitated, then decided it was unlikely Stephanie would take that route anytime soon. "She's kind of in charge of the surprise, and I told you not to ask questions."

Stephanie still looked wary. "And you're absolutely certain he's not having an affair with her?"

Clara made a face. "Trust me. Not with that bimbo."

Stephanie leaned down and threw her arms around Clara. "Thank you! Thank you! I didn't think he would cheat on me, but you never know."

"He adores you, Steffie. Even Annabelle said that."

Stephanie's eyes opened wide. "You met her?"

"Oh, yeah. Definitely not George's type."

"How do you know what George's type is?"

"I'm looking at it."

Stephanie grinned. "Well, I think Rick is your type." She headed for the door. "I have just one word of advice for you." She opened the door and looked back over her shoulder. "Go for it." With that she was gone.

Tatters raised his head. *That's three words.*

Clara looked down him, but he laid his chin on his paws again and appeared to go to sleep. "You can shut up now." She leaned down to pat his head. "But thanks for rescuing me."

He answered her with a snore.

———

Dan called Clara the next morning, waking her up out of a deep, dreamless sleep. Still woozy, she struggled to make sense of what he was saying.

"Ray confessed to everything," Dan said as she made an effort to sit up. "His mother was the driving force behind the whole thing. Apparently he's been under her thumb all his life. It's a pretty strong thumb."

Clara shook her head to clear it. "He did kill Scott, then?"

"Yeah. Apparently Scott was in Thelma's kitchen, repairing her dishwasher. Ray walked in the house, didn't realize Scott was there and called out to his mother. He said something about her needing to have an alibi for him when he was ready to rob the bank."

"Oh, wow. I bet that made Thelma happy."

"I guess Scott tried to pretend he hadn't heard, but Thelma ordered Ray to help her kill him anyway. He left a message on Scott's cell phone to meet him after work, and hit him over the head with a two-by-four. Then he and Thelma took him up to the top of the scaffolding in the lift and shoved him off."

Clara closed her eyes. "Does Karen know?"

"Yeah, I called her a while ago and told her. She took it pretty well."

"I'll stop by and see her tomorrow." She hoped that knowing the truth about what had really happened to Scott had put Karen's mind at rest.

"How are you feeling, by the way?"

"I'm fine." Clara looked at her alarm clock. "In fact, I'm just about to get ready for work."

"Okay." He paused, then added, "I didn't mean to be so hard on you, Clara. I don't have the faintest idea how you knew that Scott was murdered, but I should have listened to you. The M.E. was so sure there were no signs of foul play."

"It's okay. I'm just happy that you caught them and that they'll pay for what they did."

Dan hung up and she slipped out of bed, anxious now to get back to the bookstore and a normal routine. The last few days had been exhausting, and she was glad it was all over. Last night, going over everything with her mother, she'd realized the chances she and Stephanie had taken. They could have ended up in real trouble, if it hadn't been for luck and a dash of the Quinn Sense.

Jessie had been more understanding and sympathetic than Clara had expected, and for the first time in a very long time she'd felt closer to her mother. When Jessie had asked questions that were difficult to answer, Clara had even considered telling her mother that she had inherited the Sense.

She'd managed to hold on to her secret, but now she was wondering if it would make things a whole lot easier if Jessie knew the truth.

Ten minutes after she got to the Raven's Nest, Rick came in to ask how she was doing. Aware of her cousin and Molly lurking in the background, she was careful what she said to him. When he asked her out for dinner that evening, however, she was quick to respond.

"I'd love to go." She smiled at him. "Somewhere quiet and peaceful."

"I know just the place." He started for the door. "I'd better be off. I have grocery shopping to do."

"You're going to his place," Stephanie said after he'd left.

She'd made it sound decadent, and Clara grinned. "I am. I'm taking your advice for once. I'm going for it."

The look on Stephanie's face convinced her she'd made the right decision.

Turn the page for an excerpt
from the first
Raven's Nest Bookstore Mystery . . .

Mind Over Murder

*Available in paperback from
Berkley Prime Crime!*

"Stephanie Quinn Dowd, you've got to be kidding!" Clara Quinn stared at her cousin's serious face and suppressed an urge to laugh. "I've never worked in a bookstore. Or any store for that matter. Why in the world would you want me to manage yours?"

The other woman puffed a strand of fair hair out of her eyes and dumped a pile of books onto the counter in front of her.

"Because you're smart, you're personable and you have a degree in literature. I need someone for the afternoon shift. Twelve till eight. I'll be here most of the day. Besides, you need a job, and I desperately need help. Look at this!" She swept a hand around her in a wide arc.

Clara gazed around at the rows of shelves loaded with books, the tables displaying classic titles, the posters on the walls and the cozy corner with its deep armchairs and large coffee urn.

It didn't look much different from the last time she'd seen it, shortly after Stephanie had opened the store three months ago. Except for the sinister-looking stuffed raven perched on a light fixture and the sparkling colored crystals slowly spinning from the ceiling on golden cords. Oh, and maybe the life-size figure of a fortune-teller hovering over a crystal ball. Clara grinned. "I didn't know you still had Madam Sophia."

Stephanie's laugh seemed to echo along the shelves. "Do you remember when we rescued her from that awful carnival?"

"How could I forget? I was the one who climbed up that huge pile of trash to get to her."

"We were so excited. Then my mom saw us carrying it upstairs to my room and just about went berserk."

Clara shook her head. "Poor Madam Sophia. Relegated to a cold, drafty garage."

"We didn't sleep all night worrying about her."

Clara joined in her cousin's laughter. "Well, she looks healthy enough now."

Stephanie's grin vanished as the sound of angry voices erupted on the street outside. "What's going on out there?"

"Sounds like someone's upset about something." Clara glanced at the old-fashioned grandfather clock by the door. "I'd better get going. I'm supposed to be looking for an apartment."

"Wait! Are you going to help me out or not?"

Clara paused, reluctant to give an answer. It was true she needed a job. She just wasn't sure this one would be a good idea. For a lot of reasons.

"Please?" Stephanie looked worried. "Ever since I started serving coffee and snacks in the Reading Nook, we've been swamped with customers. Molly's been doing the afternoon shift now that Jonathon has gone back to college, but I really need her here in the mornings, and I must have someone reliable to take over for her in the afternoons."

"Have you tried advertising the position?"

"Of course, but this is a small town, and it's hard finding someone suitable for the job. My mom's been taking care of the kids while I'm here, but once school starts next week she'll be back at work, and I can't rely on George; he has his own job to worry about. I'm pretty desperate, Clara."

Again Clara struggled with her conscience. "I'd like to, Stephanie, but I don't really have the time." Seeing her cousin's face freeze, she hurried on. "I'm still getting settled in, I'm looking for an apartment and I have to find a teaching position—"

Again the raised voices interrupted her. Glancing at the window, she puffed out her breath. From the day they were born, just two months apart, she and Stephanie had shared everything from baby formulas and childhood nightmares to adolescent dreams. Since neither of them had siblings, they'd turned to each other, forming a sisterhood that had lasted thirty years and would continue,

Clara hoped, for as long as they lived. They trusted and relied on each other as only close family can.

She would do almost anything for Stephanie, and now her cousin needed her. She just couldn't see any way she could refuse without seeming selfish and heartless.

Swallowing her reservations, she held up her hands. "All right. I'll do it. On the condition that it's only until you find someone permanent."

"Great!" Stephanie's face glowed with excitement. "Can you start tomorrow? Perhaps come in a little early? I could use the extra help for the sale."

Clara gave her a reluctant nod. "Okay."

"Thanks. It'll be fun; you'll see."

"I'm not so sure." Clara waved a hand at the shelves. "You know how I feel about all this magic and spiritual stuff."

"I know you used to love it as much as I do. Until you found out you have the Quinn Sense."

And there it was. Clara waited a full five seconds before answering. "We've talked about this before. That's why I left Finn's Harbor in the first place. To get away from all that."

"And now you're back." Stephanie came out from behind the counter and laid a hand on her cousin's arm. "I don't know why you're so determined to ignore the fact that you have the gift. It's a family heritage, and I'd give anything to have it."

"I'd give anything if you had it instead of me."

"I know. That's what makes it so frustrating." Stephanie dropped her hand and frowned at the window as the sound of angry voices outside intensified. "I'd better go and see what all that is about."

Heading for the door, she threw words over her shoulder. "Be a dear before you leave and go to the stockroom for me? I need the box marked 'High School.' The books are required reading for the students, and I need to get the rest of these tables set up if we're going to start our back-to-school event today." She disappeared, leaving her cousin no chance to answer.

Shaking her head, Clara set off down one of the aisles to the back of the store. Talk of the gift had unsettled her, as it always did. Most members of the Quinn family had some psychic ability, and she wasn't happy about being included in that favored circle. In fact, it had become such a burden that she'd left Maine in the hopes that she could forget all about the family curse, as she called it, and feel less of a freak.

At first, in the excitement of attending college in New York, she'd managed to ignore the odd moments when she could read people's hidden thoughts or have a momentary glimpse into the future. For a while she'd almost felt normal.

But life in New York was so different from the life she'd left behind in Finn's Harbor. She missed her family and friends, and Stephanie most of all. Each time she'd visited, it had gotten harder to leave.

There was a time when she'd resented the small-town community, where it seemed that everyone knew everybody's business. She'd found out, however, that a big city could be incredibly lonely, and true friends were hard to make. In her need for companionship, she'd sometimes been too quick to trust, and it had backfired on her. Big time.

Coming back to Finn's Harbor, however, meant facing the same demons that had sent her away in the first place. Pushing open the stockroom door, Clara sighed. All she could hope was that she'd made the right decision to come back to her hometown. Only time would tell.

Inside the crowded room, she gazed in awe at the piles of boxes stacked against the walls. It looked like she'd arrived in the nick of time. Stephanie sure had her hands full, now that the Raven's Nest bookstore had become one of the most popular social centers in town.

Catching sight of the bust of a man, she moved over to the table to inspect it more closely. The face looked vaguely familiar, and she studied it for a moment before bending closer to read the inscription. Of course. Edgar Allan Poe. She should have guessed. Stephanie crammed her shelves with anything remotely connected to the author.

Gently, she laid a hand on the smooth surface of the head. So many nights when she and her cousin were kids, they'd spent sleepovers watching horror movies and pretending to be psychics.

They'd filled hours reading each other's palms and

predicting wild, adventurous futures for themselves. They'd eagerly discussed how they would use the Quinn Sense once they developed it.

Even then she'd felt uneasy about it, though she'd never admitted as much to Stephanie. Her cousin had loved every creepy moment, while Clara had been scared they would conjure up some terrible evil spirit who would steal their souls.

At first, when she'd realized she had inherited the family's psychic powers, it had seemed thrilling and even empowering, but as time went by, the voices she heard became an intrusion. It hadn't helped matters to learn that somehow the gift had bypassed Stephanie.

Clara sighed and patted the bust. How ironic that she should be the one to inherit the Quinn Sense, as everyone called it, instead of her spook-happy cousin.

The sudden tingling in her hand took her by surprise. She snatched it back as a wave of darkness seemed to cloud her mind. Evil. She could sense it in the room, cold and menacing.

For a moment she felt rooted to the spot, unable to move a muscle. Then she forced her mind to clear, and everything settled back into place.

Heart still pounding, she quickly scanned the boxes until she found the one marked "High School" in uneven black letters. She grabbed it up and charged out the door, not even bothering to close it behind her.

She reached the counter just as Stephanie walked in through the front door, followed closely by a young woman with tangled red hair and flushed cheeks. Both of them stared as Clara came to a halt, breathless and shaking.

Her cousin was the first to speak. "Are you okay? You're looking a bit weird."

Clara gulped in air. Glancing out the window, she could see Ana Jordan, the owner of the stationer's next door, glaring at the bookstore, her short, chubby body still in fighting mode with feet planted apart and hands on her hips. The furious woman threw her hands in the air, then ran them through her cropped bleached hair before turning and stomping back to her store.

"I'm fine." Clara gestured at the window. "I thought I heard someone yelling."

"You did." The redhead held out her hand. "I'm Molly Owens, Steph's assistant. I've heard a lot about you."

"All of it disgusting, I suppose." Clara shook the firm fingers.

Molly grinned. "Let's just say you two must have had a dynamite childhood."

Clara gave her cousin a sharp glance. Stephanie had promised long ago not to tell anyone, including their own family, that her cousin had the gift. She was reassured by Stephanie's firm shake of her head and answered Molly with a smile. "You've got that right."

"Well, Steph told me you'll be working here." Molly tilted her head to one side, her green eyes sparkling with mischief. "I have to say, it'll be fab to have someone here tall enough to reach the top shelves."

Stephanie laughed and walked over to the counter.

"Just don't ask her how tall she is. The kids in high school drove her nuts with that question."

"Oh, bummer." Molly paused. "So, how tall are you, then?"

"Tall enough to thump you on the head if you ask that question again." Clara glanced at the window again. "So what was all the shouting about out there?"

"Oh, that was me." Molly sighed. "I was screaming at that old bat next door. I tell you, that woman is nuts. You know her, don't you?"

"Of course I know her." Clara rolled her eyes at Stephanie. "Most of these shops have changed hands so often I don't know anyone anymore, but Jordan's has been here since we were kids. Is Ana still causing trouble for everyone?"

Stephanie shrugged. "Nothing we can't handle."

Molly made a guttural sound of disgust. "That woman should be run out of town. She hates Steph, she hates the bookstore, she hates the fact that we're successful and she'd do anything to shut us down."

Clara stared at her cousin. "Really? What's her problem?"

"She says I'm poisoning young minds with my occult books and turning our children into demons."

"Whoa, heavy stuff." Clara nodded at the nearest table. "Those don't look like occult books."

"They're not!" Molly's cheeks turned red again as she gestured at the tables. "Look at the titles. They're books the high school asked us to carry, and what about those?" She pointed to several rows of colorful hardbacks. "Craft books and cookbooks. There's lots of choices, and it's not like we're forcing people to buy the occult stuff."

"There's a lot of interest in it right now, though," Stephanie put in. "I'm not endangering anyone—I'm just supplying what the public wants."

"Yeah, well, Ana doesn't think you have any right to do that." Molly jerked her hand at the window again. "She keeps putting up signs advertising Big Books, that new chain bookstore that opened up last year. She's doing her best to put us out of business. I saw the poster and tore it down, and of course, she saw me do it. She came screaming out of the store, and she's like, 'I'll have you arrested!' and I'm like, 'Just try it, you old witch, and I'll burn your broomstick and you along with it.'"

"I told you just to ignore her." Stephanie picked up a pile of books and hurried over to one of the tables.

"If you ignore her, she'll get what she wants and shut you down. You have to *do* something about that woman." Molly turned to Clara, green eyes pleading. "You tell her."

"She has a point," Clara said mildly.

"I know what I'd like to do," Stephanie muttered, "but I can't afford any trouble. Not today." She carefully stood an opened book on top of the pile. "We have teenagers coming into this store today for our back-to-school sale. The last thing I need is a screaming match with Ana Jordan."

Molly muttered something under her breath. "If you won't do anything, then I will. I love this job, and I'm not going to let a miserable old hag take it away from me."

"Well, I appreciate you coming in early to help." Stephanie hurried back to the counter for more books. "I'm going to need more boxes from the stockroom. I'm counting on this sale to buy school clothes for my children."

Molly sighed. "I'm going. But don't think I'm going to forget about it. Ana Jordan has a nasty shock coming her way, sooner or later."

She rushed off toward the back of the store, leaving Stephanie to stare after her with a worried frown. "That girl is a good worker, but she's got a temper that would curl the devil's toes."

Clara laughed. "I seem to have heard that somewhere before."

"You know as well as I do that I've gotten a lot better at controlling my temper." Stephanie carried more books over to the table. "Though my kids do know not to push me too far."

"I bet they do. Well, I'd better get over to the rental agency." Clara headed for the door. "They've probably rented that apartment by now."

"You don't like living with Aunt Jessie?"

Clara hesitated. "It's okay, I guess. It's just that I'm used to living on my own. So is my mother. She's gotten a lot more independent since Dad died."

"I know. It's sad. They were so happy together. I miss Uncle David and his silly jokes."

"We all miss him." Clara pulled the door open, jingling the bell and letting in the warm sunshine.

"Clara? Did anything . . . weird happen in the stockroom?"

Clara paused, one hand on the door handle. "Weird?"

"You know. *Weird.*" Stephanie looked uncomfortable. "You had that odd look on your face you always used to get when—"

"Nothing happened." Clara made an effort to soften her tone. "Good luck with the sale. I'll see you in the morning." She didn't wait for an answer.

Once outside, she pulled in a deep breath of the fresh, salty air. Main Street stretched ahead of her for several blocks, sloping down toward the harbor.

In summertime, the town was always crowded with tourists, and today was no exception. On either side, people strolled along in front of the quaint shop windows, peering under the colorful striped awnings at souvenirs, antiques, artwork and beach supplies.

At the bottom of the hill, boats bobbed around in the bay, their white sails gleaming in the sun, while behind them a thin line of fluffy white clouds separated the pale blue sky from the deeper blue of the ocean.

Clara's heart warmed at the sight. This was what she'd missed so much—this little town with its friendly people; its unique little shops and charming, narrow streets; the bustling activity of the picturesque bay. Here she could find peace and put all the problems of New York behind her. This was Finn's Harbor, Maine, and this was where she belonged.

Glancing across the street, she saw a man standing in front of the hardware store, one hand shading his face as he gazed at something farther down the street.

He didn't seem to be a tourist, and Clara stared hard for a long moment, trying to recognize the rugged features that were half hidden behind his hand.

Deciding that she didn't know him, she was about to turn away when he twisted his head in her direction. He apparently realized she'd been staring at him, as he touched his fingers to his forehead in a mock salute.

Embarrassed, she ducked her head and took off down the hill. Things had changed a lot since she'd left, twelve years ago. People had gone, and others moved in, and although she'd come back to visit several times every year, it wasn't the same as living there. She felt like a stranger now in her own hometown.

She wondered if the man across the street was a stranger or if he had lived there long enough to become a familiar member of the community. Then, wondering why on earth she was still thinking about him, she headed for the rental agency.

———

The following morning, Clara arrived on the doorstep of the Raven's Nest just as Stephanie was opening up the store. "I couldn't sleep," she explained, in answer to her cousin's raised eyebrows. "I thought I might as well come down early and give you a hand."

"Well, good. That will give me time to show you the ropes." Stephanie walked in ahead of her. "It will be a long day, though, and you'll probably regret coming in early by the time it's over. Molly won't be here for another hour. She stayed late last night to clean up, and I told her to sleep in. As you can see," she said, and flapped her hand at the neat tables, "she did a great job."

"She sure did." Clara studied the stack of books on the table closest to her. "You should have called me. I could have helped. I wasn't doing anything."

"Did you find an apartment?"

"Nope. The one I saw was too small and didn't have a dishwasher. I've got to have some place to hide my dirty dishes."

"You only saw one apartment?"

Clara made a face. "This is Finn's Harbor. There's not a lot of rentals to choose from."

"Well, it's not New York, I give you that." Stephanie took a bunch of keys out of her purse and unlocked the cash register. "You'll just have to be less fussy about where you live."

"After looking at what's available out there, my mother's house is beginning to look a lot more comfortable. Even with her in it."

Stephanie laughed. "You'll be good for each other. Now come over here, and I'll show you how to ring up purchases."

Clara did her best to remember everything, jotting down notes as Stephanie explained her duties. The next half hour passed quickly, and by the time they were done, Clara felt reasonably confident she could handle anything, barring an unforeseen emergency.

"You can always call me if you're in doubt," Stephanie

told her as she closed the file that held customers' new-book reservations. "I can be down here in a few minutes if you need me."

"I'll be fine," Clara assured her. She looked around, smiling as her glance fell on Madame Sophia. "I think this will be fun."

"I hope so. I want you to enjoy working here; then, maybe you'll stay." Stephanie grinned. "Now, I need you to go to the stockroom. The copies of Wayne Lester's new astrology book came in yesterday, and we need to get them out on the shelves. A lot of customers are waiting for that book."

At the mention of the stockroom, Clara felt a stab of uneasiness. She nodded, carefully keeping her expression blank.

Her cousin, however, knew her too well. "What's the matter?" Stephanie frowned. "Am I being too bossy?"

That made Clara smile. "You've always been bossy, but it's okay. You're the boss. You're entitled." Before Stephanie could probe anymore, she took off down the aisle and headed for the stockroom.

The disturbing sensation she'd felt the day before came back to haunt her as she opened the door. It didn't mean anything, she assured herself. She had moments like that all the time. Most of the time they went away without her ever knowing what was behind them. This was just one of those times. Even so, she braced herself as she pushed open the door and flipped on the light.

She had taken only two steps into the room when

she saw the huddled figure on the floor. Shock slammed into her chest, making it hard to breathe. She tried to shout for Stephanie, but no sound would come out of her mouth.

She took a wobbly step or two forward and uttered a whimper of horror. The shattered pieces of Edgar Allan Poe's bust were scattered on the floor. In the center of them, Ana Jordan lay face-up, a puddle of dark blood spreading out from under her head.